A Dan

MW01140475

H.L Day

Also, by H.L Day
Time for a Change

A Temporary Situation (Temporary series;
Tristan and Dom #1)

A Christmas Situation (Temporary series;
Tristan and Dom #2)

Kept in the Dark

Refuge (Fight for Survival #1)

Taking Love's Lead

Edge of Living

Love can be dangerous!

Valentin Bychkov, rising star of contemporary Russian ballet, appears to have everything: wealth, talent, success, and a face and body to match. Not that anyone can get close. Bypass the entourage and there's still Valentin's sharp tongue and acerbic wit to deal with. He may give his body freely, but his emotions are kept tightly locked away.

Max Farley's life is a simple one. All he's interested in is work, drinking, and picking up the latest in a long line of one-night stands. The way he chooses to live may not be to everyone's taste but it suits him down to the ground. He's never met anyone who's made him want to confront the demons from his past. Until now.

A show in London brings the two together. Lust brings them closer still. But if rumors of Bratva connections turn out to be true, then dangerous men wait in the wings. One dangerous man in particular, who's used to people following his orders without question.

Difficult choices need to be made on both sides. Valentin and Max need to stop playing with fire and let each other go, or face the consequences. But letting go isn't that easy where love is concerned.

And some things are worth the risk.

Warning: This book contains a snarky ballet dancer with an aversion to clothes, a little too much wall sex and an overabundance of Russian heavies.

Copyright

Cover Art by H.L Day

Edited by Diane Nelson

Proofread by Judy Zweifel at Judy's Proofreading
http://www.judysproofreading.com/

A Dance too Far © 2019 H.L Day

Foreword

This book came from one thing. I saw the gorgeous cover picture on a stock photo site and knew that I had to write the story, and Valentin was born. Okay, maybe two things, I was also watching whichever season of Arrow has Bratva in, so a few influences from that may have leaked into the story, just ever so slightly.

Dedication

To all the people who read and enjoy my books, and look forward to the next one.

You know who you are.

Thanks

A huge thank you to my beta readers for this book, Jill, Fiona, Barbara, T.A, Tanja, Karen, Anarra, Belinda and Sherry.

And a massive thank you to Diane Nelson who stepped in at the last moment to provide editing in order for me to get the book out on time.

Table of Contents

Chapter One

Max

Just when I was convinced that escape from the bedroom was going to be possible without him waking up, he sat up in bed. Bleary eyes searched the room, eventually focusing on my location and watching intently as I fastened my belt while avoiding looking his way. "You're leaving?"

I went to nod, stopping mid-action when the pounding in my head due to last night's overindulgence made it clear it wasn't a good idea. "I'm late for work."

The man in the bed ran a hand through his rumpled blond hair. "But you can stay for breakfast? Or a cup of coffee at least?"

I recognized that expression. It was the "I can't believe that after everything we did last night, you're going to leave just like that" look. I recognized it because I'd been on the receiving end of it far too many times to count. Why couldn't he have stayed asleep? Five more minutes and I'd have been out of there, and we could have avoided this conversation altogether. "Listen, Aaron..." At least I remembered his name. "...I'm really late. I'm not just saying that." I checked my watch, wincing at the time. "I'm meant to be across the other side of London in ten minutes to start a new job, so..." I let the rest of the sentence hang there.

His eyes turned cold. "My friends warned me about you."

I bit back a sigh. It appeared as if my hangover was going to come with a free dose of early morning drama. The temptation to simply ignore the comment and leave was strong, but I guessed I wasn't quite as much of a dick as I liked to think I was. Turning to face him, I kept my voice as even as possible. It might be drama, but it didn't need to escalate any further. "Did they? What did they say?" I could probably guess, but sometimes it was better to hear it straight from the horse's mouth rather than fill in the gaps yourself. Who knows, maybe it would be something I hadn't heard before.

His face turned belligerent, the sheet dropping to reveal several red marks on his neck that I guessed I'd been responsible for. "That you don't do relationships, that you're more the 'fuck 'em and leave 'em' type."

I shrugged my shoulders into my jacket. It was lucky that last night's undressing hadn't started till we'd gotten to the bedroom. Not that I could remember. The whole night was pretty much a blur. "Yet you still chased me." He had. For weeks. Everywhere I'd gone, he'd popped up, offering himself up like some sort of tasty appetizer. He'd even gone as far as cock-blocking me a couple of times when I'd had someone else in my sights. I'd made it clear I wasn't interested. But at some point after the third or fourth

8

tequila, his sex appeal had increased exponentially, and I'd gone home with him against my better judgment.

"I thought..." He looked embarrassed, his cheeks taking on a distinctive rosy blush.

I rolled my neck from one side to the other, trying to ease some of the stiffness out of it from sleeping in an unfamiliar bed. He was a good-looking guy with a good body. There was nothing wrong with him. But there was nothing that stood out about him either. Not to me anyway. But then you could say that about all the men I slept with. They scratched an itch. Gave me a physical release. Nothing more. I didn't need anything more than that. I didn't *want* anything more than that. "You thought you might be special?"

He shrugged, unwilling to admit that what I'd said was the truth. "Why don't you do relationships?"

It was my turn to shrug. I knew. Of course, I did. But it wasn't something I was willing to discuss with a near stranger simply because our bodies had gotten intimately acquainted for a few hours. I offered a tight smile. "Maybe listen to your friends next time. They were trying to help you."

He looked hopeful for a minute, his lips curling into a smile far more genuine than mine had been. "Okay. No relationships. I get it. But everyone needs a fuck buddy, right? I can give you my number."

I shook my head, the pounding having eased off enough that it wasn't too painful. *Bloody tequila!* "Thanks, Aaron, that's sweet, but I'm going to have to turn down your generous offer." I took another pointed look at my watch. "I've got to run. See you around."

I didn't wait for his response before hightailing it out of the bedroom and managing to find my way out of the unfamiliar house.

* * * *

I slid down lower in the seat and laid my head back as the tube train approached Covent Garden. As a freelance sound engineer, I was used to working in many different venues. The Royal Opera House was a first though. Apparently, the person lined up to do the job had had to pull out at the last minute. Something to do with a family emergency triggering a trip to New Zealand. The head of set design, and a long-term friend of mine, had put my name forward as a possible replacement. So there I was, on my way to hang out with a load of ballet dancers for the next few weeks. I wouldn't normally have been available, but I'd been planning on taking some time off. But with the money they were offering, plus an additional bonus for taking the job on such short notice, it was too good to turn down. The planned trip to a sun-soaked beach somewhere exotic would have to wait. It was for that reason that I wasn't too concerned about turning up late. If they were desperate enough to pay me almost double what I was used to, then they were hardly likely to turn me away for being a bit late. I checked my watch again, my mouth twisting. Okay. More than a bit — an hour late.

I sat up as the tube train slowed to a stop, the man in the seat opposite catching my eye and making a point of letting his gaze travel slowly down my body. *Jesus!* He must be desperate. I hadn't looked in a mirror, but given the way I felt, and the fact I hadn't showered or shaved, I knew I was hardly looking my best. Perhaps he dug the homeless look. I averted my gaze and headed for the door farthest away from him.

It took another fifteen minutes to reach the imposing white stonework and intricate masonry that made up the Royal Opera House. I navigated my way between the columns that fronted the building, wishing I'd had time to stop for something to eat. Or at least a coffee. I'd kill right then for a coffee. I doubted there was going to be much on offer inside. Particularly for a latecomer reporting for duty on his first day. A further ten minutes was wasted while security checked out my story. It seemed that nobody had thought to change the name of the previous employee to mine: a glaring oversight on someone's part. It took multiple phone calls and conversations before it was finally sorted and I was issued with a pass and a set of directions to where I needed to go.

I wended my way down the corridors, attempting to recall the barrage of "left, right, right, left" instructions I'd been given, and thankful for the occasional sign that told me I was on the right track. After a long trek, I finally reached the side door that would take me into the auditorium and therefore to the sound booth next to the stage.

I'd barely gotten a foot inside when my arm was grabbed and I was hustled back out into the corridor, the door banging shut loudly behind us as Noel's furious face glowered into mine. "For fuck's sake, Max! Do you know what time it is? They've been asking where the hell you are. I put a good word in for you to get you this job. So you being an irresponsible dick reflects badly on me. As well as you. Not that you probably give a damn. But I do."

Noel and I went back years, ever since school, but I couldn't remember ever seeing him this pissed before. Not at me anyway. I removed my arm from his grasp. "I had a problem getting through security. They were still expecting the other guy."

"For two fucking hours? I don't think so." His nose wrinkled. "You stink of booze, and you look like shit. What happened?"

"I woke up late."

His eyes narrowed. "In whose bed?" He huffed when I made no effort to dispute the assumption. "Fuck! Just for once, couldn't you have..." He sighed dramatically. "Never mind. You're here now. If you weren't so good at your job, I swear..." He pulled me back through the door, gesturing at the sound booth at the side of the stage. "Down there. Get yourself acquainted with the equipment. The dancers are due onstage at any time for rehearsals, so you've got little to no time to get your shit together." He backed away a couple of steps. "Don't let me down, Max, please. You might be able to float around and pick and choose your jobs whenever you feel like it, but the rest of us rely on consistent money coming in."

I resisted the temptation to point out that I hadn't asked for his recommendation, offering a wholly unconvincing "sorry" instead.

In return, I got a weary headshake, the beginnings of another sigh, and then the view of his back as he walked away to go back to whatever he'd been doing before he'd felt obligated to lie in wait for me. He'd be fine once he'd calmed down a bit. I headed for the booth, the small dark space I'd share with a couple of other people for the next few weeks. Being a sound engineer sometimes felt like living underground.

I glanced at the stage on my way past. It was still a hive of activity, which meant it hadn't been cleared for the dancers yet. That still gave me some time to get my head around whichever sound console they used, and quickly read through what they required. If I was lucky, I'd also get a chance to test audio levels and start turning acceptable into something that sounded great. It should be child's play for someone of my experience. I'd rather have done it with coffee and breakfast inside me, but I supposed that beggars couldn't be choosers. I should have asked Noel to get me something. I chuckled to myself as I imagined the earful I'd have gotten in response if I'd dared to raise the subject that I was running on empty.

In the end, I got twenty minutes before rehearsals kicked off. More time would have been useful, but I guess I'd sacrificed that the moment the first tequila had slipped down my throat the night before. Everything went smoothly for the first three dancers, Noel appearing by my right shoulder just as the third finished their routine. He looked a hell of a lot calmer than he had earlier. I quirked an eyebrow at him. "See! Everything's under control."

He pulled a face. "Thank God for that."

I gestured toward the stage. They'd called a halt while they discussed some sort of issue with the last dancer's performance. It had looked fine to me. But then what did I know about ballet dancing. "Where're the female dancers?"

Noel laughed. "You don't do any research at all, do you?"

I shook my head, pausing to smile and give thanks to the stagehand who'd taken pity on me and magicked up a coffee from somewhere. He blushed and scurried away. I was beginning to think I needed to adopt the rough-and-ready look more often. If you counted the guy I'd woken up with, that was the third expression of interest I'd had in so many hours. I rubbed a hand over my chin, the stubble rasping under my palm. "What was I supposed to research?"

14

Noel rolled his eyes. "This show is all-male contemporary ballet. So if you're waiting for the women to pop up, you're going to be waiting an awfully long time."

"I see." I let my gaze rove slowly over the muscular physique of the dancer still onstage. The job was starting to seem too good to be true. Extra money, and I got to ogle muscular men on top of that. I wondered how many of them were gay.

Noel's gaze followed mine, his brow furrowing. "And don't even think about chasing any of the dancers. Leave them alone."

"I don't chase." It wasn't arrogance talking, it was the truth. I didn't need to. On the rare occasion I expressed interest in someone who didn't reciprocate, I moved on. There were plenty more fish in the sea.

The dancer left the stage, making way for another to walk on seconds later. I found myself staring, something about him immediately commanding my attention. I didn't know whether it was his sheer presence, the graceful way he walked, the way he looked, or a mixture of all three, but I couldn't tear my eyes away. After the first three dancers, I'd grown somewhat accustomed to the extremely revealing ballet tights. But none of the others had filled them out in quite the same way this guy did. My scrutiny started at his bare feet before traveling over every inch of his muscled calves and thighs encased in tight Lycra.

I swallowed with difficulty as I reached the distinctive bulge of his crotch. The similarities between how he and the other dancers were dressed ended at that point. Their costumes had all been full body. This guy though, was bare-chested — unless you counted the scrap of black, lacy material fastened around his neck. Matching material also adorned his forehead, the color the same as the short, cropped black hair.

Every inch of skin on display — and there was a lot — was flawless. And yet it still was not as beautiful as his face. I'd never gone for makeup on men. There was nothing wrong with it, it just had never been my thing. But on this guy it worked, the blue eyeshadow and eyeliner gave his eyes an exotic slant, while the lipstick and blusher drew attention to the perfection of the features they highlighted. He wore no jewelry. Although, that may have been because he was onstage. Whatever the reason was, he didn't need it.

"Who's that?" My voice came out breathless, my eyes still glued to the stage as he took up position in the center.

Noel snorted. "The star of the show of course. Rising star of the ballet world, Valentin Bychkov."

"Valentin?" I tasted the name on my lips. It suited him. An exotic name for an exotic man. "He's Russian?"

"Father was Russian. Mother was English. Why do you..." Noel finally seemed to clue into the reason I was asking, his head swinging around to peer into my face closely. It was clear that he didn't like what he saw. "No. No. No. Don't you dare. I said the

16

dancers were off-limits, but *this one* is most definitely off-limits. Don't even think about it. Don't go near him. Don't even mention his name. I'm not joking, Max. There are lots of rumors about the sort of people he's mixed up with, and they're not the sort of people you want to get on the wrong side of. So, I take back what I said earlier. Chase the other dancers to your heart's content. Fuck them all if you want to. But not Valentin. Stay away from him. He's not worth getting your kneecaps broken over."

Amusement over Noel's rant fueled the smile on my lips. "That's one hell of an overactive imagination you've got there."

He shook his head. "Nothing to do with imagination. Stories I've heard. You've heard of Bratva, right?"

I shrugged. "Vaguely. Russian organized crime, right?"

"Right. And Valentin's... mentor" — I frowned at the pause, wondering what word he'd been going to use before changing his mind — "is rumored to be a member of Bratva. He certainly has both the money and the entourage to suggest it's true."

I started the music. "How do you know all this?"

Noel stopped halfway to the door, his eyes darting to the only other person in the sound booth at that moment. Given that he was wearing headphones and not looking our way, Noel must have decided it was safe to continue with what he'd been about to say. "Unlike you, I do my research. Just... take my advice, Max. Please."

I kept my eyes on the stage, offering only the merest glance of acknowledgment to my friend. "You don't need to worry. Even if I *was* interested, it's not like I'm going to get anywhere near him, is it? Or that he's going to have any interest in the hired help."

He nodded, seemingly placated. "True."

With him gone, I was able to turn my full attention back to the stage. I knew nothing about dance, especially ballet, but even I could tell that what I was witnessing onstage was something special. The other dancers had been good, but this guy — Valentin — was something else. It was easy to see why he was the star of the show. Every movement. Every twist. Every turn was pure beauty in its precision, his muscles flexing and bending effortlessly in ways that could only have been the result of years of hard practice. He was strong, yet graceful. Aggressive, yet playful. The contradiction provided a contrast at the same time as it fit seamlessly together. My concentration waned as I found myself caught up in the beauty of the dance, my fingers occasionally managing to fumble at buttons I was meant to be pressing.

He pirouetted across the stage, each movement as perfect as the last. Then with one last death-defying leap in the air, landed as if he'd barely left the ground, the routine came to an end. As he stood stock-still in the middle of the stage, an officious-looking man, presumably the theater director, applauded while saying something in a language that had to be in Russian.

Valentin didn't bother to offer any response to whatever feedback he'd just been given. His head suddenly turned, his gaze sweeping over the sound booth where I stood. I fought the urge to step back out of view, the searching gaze having a strange effect on me. "The music was wrong. It needs fixing." His voice fit him perfectly, English with just a hint of a Russian accent to add richness to the sound.

Fuck! My heart jolted, my mouth going dry. He was right. I'd been so transfixed by his performance that I'd messed up some of the transitions, way beyond anything I could put down to first-day teething problems. I didn't know whether it was guilt for not doing my job properly or the fact that he was looking straight at me causing it, but there was no doubt that I felt unusually out of sorts. I opened my mouth to say something, but he was already turning away, apparently not interested in any sort of explanation.

He left the stage the same way he'd entered, my eyes automatically dropping to the muscled tightness of his ass. An ass you could crack walnuts with. And an ass that I'd give anything to get better acquainted with. I had a serious case of lust bubbling through my veins.

* * * *

The rest of the day passed smoothly. I seemed to have gotten away with the mistakes I'd made earlier when my cock had momentarily taken over from my brain. Either they hadn't been as obvious as I feared, or they just hadn't had time to come and speak to me about it. I needed to make sure it didn't happen again. Valentin had only danced once. The word on the street from the few people I'd chatted to during my breaks that day was that he was on partial medical rest, so an understudy had stood in for him during the rest of the rehearsal. It seemed a good gig to me. Come on. Dance for five minutes, and then get the rest of the day to do whatever it was that contemporary ballet dancers did during their downtime.

The same blushing stagehand that provided me with coffee earlier had showed up at midday with a sandwich. I wasn't entirely sure whether it was his job or I was getting special treatment. But from the looks he gave me, I suspected it was the latter. I'd felt sufficiently human enough by that time to look him over with a bit more interest. He was cute. There was no arguing with that, but everything about him screamed innocence. The poor boy probably wanted to be wined and dined, not fucked and chucked. In spite of what people thought — or said — about me, I did have some limits. My one-night stands were always mutual, and I never made false promises. It was just that some guys chose not to hear it. Like Aaron that morning. No, he was definitely one to put on the "do not touch" list. It wouldn't hurt to flirt a bit though. It'd give him a bit of an ego boost while keeping me well supplied with drinks and food while I was working. That way everyone was a winner.

It was nearly three by the time I finally exited the theater onto the street. I looked forward to getting home, taking a much-needed shower, and perhaps even indulging in a bit of the "hair of the dog that bit me" to eradicate the last traces of the hangover that hadn't quite gone away all day. I was about to head for Covent Garden tube station when I became aware of a familiar figure slouched against the wall, smoking a cigarette. He was in the same outfit as he'd worn onstage earlier, despite a big chunk of time having gone by since. His only concession to being outside was the addition of an open jacket to partially cover his bare chest. His feet were still bare, his toes appearing even more naked against the backdrop of the street tarmac.

Keep walking, Max. Just keep walking. Spurred on by Noel's earlier words of warning, it was excellent advice that my subconscious was offering. It was a shame then that I didn't pay the slightest bit of attention to it. I drew to a halt next to him. He continued to stare straight ahead, either deliberately ignoring me or unaware of my presence. "I thought dancers were meant to be healthy? Isn't smoking bad for you?"

There was a long pause while he took a drag of the cigarette and exhaled the smoke. I took the opportunity to examine his face in profile. Up close, he was equally as stunning, if not more so than he'd been onstage.

Valentin finally answered, his voice crisp and cool, the Russian accent more pronounced than it had been earlier. "Keeps my weight down."

He still hadn't spared me so much as a glance, as if I was of such inconsequential importance that I barely registered on his radar. I probably didn't. He didn't even know who I was. In his eyes, I was probably just some busybody of a passerby who'd recognized he was a dancer from his outfit and wanted to stick my nose into his business.

His head suddenly swung around, his gaze cool and assessing as it swept over me. "Is that okay with you, Max?"

There weren't a lot of situations that could throw me for a loop, but him knowing my name did. I gawped at him. "How do you... I don't..."

His lips quirked at the corner as I floundered over my words — the son of a bitch obviously found it amusing that he'd managed to catch me off guard. He took another drag of his cigarette, the smoke going in my eyes as he exhaled. "You *are* the one that ruined my dance? Correct, yes? I made a point of finding out your name."

The words felt like a slap, yet my brain chose to focus on his use of the word ruined. "Your dance was... it was — "

"Better with the correct music transitions." He levered himself away from the wall, even managing to perform that movement with a great deal of grace. *What would he be like in bed?* When he'd

22

danced, there'd been parts that were slow and graceful, and parts that were fast and furious. Which one would he be? Or would he be both, depending on his mood? Heat filtered through my body as I was bombarded with a series of arousing images.

I needed to calm down. There was no way in hell I'd ever get to find out, so it was a waste of time taunting myself with scenarios that couldn't happen. He dropped the cigarette butt on the ground and turned to face me. I was surprised to find that we were roughly the same height. He stepped closer, raising his chin and looking me straight in the eye. "What's *my* name?"

"Valentin," I answered automatically, regretting it immediately as a smug smile slowly spread across his face. "I mean... you're the star of the show, right? Everyone knows your name."

He didn't look fooled for one minute by my feeble attempt at a cover-up. "You're going home?"

I nodded.

He stepped closer still, and I did my best to pretend that I wasn't affected by his close proximity. What the hell was wrong with me? It must have been the combination of a hangover and lack of sleep. He leaned forward, his lips mere inches from my own. My breath caught, and the world stood still. Was he going to kiss me? If so, I didn't care that we'd only just met. I didn't care that we were in the middle of the street. I'd kiss him back, and I'd probably thank him afterward. He pulled back slightly, his nose wrinkling. "Good! You are in need of a shower. You smell like a distillery."

Then he was pushing past me on his way back into the theater, a full smile on those delightfully shaped lips, and I was left feeling like something momentous had happened when nothing had happened at all.

Chapter Two

Valentin

The smile from baiting the new guy didn't last long, fading as soon as I caught sight of the twin walls of muscle waiting at the end of the corridor. Both men topped my six-foot frame by a good five inches. Both wearing equally expensive and fitted suits. To most people, they were my bodyguards, but I knew better. They were paid to keep a close eye on me, but it wasn't about protection. It never had been.

Igor crossed his arms across his massive chest, watching my approach with an impassive stare that gave nothing away. Mikhail, however, was less willing to hide his displeasure, the angry scar down one cheek creasing as he glowered.

I slowed down to a saunter, making them wait even longer until I reached them. Mikhail tilted his chin, the glare growing more pronounced. "Where have you been?"

He'd spoken in Russian. They were both far more comfortable conversing in their native language. Therefore, naturally I responded in English. "I went outside for a cigarette." I smirked as a muscle ticked in Igor's cheek, the first sign that he was as annoyed with my actions as his colleague was. "I thought you were with me." I hadn't. I'd known that they weren't used to the layout of the theater and I'd taken advantage of that, slipping through a side door I'd spotted and skirting the building to reach the front of it.

Mikhail reached out, his fingers almost making contact with my arm before he thought better of it, his hand pausing in midair and then dropping back to his side. "You think Dmitry will be happy when he hears that you were alone outside the building."

I leaned my head to the side, pretending to give the question a great deal of thought. Apart from dancing, one of the few pleasures I got in life was winding up my two perpetual shadows. "I doubt it. But then when is Dmitry ever happy?"

"You think we will not tell him?"

I walked in the direction of my dressing room, knowing they'd follow. They followed me everywhere. That was the problem. They weren't the first, and they wouldn't be the last. When I was younger, it hadn't bothered me as much. But I was twenty-five now, and I still had to justify my whereabouts on a minute-by-minute basis. It was suffocating, and I'd long since grown tired of it. But what Dmitry wanted, Dmitry got. I was his prized possession and, as such, he kept tabs on me. Day and night. I sighed. "Do what you want. Tell Dmitry. Don't tell Dmitry. I don't care."

"You are ungrateful... brat."

That was Mikhail, always more outspoken than the silent, brooding Igor. I swung around, shoved my face close to his and switched to Russian, unable to keep the anger out of my face and voice. "You need to remember who you work for. Dmitry may need someone to do your job, but you're hardly indispensable. There are at least twenty people who preceded you, and when you're gone, there'll be twenty more after..." Something died inside me as I said the words aloud. It didn't take a genius to work out that Dmitry would have me escorted for the entire duration of my dance career. As I had every intention of continuing well into my thirties, that was a long time to have to endure. "One word from me, and Dmitry will have you replaced. So you might want to think carefully before you go admitting to him that you can't do your job properly."

The anger faded as quickly as it had begun, replaced by a mixture of exhaustion and pain. I'd hoped the nicotine would help. It had, but only for about five minutes. Now the throbbing in my ankle had worsened again. I shifted position, placing the majority of the weight onto my other side.

Igor finally found his voice. "Dmitry arrives next week."

"Does he? Great!" I forced a smile, even while my heart sank. I'd been counting on having a couple of weeks to myself before he flew over from Russia. His business must have concluded quicker than he'd expected. "So there's very little point in telling him anything then, is there?"

Neither man responded. I turned and opened the dressing room door.

"When do you want to go to the hotel?"

I reluctantly turned back. "Soon. I'll let you know. Don't worry, there's no secret back entrance out of *this* room, and I'm sure you're going to wait right outside? Correct?" They both nodded. I closed the door in their faces and finally allowed myself the luxury of limping. I hobbled over to the closest chair, sinking into it and pulling my sore ankle onto the opposite leg to examine it. Apart from a slight puffiness, there were no external signs that I'd aggravated the injury any further, but the increase in pain said otherwise.

I made a call, waiting for the other man's greeting before I spoke. "Dr. Chambers, it's Valentin. I need you to increase the strength of the painkiller shots you're giving me. Either that, or I need more than one in a day."

The doctor's sigh was audible over the phone line, as was his irritation at the request. "We already had this conversation, and I told you that would not be possible. You were advised not to dance for three months to give the injury a chance to heal. You have Achilles tendonitis. Every time you go against medical advice and dance on that ankle, you stop it from healing and risk aggravating it further. It—"

I cut him off, knowing it was pointless arguing. "Fine. I'll see you in the morning for the next injection."

"You need to rest it. You really shouldn't be dancing on it. These things—"

"Thank you, Doctor." I hung up. I'd heard it all before, from more doctors than just him. The ones back in Russia had said exactly the same. It suited Dmitry to let them believe that it was my choice to carry on dancing against medical advice. As if I'd be stupid enough to risk my whole career for the sake of one show, no matter how important that show might be. I'd all but begged Dmitry to let me sit this one out, but he was adamant that wasn't going to happen. As far as I'd been able to work out, there were a multitude of reasons behind his bull-headed attitude. Dmitry never liked anyone telling him what to do, including doctors. He was arrogant enough to believe that he knew better—the need to keep control overruling common sense. Then there was the fact that he'd told me on more than one occasion that I was exaggerating the injury for attention. I suspected he thought that I'd even had a word with some of the doctors in an effort to get them to say that it was worse than it was. As if I'd do that. This was my big break. It was by far the most high-profile show I'd been involved in to date. The Royal Opera House in London wasn't anything to sneeze at. If the reviews were good, it would open doors for me across the world and finally push my name into the ranks of dancers who were so in demand they could pick and choose when and where they performed, at the same time as commanding a serious amount of money for considerably fewer shows.

And then there was the financial aspect, and I suspected the real crux of the matter. I had no doubt in my mind that his investment in the show was very much a cover for two things: it gave him all the appearances of being a professional businessman and manager, which he loved, while offering a perfect opportunity for the money laundering that I knew he was involved in and had been for years. One of the reasons he was so hell-bent on raising my profile and opening up opportunities in other countries was that it provided a legitimate reason for visiting and stopped the authorities from asking too many questions. He liked the attention that my dancing brought, but he liked money more. I was under no misapprehension about that. Whatever the reason, and it was probably a combination of all three, there was no arguing with him. Lord knows I'd tried, and it had simply fallen on deaf ears,

I massaged my ankle, the pain not quite so severe now that I'd taken the weight off it. It was very concerning though, given that I'd done no more than a ten-minute warm-up and a rehearsal for my solo onstage. Fifteen minutes in total and I was still suffering for it. I fumbled in the drawer, pulling out the bottle of painkillers

I'd been warned not to take on top of the injections. I unscrewed the top, tipping two tablets out onto my palm and swallowing them dry.

I lowered my ankle to the floor and stared at my reflection in the mirror. I'd chosen to go with full makeup today, a fact some of the other dancers had clearly found strange, going by the furtive looks they'd given me. Not that any of them had dared to voice their thoughts aloud. It wasn't necessary for rehearsals, but what none of them realized was that I used makeup as emotional armor. It was the veneer I used to project the toughest version of Valentin to the world that I could. That Valentin didn't care that he was constantly accompanied by two babysitters masquerading as bodyguards; he didn't show an iota of the discomfort that it took to dance the simplest steps; he wasn't bothered that some drunken idiot couldn't even get his music right or that he only had a few days left before Dmitry's arrival. He was tougher than that and didn't let anything permeate the outer layer.

I reached for the wipes, my hand pausing halfway. The makeup could stay on a bit longer. At least until I was back at the hotel and safe in the knowledge that I didn't have to deal with anyone else. Closing my eyes, I made an effort to relax, breathing evenly and waiting for the painkillers to kick in enough that I could walk without limping. I hobbled over to the fridge and got an ice pack out, sitting back down before pressing it to the inflamed skin of my ankle. Hopefully between that and the painkillers, it would be enough to ease the pain enough for me to at least get back to the hotel.

* * * *

If it wasn't for my ankle, I would have complained about the need to take a cab to travel the grand total of three blocks. But as it was, I was grateful for the chance to sit back and rest, even if it was sandwiched between Igor and Mikhail. I could tell from the looks they kept exchanging that they were finding it odd that I wasn't kicking up a fuss about something. I would have been tempted to put on an act if drowsiness from the painkillers I'd taken hadn't rendered me almost useless.

Mikhail shifted in his seat, his gaze sliding my way. "Dmitry called. He says you have not been answering your phone. He says you must pick up next time."

Three days. That's how long it had been since I'd last spoken to him. It wasn't as if I had anything new to tell him. "I dropped my phone. I think it's broken." I hadn't. But it was as good an excuse as any to explain why I'd been avoiding Dmitry's calls. I'd known I couldn't get away with it forever. But the temptation for a respite from constant instructions, reminders, and threats dressed up as Dmitry having my best interests at heart had been too tempting.

"I will get you a new one. Then you must call him

immediately."

I nodded, looking past Igor to stare out of the window. It wasn't my first time in London, but I assumed that just like the previous time, sightseeing was going to be out of the question. Not unless I dragged these two brutes along, and that thought alone was enough to put a dampener on any possible trip. I'd rather stare at bare walls.

The cab drew up in front of the hotel. Five-star, of course. Dmitry wouldn't have it any other way. Igor got out first and I followed, careful to avoid showing any signs of discomfort as I placed my weight on my injured ankle. I'd convinced myself that I'd landed awkwardly during one of today's jumps. A few hours' elevation and it would be as good as new tomorrow. If not... well, that didn't even bear thinking about. Not dancing wasn't an option, so it had to be all right.

The three of us walked through the lobby and into the elevator that would take us up to the top floor that consisted of only three suites. One was mine, one was occupied by Igor and Mikhail, and the last stood empty waiting for Dmitry's arrival. The door to the elevator opened, and I made my way to my suite, using the keycard to open it. I paused for a moment in the doorway. "I won't be going out, so you two can do whatever it is you normally do. You don't need to hang around." I knew it was a pointless request, that they'd take it in turns to station themselves outside my door for the entire night, but I said it anyway. If only because it made it sound as if I had a measure of control. They didn't take orders from me. They took them from Dmitry, but I could still dream.

Then I was alone in the suite, the door firmly closed to shut out the outside world. Apart from accepting room service, it would stay that way until morning, where I'd start a day almost identical to the one I'd just lived. There'd been one difference today though: the man I'd met outside the theater. The man who'd virtually undressed me with his eyes, his expression clearly broadcasting all the things that he'd like to do to me, given half a chance. I wondered what his story was. What sort of person turned up to a new job reeking of alcohol from the night before and looking as if they'd tumbled out of someone else's bed, yet didn't seem to give a fuck what anyone thought? It had been strangely refreshing. Underneath the rumpled and disheveled exterior, and despite not being exactly fragrant, he'd still been hot, the bloodshot eyes and scruffy stubble doing nothing to hide the fact. He was certainly the only thing that had provided entertainment. His shock at finding out I knew his name, and the way he'd looked as if he wanted to bite his tongue off at the admission that he knew mine, shone a ray of light on an otherwise unremarkable day.

I'd like to have been in a position to find out more about the mysterious Max. Something about him intrigued me. It was just a shame that wasn't going to be possible.

Chapter Three

Max

I offered a nod in passing to the theater manager, Yakov Komilov. It had taken some time to grow accustomed to the large number of Russians involved in the production, but the majority spoke good enough English for it not to be a problem. Unless tempers were frayed, and then everyone seemed to launch into quick-fire Russian at the same time, with those of us who didn't speak it left staring at each other completely bemused. I hadn't been able to get anywhere near Valentin. Apart from when he was onstage, he was never alone, and his two bodyguards weren't exactly approachable. Who needed *two* bodyguards anyway? If he needed any at all, which I seriously doubted. Wouldn't one suffice? There were Hollywood actors and actresses with less security. And where had those bodyguards been when I'd seen Valentin out on the street? Wouldn't there be *more* need for protection outside the building, not less? It all seemed a bit pretentious and unnecessary, and should have provided yet another reason to stay away from him.

There was something about Valentin that I couldn't get out of my head, besides the fact that he was so easy on the eye. Maybe it was something to do with how prickly and rude he'd been. I wasn't used to men speaking to me like that. It made me wonder whether that was his usual manner or if I'd simply caught him on a bad day.

A sudden thought occurred to me. What if the bodyguards were a Bratva thing? I laughed to myself and dismissed it immediately. Noel might be stupid enough to believe any crazy rumor doing the rounds, but that didn't mean I had to.

I'd managed to avoid making any more mistakes with the music, balancing the need to follow Valentin's every movement onstage with still being able to do my job properly. Noel had been too busy barking orders at his team of set designers to spend any time worrying about what I was getting up to, so I'd managed to settle into a nice routine. The job wasn't too taxing and came with the added bonus of watching half-naked muscular dancers strut their stuff. What more could I possibly want?

I swerved at the sight of Glenn coming toward me, ducking down a corridor I'd never ventured down before. The rosy-cheeked stagehand was becoming increasingly clingy, to the point where I was faced with either giving him what he wanted or letting him down gently. But that was a decision for another day, hence the fact I was avoiding him. When the sound of his footsteps had faded, I lifted my head, only then registering where my detour had taken me: right outside Valentin Bychkov's dressing room. I knew it was his because his name was emblazoned across the door in large gold letters.

Before I could consider what the hell I was doing, I raised my hand and knocked. The door flew open, and there he was in all his glory—bare-chested, barefoot, and fully made up like every other time I'd seen him. He frowned, his gaze scanning the length of the corridor. He was probably wondering where his bodyguards were, seeing as they were employed to keep riffraff like me away from the star attraction.

I found myself entranced by the curve of his collarbone, and the sheen of his skin, my gaze traveling slowly over his body. It traversed his shoulders, his nipples, all the way down the smooth, mostly hairless chest to where the stubble of what would be a tantalizing treasure trail if he didn't shave disappeared into the ballet tights, and then to the promising bulge below. Men didn't normally have this effect on me. But then I didn't really know any others with a body like this who were in the habit of walking around half-naked. Surely that was as good as an invitation to stare. Only problem was, I'd been so busy doing that—invitation or no invitation—I'd forgotten to speak. Given that I was the one who had knocked on *his* door, it must have looked decidedly strange.

I made an effort to drag my gaze back up his body until it was his face in my field of vision. The knowing expression and the condescending arch of his eyebrow instantly filled me full of regret that I wasn't still staring at his crotch. At least there'd been no judgment there, just the delightful curve of a barely concealed cock. I tried to bury the surge of lust while I struggled to find words. "I came to check that your music has been okay for the last few days? You know... since I *ruined* it on the first day."

He tilted his head to the side, his scrutiny giving the appearance that he was considering something. "The music has been... acceptable."

He took a step back, and I braced myself for the door to close. Therefore, the next words out of his mouth came as quite a shock.

"Come in."

I hesitated, unsure of what I was supposed to do. A glance back to the corridor revealed it to be empty of irate bodyguards. In fact, empty of anyone who might have been tempted to tell me to stay away from Valentin. I stepped inside, scanning the room out of curiosity. I hadn't set foot in any dressing room before, never mind one belonging to the star of the show. There wasn't a lot to see: a dressing table covered with makeup and hair products, a sofa, a few items of clothing hung up around the room, and a small fridge humming away in a corner. I'd expected more. If this was the dressing room for the number one attraction, then what did the rest of them look like? They must have been nothing more than cupboards.

"Do you have a condom?"

"What?" I swung around to face him, examining his face for signs that he'd cracked some sort of Russian joke. He stared back at me, his facial expression remaining the same while I struggled to process if he'd actually said what I thought he had. "Why would I... what?"

Valentin strolled to the other side of the room, examining himself in the full-length mirror that stood along one wall, his implacable gaze meeting my considerably more shocked one in the reflection. "It's a simple enough question. You either do, or you don't?"

"Yeah... I do, I just—"

He nodded. "I thought so. You strike me as a man who carries at least three around in his wallet."

I couldn't help but feel that there was a thinly veiled insult there somewhere. I might have said so if it wasn't for the knowledge that currently in my wallet, there were exactly three condoms. I knew that because I'd replaced the one I'd used during the tequila-influenced one-night stand. Therefore, his insight was uncanny.

I shrugged, reluctant to admit that he could read me like a

book when our interactions hadn't yet reached the five-minute mark. This man was younger than I was. Yet he seemed able to trigger a constant feeling of being caught off guard with a single comment or a scathing look. I reminded myself that I was twenty-eight years old and fully capable of handling a conversation, no matter what strange turn it might take. Looking him straight in the eye, I was determined to ask a direct question, but he got in there first.

"You don't want to fuck?"

I felt as if I'd been sucker-punched in the gut, like I couldn't breathe. The best course of action would be to leave. To walk out of there and put some distance between myself and this strange but alluring man. What kind of person made an offer like that on the second occasion of meeting someone? Maybe in a bar where both participants were out looking for a no-strings sexual hookup. But I wasn't in a bar. I was in a dressing room in the Royal Opera House, alone with the star dancer. Noel would kill me if I touched him. Hell, the pair of Neanderthals who were usually glued to Valentin's side would probably do it before Noel could.

My cock throbbed, already half-hard at the mere suggestion of getting some action. Without conscious thought, I reached down, readjusting myself. Valentin followed the movement with a smirk before sauntering over to the other side of the room. He turned around to face the wall, one hand bracing against it while the other moved back to grasp the waistband of the ballet tights.

My heart thudded as he gradually eased them down, revealing his bare ass inch by tantalizing inch. Underneath the ballet tights was something resembling a thong. I guessed it was actually something more specialized than that — specifically designed for a dancer. Whatever it was, I was given very little time to contemplate it before that was pushed down too, and I was left staring at the muscular lines of his back as it tapered down to one of the most toned asses I'd ever had the good fortune to be anywhere near. He looked back over his shoulder, his gaze finding mine, the smirk still in place. "Make a decision, Max. Either get over here and fuck me. Or get out."

My throat closed up, making swallowing difficult, my senses screaming at me to do the latter. Nothing good could come of touching him. Not with the stories I'd heard and the fact that he was so damn aggravating and arrogant. I was immensely proud of my brain for dredging up cold, hard logic while a fuckable ass flexed in front of me. But my hands, well, they weren't listening to my brain. They were already fumbling in my wallet and extracting a condom. My feet must have been in on the conspiracy too because they were already walking toward Valentin.

He'd already turned back to face the wall as if there'd been no doubt in his mind whatsoever about which option I'd choose. I unzipped and pulled my cock out, not bothering to unfasten my trousers completely. I gave it a couple of strokes, even though it wasn't necessary. One glimpse of that ass, and I'd been good to go. Foreplay didn't seem to be on the menu, so I rolled the condom down my cock, adding extra lube from a packet I always carried around.

Reaching out with both hands, I hesitated briefly before my fingers made contact. He was all warm and sleek, the skin goose-bumping beneath my fingertips. I traced his shoulder blades before dipping down, following the sinewy lines of his back muscles until my hands came to rest at his waist. I felt dizzy, forgetting to breathe, such was my arousal. I paused to get myself back under control, my palms itching with the overwhelming desire to squeeze the muscular globes that lay beneath.

"I don't have all day. I have a meeting to attend."

The words should have hit me like a dose of cold water, making me think twice about what we were about to do, particularly given the haughty way they were delivered. They didn't. I was being given permission to go fast and hard, to treat him like nothing more than a sex object. No pretending that he meant more than he did. No false assurances. No whispering endearments I didn't mean. Just two men fucking until they both came. It was like all my Christmases had come at once. It might be a bad idea, but it was the best bad idea I'd ever had.

I palmed his ass, using my grip to push the two firm cheeks apart to glimpse the prize that lay in between. At the same time, I moved forward, lining my cock up with the tight, puckered hole

I'd uncovered. I pushed forward. Not enough to penetrate. Just enough to make my intent clear. If he wanted to change his mind, or he needed something more before I fucked him, then this was his chance to object, to demand whatever he needed.

He not only stayed silent, but he also squirmed, balancing against the wall to tip his ass up to a more inviting angle. I didn't need asking twice. Wrapping one arm around his waist to keep him flush against me, I pushed slowly forward, the head of my cock entering him. His body stiffened beneath my hands, the muscles tensing at the initial sting of penetration. I stopped immediately, not wanting to risk hurting him. "Do you need—"

"Do it!"

The words couldn't have been clearer, but still I hesitated, until Valentin's ass pushed back against me, the decision taken out of my hands as my cock slowly slid inside him, our bodies pressed together, and a fine sheen of sweat breaking out on his skin. This was everything I'd dreamed of and more. And once we'd fucked, well, at least I'd be able to get him out of my head.

A loud hammering at the door started up, Valentin's name being called in a heavy Russian accent. In a panic, I started to withdraw. I was halfway to doing so when a strong hand reached back, anchoring me firmly in place inside his body.

"Don't move. They won't come in without my permission. They want to check that I have not gone anywhere."

He called something out in Russian, and there was an answering response in the same language. Then there was silence. Had he told them what he was doing? How had he phrased that? *Hang on, I'm just getting the sound engineer to fuck me up the ass.* Maybe this was a habit of his. Maybe he always fucked his way through the behind-the-scenes crew. Somehow though, I couldn't see it. He was too cold. Too aloof. This was more a case of opportunity presenting itself. After all, it wasn't as if I'd made any attempt to hide my desire when I'd looked at him.

"Are you going to finish what you started?" His voice sounded cool and collected. Anyone listening to him would have found it hard to believe that he was splayed against a wall with a cock inside him.

Was I ever? Despite the interruption, my erection had never waned, snug as it was inside the tight Russian ass. I adjusted my balance, filling him to the hilt as I began to thrust, forcing an exhalation of breath from his mouth as I worked myself deeper. Valentin's back muscles flexed with each of my thrusts, and I found myself mesmerized by the sight, unable to believe that he was actually allowing me to do this to him. I dug my fingers into his skin, leaving fingermarks behind as I thrust deep. Heat built quickly in my balls, the wet slap of my body against his and our sweat-slicked skin rubbing together only serving to fuel it further.

I slid my hand over his hip, unsure what I'd find. Given how remarkably cool he'd kept and how quiet he'd been, I would have

44

been less than surprised to find him soft. *Would I have stopped?* It was doubtful. I was way beyond that point, the first stirrings of orgasm already making themselves known. I groaned as a hard cock filled my hand. I wrapped my fist around him, jacking him off as I thrust harder, my nose buried in his hair. I changed the angle, wanting to hit his prostate, the small gasps coaxed from his mouth, as well as the twitch of his cock in my hand, letting me know when I'd hit the target. I pegged the same spot over and over again, Valentin's breathing growing louder and more desperate, sweat dripping down his back as his balls tightened. I leaned over his shoulder, wanting to kiss him, wanting to feel his tongue against my own as I brought us both to completion.

He wrenched his head away, and I had to make do with kissing his neck, my tongue darting out to taste the sweat on his skin. My hand moved faster, in combination with my hips, until he cried out, his cock pulsing and shooting cum all over my hand as well as the wall. I dragged him back against me, soaking up the feeling of his orgasm as it reverberated through his body, massaging my cock. Only when the twitches had all but subsided did I let go, my cock pulsating as I filled the condom. The thought sprang to mind that I wished there were no barriers between us, that I wanted to see my cum leaking from his ass. I breathed heavily into his ear, enjoying the sensation of having the tall, lithe body wrapped in my arms and contemplating how something so quick could have been so good. It was so strange that he felt so right in my arms. I could have stayed like that for hours, but Valentin clearly didn't share the sentiment.

He wriggled out of my grasp, my spent cock withdrawing from his ass, and walked over to the dressing table where he picked up a tissue. He reached behind, using the tissue to wipe up the remainder of the lube before discarding it into the wastepaper basket. Then he pulled up his underwear and ballet tights as if nothing had happened. I didn't know what I'd expected to happen after, but it wasn't this. Finally, he turned to face me, his gaze dropping to where my limp cock still hung outside my trousers. I must have looked ridiculous.

He walked forward, holding out the wastepaper basket. The smirk was back on his face. Or perhaps it had never gone away. "I wouldn't go out like that if I were you. People will stare."

I took the hint, removing the condom and dropping it into the proffered basket before tucking myself in. With no offer of a tissue, I had no option but to wipe my hand on my own trousers. That was going to be a fun journey home, smelling of cum. Only then could I bring myself to meet his gaze. It was strange. We'd done one of the most intimate things two people could do together, yet there was a huge chasm between us. I glanced over to the wall, using the clearly visible stain of Valentin's cum to reassure myself that we'd had sex and it wasn't just a figment of my overactive imagination. I cleared my throat. "What happens now?"

Valentin's brow furrowed. "What do you mean?"

"I mean..." *What did I mean? What was wrong with me?* I'd walked away from more one-night stands than I could count with barely a backward glance. So what was I expecting here? Reassurance? Something else? "I don't know."

The pink lips, accentuated with lipstick, curled up into a smile. I'd been robbed of tasting those lips. Maybe that's why this whole scenario felt horribly incomplete. My body was sated, but my mind was insisting that there was still unfinished business. As I stared at those lips, they twisted, and I braced myself for the stinging barb which I knew would be on its way.

He didn't disappoint. "What? You want to date? Get married maybe? Adopt children together? Maybe you want to introduce me to your parents. I can't introduce you to mine, I'm afraid. They are both dead." He crossed his arms over his chest. "Where shall we get married? Is Russia okay for you? There's a little church close to where I grew up. How many children do you want? I was thinking one of each? Any thoughts on names? For a girl, I was thinking, maybe—"

"Stop!" I didn't need to hear any more of his mocking. I was getting the message loud and clear. I may have fucked him, but he was just as unattainable as he'd ever been, and I had no idea why that thought rankled so much. I didn't do relationships. Hadn't done for years—ever since the one I didn't like to think about. So everything he was saying should have been music to my ears. That same speech from the guy I'd picked up the other night would have been exactly what I wanted to hear. "I get it. You didn't bring a dildo with you to England, so you used the next best thing."

He shrugged, but there was no denial. He inclined his head toward the door in a pointed instruction.

"What if your bodyguards see me leave? Is that okay? They might guess what we were doing."

There was a chink of something in his expression, and I felt as if a little bit of the real Valentin was seeping through. Before I could analyze it properly though, it was gone and the impassive mask was back in place. "Darling, they've been outside the door the whole time. You may as well get it over with because they're not going anywhere."

I nodded and walked toward the door, pausing with my fingers on the handle. "What did you say to them when you were speaking Russian?"

Valentin lifted his chin. "I said"—he hesitated just that little bit too long for me to be able to tell whether the words that were about to be spoken were the truth or a lie—"listen to how loud this one moans when he comes."

I opened the door and left, shouldering my way between the twin slabs of muscle stationed on either side. There was a lesson to be learned somewhere, but right now, I had no idea what it was.

Chapter Four

Valentin

I sat back and closed my eyes, letting my mind drift back to the events in my dressing room a few days ago. Max Farley had proved himself to be quite the stud. The man certainly knew how to fuck. There was no doubt about that. Snatching sexual interludes where I could often meant that I couldn't afford to be that choosy. So what was I supposed to do when a good-looking man happened to knock at my dressing room door, especially coinciding with the mysterious absence of my twin shadows? After all, I was only human. And he'd given me that look again—the one that said he wanted to lick me all over. If I hadn't propositioned him, then it would only have been a matter of time before he'd noticed the effect he had on me anyway. Ballet tights weren't exactly conducive to hiding a stiff cock. It was rare that I came across a man who was prepared to fuck me the way I liked to be fucked. But Max had done that in spades. And then he'd had to go and ruin it, he'd had to go and look at me like he expected something more, as if I'd disappointed him in some way. At that point I'd needed to get rid of him. There was no room for someone like Max Farley in my life, even if I wanted there to be.

When the door to my suite flew open without any prior warning, there was only one man it could be. There was only one person in my life who believed it was their God-given right to enter any room they desired without knocking first. As the person paying for all three suites, he'd no doubt demanded a spare keycard from reception, with the intention of catching me off guard. Which he'd done. I steeled myself and stood, regretting having already removed my makeup. It left me feeling naked and vulnerable.

Dmitry Gruzdev, dressed in his usual expensive designer suit, quickly closed the space between us, his arms outstretched. "Valentin, my love! I have missed you." I allowed myself to be swept up into his embrace, keeping my head still as he delivered a kiss on both cheeks, his cold lips lingering. He pulled back to hold me at arm's length, keen blue eyes raking over my face. "Nothing to say to me, my love? First, I cannot get hold of you on the phone, and then I do not even get a greeting from you. It is a sad day."

I answered in Russian, the same language Dmitry had spoken. "S-sorry..." I slowed as I stumbled over the words and forced myself to smile. "You surprised me, that's all. Igor said you weren't getting here until tomorrow." *I thought I had one more night of freedom.* "Of course I am happy to see you. I am very happy that you have finally arrived in England."

His eyes bored into me for a few seconds longer as if he were waiting for my facade to crack. His hand reached out, his thumb smoothing over my cheekbone. I swallowed but didn't try to pull away. He frowned. "That explains why you have not bothered to look pretty for me." He grabbed my chin, turning my face from one side to the other while he squinted disapprovingly. "You look so much better with makeup on, my love."

"I know. I'm sorry. I was planning on an early night. Had I known you would be arriving, it would have been different."

He let go and walked over to the floor-length windows to stare out onto the London street. "Yakov says that the show is going well. That you are dancing beautifully."

"My ankle..."

He swung around, the look of displeasure on his face making the words in my throat dry up. "What about it? Is the doctor who I organized for you not doing his job properly?"

"He is. It's just that... it's getting worse. I'm in more pain than I was before. The injection helps for a while, but it seems to be wearing off quicker each time. I'm worried that I'm going to do irreparable damage if I keep dancing."

He patted the pocket of his jacket, pulling a cigar out. "Pffftttt. I will talk to the doctor. He will give you more injections or a stronger dose. You know how important this show is. A bit of pain is not something you can't overcome. You are stronger than that."

The conversation was pointless. I had no chance of winning, but I pressed on regardless, the constant anxiety about my ankle giving out altogether, making me give it one last-ditch effort. "I asked him for that. He said he couldn't. I thought maybe I should sit this show out. It—"

Dmitry's eyes blazed fire. "I have told you that is not an option. The investment contract is contingent on you dancing in the show. I stand to lose a lot of money, not to mention that I will look bad, if you do not dance. You wouldn't want that, would you, Valentin? For me to look bad. I will talk to the doctor. He will fix it."

I nodded, knowing there was nothing I could say or do that would sway him. I needed to get him back in a good mood. An amiable Dmitry was so much easier to handle than an irritated one. "Did you want me to order something from room service for you? You must be hungry after your flight."

He shook his head. "No. I have business to attend to tonight. Contacts in London that I need to check on, see that they have not gotten lazy during my absence in Russia. They are like you. They need my attention, or they go off the rails. It will take a while. I will be taking Mikhail, but I will leave Igor with you."

"You can take them both. I'm going to eat and then go straight to bed."

He considered it for a moment. "Perhaps. An extra pair of hands could prove useful." A slow smile spread across his face. "Then tomorrow we will celebrate our reunion. A party perhaps? You can tell me which other dancers I should invite."

My heart sank at the thought of a Dmitry-organized party. But what Dmitry wanted, Dmitry got, and everyone else agreed or was forced to pay the price. So even though he'd phrased it as a question, I knew the notion wasn't up for debate. I forced another smile, the muscles in my face starting to feel the strain. "That sounds good." It didn't. It sounded like hell. It would be hell. But I knew the drill. I knew what Dmitry's expectations were. I'd also known that him staying in Russia while I flew to London was only ever going to provide a temporary reprieve. He never let me out of his sight for too long.

He tapped the cigar on his hand while he studied me. At least he hadn't lit it. That would save my suite from stinking of cigar smoke all night. "Are you really pleased to see me, Valentin? I'm sensing a certain coldness from you. A certain reticence that I'm not used to seeing."

I forced myself to my feet. A few days of relative freedom and I was already out of practice at playing the bullshit game that the two of us had been playing for years. My feet sank into the luxurious carpet as I crossed the floor toward him, careful not to put too much weight on my injured ankle. I hadn't been exaggerating when I said it was worse. I had no idea how I was

54

supposed to get through a full show when I was in this much pain after only doing one or two dances. I draped myself over Dmitry, squeezing him tight while I stared at the wall over his shoulder. I didn't have to worry about my facial expression, safe in the knowledge he couldn't see me. "I missed you." Then I kissed him on both cheeks, imitating Dmitry's action from earlier. "I'm tired. I apologize if I seem underwhelmed at your arrival."

He stroked my hair, his face relaxing. "Ah, my beautiful Valentin. We will have so much fun tomorrow night. There is a *long* list of people who are dying to meet the new star of London." He checked his watch. "Unfortunately, that is tomorrow. I must go now. Do not wait up, and I shall see you for breakfast in the morning."

I pasted another smile on my face as he turned to leave, only sinking into the chair and letting out a sigh of relief once the door had closed. I waited until the sounds outside the door had died down before venturing over to it. I opened it cautiously, half expecting to see the familiar bulk of Igor stationed outside it, but the corridor was empty. For once Dmitry had listened to me and taken both men. I closed the door again, my mind already conjuring up various ways that I could use this rare gift to my advantage.

I pulled up a number on my phone and stared at it. It was amazing the pull you could have when you were the star of the show. Ask, and it shall be given to you. Including the phone numbers of people who probably wouldn't be at all happy to find it had been given out without their permission. Making the call was a crazy idea. It would be asking for all sorts of trouble—in more ways than one.

My finger hovered over the button, and I lost the battle against temptation, pressing it and raising the phone to my ear. It was answered on the third ring. For a moment, there was only background noise: people talking, the clink of glasses, and faint music. He was in a bar. No surprise there. He said hello, and I found myself smiling at the distinct irritation in his voice. And that was before he knew who was on the other end of it.

"Come to my hotel."

A long pause. "Who is this?"

"How many Russians do you know?"

"Too many of late." The background noise faded as if he'd found somewhere quieter to move to. "What do you want, Valentin?"

He sounded less than friendly. I guessed that I couldn't exactly blame him, given how we'd left it after our last encounter. "I told you, I want you to come to my hotel room. The Piccadilly London West End Hotel. Suite number 4."

Another pause, this one so long that I had to check the phone screen to see whether he'd hung up. "You seriously think that you can just call me out of the blue to demand I come to your hotel and that I'll actually consider it? How the hell do you even have my number anyway? I didn't give it to you!"

I let him rant, his angry words acting as a strange sort of salve after the shock of Dmitry's early arrival. Max was real. He didn't hide his feelings. He didn't play games—as far as I knew anyway. He was exactly what I needed, and to hell with the consequences. "Don't be long, Max." Then I hung up.

I was ninety-five percent certain that he wouldn't be able to resist the invitation. However, I was less sure how long it would take him to get to the hotel from wherever he was. I could have asked, but it was highly unlikely that he would have volunteered the information anyway. I caught sight of my reflection in the mirror. My makeup-free reflection. Well, that wouldn't do. That wouldn't do at all. I hurried over to the dressing table and started applying foundation, ignoring the continuous ringing of my phone, which I assumed was Max trying to call me back.

Forty minutes later and I was starting to think that my reading of Max Farley had been less than accurate. I'd made the assumption that he'd been alone—based on nothing. He was a good-looking man though. For all I knew, he could have been sitting there with some nubile twink who he'd picked up. Either that or he wasn't as interested in me as I'd like to believe. He'd had me once. Maybe that was enough.

The heat in his eyes when he looked at me though said

otherwise. And then there was the fact that he'd fucked like he couldn't get enough. I suddenly felt ridiculous. There I was, standing in a hotel room, perfectly made up, hair teased to perfection, and naked beneath a fluffy robe, waiting for a man who couldn't care less. This was what happened when you started to believe your own hype.

My head swung toward the hotel phone on the nightstand as it rang. I lifted the receiver to my ear. "Yes."

"Mr. Bychkov, I'm so sorry to disturb you, but there is a man in reception claiming to have received an invitation from you. We didn't want to send him up without checking his story with you first."

Relief and satisfaction jostled inside me. "Does he look annoyed?"

There was a long pause. I assumed the concierge was contemplating the best way to answer the question tactfully with the man standing right in front of him. "Ermm... I would probably say yes to that question. Would you like me to call security?"

I shook my head, even though the man on the other side of the phone had no way of discerning it. "No. Send him up."

Muffled voices came over the line as the concierge relayed the message before ending the call. I imagined the look that would be on Max's face when he got to my suite. He'd been annoyed, but that still hadn't stopped him from coming to the hotel. That spoke volumes.

I propped the door open a few inches before lounging back in the chair, aiming for a look of relaxed languor. I shifted my robe to the side slightly, ensuring there was an ample amount of thigh on display, the tanned skin dark against the whiteness of the robe. And then I waited. I didn't have to wait long, the knock sounding at the door, even though it was clearly open, less than a minute later. Apparently, even a Max who was pissed still had manners. I schooled my face. I might be looking forward to seeing him, but it wouldn't pay to let him know that. "Come in."

The door burst open to reveal a glowering Max. His gaze swept briefly around the suite before settling on me, his expression turning even stormier. I cocked my head to the side and studied him as his long legs made short work of the space between us, the door slamming shut in his wake. He halted a few paces away, his eyes dropping to the generous portion of bare skin I'd left on display before dragging his eyes back to my face. I arched an eyebrow in a deliberately infuriating fashion and waited for him to speak first.

He shook his head. "Who the fuck do you think you are?"

I gave the question some thought. Despite the fact that niggling him would definitely appear in my top five list of fun things to do and it was a really bad idea for him to stay, I didn't want to push him to the point where he actually left. Therefore, I needed to find the right balance between the two. "I think I am a man who picked up the phone and offered an invitation."

Max raked his hand through his hair, leaving it looking delightfully rumpled. It reminded me of the way he'd looked on the first day I'd met him. "An invitation? It didn't sound like an invitation to me. It sounded more like a demand."

I waved a hand lazily down the length of his body. "Yet here you are. And I'm so flattered that you chose me over alcohol."

His nostrils flared. "What the hell is that supposed to mean?"

"You have a drinking problem... or you're on your way to having one. I haven't quite decided which yet." The words weren't designed to provoke. I was stating a fact. During the last two weeks, he'd turned up to work looking like crap and smelling of booze more often than he hadn't. The only reason nobody had complained was that it didn't seem to stop him from doing his job. Apart from the error with my music on the first day, he hadn't put a foot wrong.

He let out a humorless laugh. "You're unbelievable! Do you know that?"

I chose to deliberately misunderstand him. "Thank you." I gestured to the empty chair arranged diagonally to mine. "Have a seat."

His eyes dropped to my thigh again. "I'm not staying. I just came to tell you what you could do with your demand."

I shifted so that the robe fell open a few more inches, the belt barely holding it closed. "You came all this way to tell me to *otva li.*"

His jaw tensed. "What does that mean? You know I don't speak Russian."

I smiled. "It means fuck off, whereas to fuck would be *ebat.* I would rather we *ebat'sya* than you *otva li.*"

He crossed his arms over his chest, his gaze dropping to his feet. He studied them as if he'd spotted something fascinating. "Is it a power thing? Is that it?"

His head slowly lifted, the blue eyes finding mine again. I was momentarily shaken by the intensity in them. It must have been for that reason that the truth spilled unwittingly from my lips. "I have no power!"

He snorted and glanced toward the door. I was losing him. He was already planning his escape. Perhaps he was right, and I was trying to exert the only power I could in a world where I had none, using my face and my body — the only attributes I had apart from my dancing talent. I should let him leave. I should never have lured him there in the first place. I didn't know how long Igor and Mikhail were going to be gone. And bringing Max into Dmitry's radar didn't even bear thinking about. It was risky. It was dangerous. It was selfish, stupid, and reckless. But right now, I wasn't thinking with my brain; I was thinking with my cock. I was remembering how incredibly good it had felt to get fucked by him. He was an aggressive lover, a man who took what he wanted, but yet was still considerate enough to think of his partner's pleasure. Our bodies had fit together perfectly, and I wanted more. One more electric sexual experience before I ghosted him. With him right in front of me, I yearned for it.

I stood up, letting the robe slip off my shoulders to pool on the floor by my feet. I lifted my chin as I stood in front of him completely naked, my obvious arousal clearly on display. "Surely, you can stay for a little while?"

His body froze. But his eyes were moving. They were darting over every inch of my exposed body as if he couldn't make a decision which part to focus on first. His gaze heated, the same way it had back in the dressing room. He wanted me. There was no denying that. It just boiled down to whether he had the strength of will to walk away. Max let out a huff of breath. "Fucking hell! You're..." He swallowed, his gaze now focused on my crotch, my cock giving an answering twitch of appreciation at the interest.

"I'm what?"

"You know."

"It would be nice to hear it."

He spoke slowly as if the words were being forced out of him by torture. "You know you're fucking hot. I mean, your body, it's amazing." He waved his hands in front of him as if he'd lost the ability to put it into words.

"Thank you." I meant it. I'd heard it before, but from the mouth of someone who'd been ready to lynch me moments before, it somehow meant more. Plus, he didn't strike me as a man who gave out compliments that readily.

He moved forward, his lips on a collision course for mine. I stepped back and shook my head, causing Max's face to cloud over with confusion. "Why do you have a problem with kissing?"

I met his stare, refusing to look away. "Why do you have a problem with alcohol?"

He laughed. "I don't. It's all in your head."

I rolled my eyes and gestured to the jeans and shirt he was wearing. "Your turn. All I got to see was your cock the other day. I want to see more."

His hands moved straight to his shirt buttons. Funny how a little nakedness had completely eradicated his will to leave. I watched without comment as he stripped his shirt off before making short work of the bottom half of his body, until he too stood there naked. I did the same to him as he'd done to me: looking my fill and taking in the hairy chest and thick biceps before letting my gaze travel down over his abs to his cock. Even semi-erect, it was a good size, but then I'd already known that from when he'd been inside me. My asshole twitched in anticipation of it happening again. Very soon. Max seemed to mistake my silence for disapproval as he looked almost apologetic. "I don't have a dancer's body."

I dropped to my knees, delighting in Max's sharp intake of breath as he realized my intention. I lifted my hand, letting my fingers graze the hair stretching from his bellybutton to where it encircled his cock. "Looks fine to me." Leaving my hand resting on his abdomen, I leaned forward, stretching out my tongue and grazing his cock before I retracted it. Despite the fact that I'd barely made contact, the muscles underneath my hand quivered wildly. I sat back on my haunches, meeting Max's gaze with a smirk. "Anyone would think you'd never had your cock sucked before."

The glower was back, but it looked forced this time as if he was trying to be annoyed with me and not quite succeeding. "I think I'll prefer you with your mouth full. At least I'll be saved from being on the receiving end of your wicked tongue."

I threw my head back and laughed. Genuinely laughed for the first time in ages. "Darling, you're about to feel the full brunt of my wicked tongue, and you'll thank me for it. Now say please, and I'll consider it."

He looked like he had no intention of doing any such thing. I leaned in, letting my tongue trail over the delicate underside of his cock, but only for a second before I withdrew again. Then I sat back and looked at him. "I'm not hearing you."

"Please." The word sounded as if it had been squeezed out through tightly pressed lips.

"Now, that wasn't so hard, was it?"

His cheeks flushed, but his eyes glittered. "I think I might hate you."

"That's probably for the best." Before he could think to question what I meant, I slid my lips over the head of his cock, my hands moving to his hips to pull him deeper. He went willingly, a shudder reverberating through his body as I took him deep into my throat. I was going to give him the best blow job he'd ever had. From the moans and shudders I was getting as I worked him expertly, my lips and tongue coordinating with the movement of my hand on his balls, I doubted very much that he'd have argued the fact.

Just at the point where the tightening of his muscles and the taste of precum on my tongue announced his orgasm to be close, I stopped. I let his cock slide out of my mouth with an obscene popping sound and sat back to stare up into his dazed face. "Still hate me?"

There wasn't even the slightest hesitation. "Yes."

I laughed and held out my hand. "Condom?"

Max crouched down, reaching across the floor to where he'd left his jeans and extracted one from his wallet. He passed it across silently, along with a packet of lube before rising to his feet again. I kept my gaze locked on his as I rolled the condom over his cock, my body twitching with the need to have him buried inside me again. I added the lube before gesturing to the chair. "Sit down."

His eyes flicked to the adjoining door. "No bedroom. Why am I not surprised?" Despite his words, he did as he'd been told, seating himself on the chair, his stiff cock pointing straight up in the air as he braced his feet on the floor. I reached behind myself, using the remnants of the lube on my fingers to add extra before straddling him. I braced my hands on his shoulders, lowering myself slowly until the head of his cock nudged my asshole. I took a deep breath and pushed down, watching the ecstasy on his face as his cock slid home. His hands trailed over my back, kneading the muscles before moving lower to grasp my ass cheeks, his head dipping so that he could nuzzle my neck. I moved forward, giving him better access at the same time my chest pushed against his. I smiled as his hair rasped over my skin. "Fuck me, Max. Fuck me hard."

His lips stilled on my neck, the words he spoke producing a pleasant vibration. "Isn't this where you're meant to tell me that you have limited time? I might start thinking that you're not as cold as you pretend to be, if you're not careful."

I gyrated my hips, easing my body almost entirely off his cock before slamming it back down. "Do I feel cold to you?"

Max's groan was long and loud, his fingers flexing against my ass as he began to thrust. I looped my arms around his neck and held on for dear life, letting him do most of the work but using my position on top to prevent him from driving too deep, too soon. My eyelashes fluttered closed, and I concentrated on feeling, wanting to imprint every moment of this experience into my memory, every pant, every moan, every flex of muscles, every slide of his cock against my prostate, every place in which our bodies touched, the heat gathering between us.

Lips touched my ear. "Hold on."

My eyes snapped open just in time to see the world tip as Max stood, his cock still embedded in my ass. It was an impressive feat, given the fact we were the same height. He took a couple of steps forward before lowering me onto the rug. His knees fit between my thighs, and then he was braced on his arms, surging back into me. I stared up at him. I hated to be on my back. There was something about the position I'd never liked. But with his hips moving rapidly, every thrust sending a spark of pleasure through my body, it was hard to summon the energy to protest.

I wrapped a hand around my cock and watched him through lowered lashes. In the heat of passion, he was gorgeous: all flushed skin and straining muscles, his teeth biting into his lip as he thrust deep. I wrapped my thighs around his waist, using the superior strength of my thigh muscles to drive our bodies together harder. He wasn't having that. He grabbed my thighs, pushing them up to my shoulders and discovering how flexible I was as he pounded into me. I came first, my cum painting my stomach as he collapsed on top of me, his body shaking with the force of his orgasm. Fingers stroked my skin as he struggled to get his breathing back under control.

I closed my eyes again, trying to force back the cold fingers of reality as they inserted themselves into my brain. I wanted to revel in the feeling of the warm body draped over mine for a few more seconds. I wanted to take time to process the fact that I'd allowed him to take charge without even a single word of argument. But it was no good. There was only so long you could keep rational thoughts at bay. I pushed him off, wriggling out from underneath him and reaching for my robe. I wrapped it around me and belted it tightly, feeling better once I was no longer naked. Then I gathered up Max's clothes and dropped them on top of him. "Time to go."

He rolled onto his back, and I averted my gaze from the sight of the condom-covered cock, his erection subsiding. His eyes widened. "Wow! I thought I'd at least get to the minute mark after coming before you threw me out. But there he is, *my cold Russian.* Back with a vengeance as soon as he's gotten what he wanted. And to hell with everyone else." Max propped himself up on one elbow, making no move to get dressed. "You should think about hiring a prostitute next time. Then you won't get all this unnecessary drama. You can just pay them, and they'll leave."

My brain had stalled on the words "my cold Russian." He'd meant them as an insult, but there was something so possessive about them, so intimate, that they'd sent a strange thrill coursing through my body, and I was alarmed to discover I liked it. I liked it a lot.

I forced myself to concentrate on the rest of what he'd said, searching for the chink in his armor that I could exploit to make him leave before Dmitry got back and shit really hit the fan. His last words provided the perfect opportunity. I strolled over to the table where I'd left my wallet, grabbing a handful of notes without bothering to count how much it amounted to — more than a hundred pounds if I had to hazard a guess, and threw them at him. "There you go!"

Max shook his head, climbing to his feet angrily, the used condom dropping to the floor. He peeled a twenty-pound note from his chest, and it fluttered to the ground to join the condom. "You really are a piece of work! Do you know that?" He bent down to retrieve his clothes, stepping into his jeans angrily. "You think you can snap your fingers and you get everything you want: money, fame" — he lifted his head from where he was fastening the buttons on his shirt — "a dick up the ass. I have no idea why I was stupid enough to come here. It — "

"Why did you?" I should have let him rant, then leave. By engaging him in conversation, I was prolonging it.

"Because..." He forced one foot into his shoe."...I keep thinking that there must be more to you. That somewhere behind that mask you wear, there's a living, breathing human being capable of actual emotions."

"There isn't." They were two of the most difficult words I'd ever had to say. I lit a cigarette, careful to make sure that my hands didn't tremble. I held it to my lips and inhaled, letting the nicotine smooth away the edges of emotions I was pretending not to feel. Max was almost dressed. A few more seconds and he'd be gone, safe from possible harm and hating me enough that he wouldn't come near me again. Mission accomplished. A burning started in my chest as I watched him head for the door.

He turned at the last minute, the anger having given way to a thoughtful expression. "Maybe you're my karma."

"What do you mean?"

"I have one-night stands" — his face twisted — "a lot of them. And they often want more when I don't. So I guess the fact that it's the other way around serves me right." He lifted his hand, revealing a twenty-pound note clutched in his fist. "I'm taking this one, by the way. Not for services rendered, but for the cab money I wasted coming here." He paused as if he was waiting to see whether I'd argue. When I said nothing, did nothing, he left.

I collapsed back into the chair, my fingers gripping the cigarette so tightly it started to bend. I wished I could rewind, back to the part where I'd allowed my lust to get the better of me. If I could, I'd make better choices. Choices that wouldn't hurt someone else and in turn myself. Unfortunately, there was no turning back the clock.

Chapter Five

Max

"Sweetheart, can you set the table?"

"Sure, Mum." I dutifully placed a knife and fork at either side of the two placemats on the dining room table. Dinner was our Wednesday night routine. My mum would cook, and we'd eat together. Just the two of us. It had started off as a Thursday, but then Thursday became *two drinks for the price of one night* at my local bar, which was not only cheaper but also had the added bonus of enticing sexually adventurous students through its doors. They were easy pickings, particularly with a great deal of alcohol in them. So we'd swapped nights. Of course I hadn't told my mum the real reason. She wouldn't approve. I think I'd said it had something to do with work, and she'd believed me.

My mum breezed in, carrying two plates full of hot food, which she deposited on the table. "Paella. One of your favorites."

I smiled at her. "It certainly is. Do you have any beers in?"

Her face fell. "I thought maybe for once you might not drink."

"What's that supposed to mean?"

Her hands curled reflexively around the back of the chair. "Just that I've noticed that you've been drinking more recently. I'm worried, Max, that's all. You never used to drink this heavily. Maybe after James left, but—"

"Don't mention his name!" The words came out unnecessarily sharp, and I immediately felt guilty. But she knew better than to bring him up. It was a subject that had never been, nor ever would be, up for discussion. Even more than ten years later, the wounds hadn't healed. "And I don't drink that much." *Christ! First Valentin and now my own mother is having a go at my drinking.* Okay, so maybe I was drinking more frequently than I used to, but it wasn't as if I was an alcoholic. People needed to get off my back about it.

I sat down, giving up on the idea of a beer with dinner to relax me. It would only make my mother think she was right. I made an effort to change the subject as my mum seated herself in the chair opposite, her expression still one of concern. "How's Auntie Felicity? Did she manage to sort out the problem with her car?"

We spent the next twenty minutes chatting about relatives and what my mum had been up to in the last week. When she'd finished telling me about her hairdresser Ned's new boyfriend and their upcoming marriage in the spring, I braced myself, knowing with a sick sense of inevitability where the conversation would go next.

Sure enough, my mum hesitated before launching into it

anyway, her fingers curling around my arm. "And guess what! Ned told me he has a friend who's gay. He's thirty, and he's just started dating again after a long-term relationship ended over a year ago. He has his own business, and he showed me a picture. He's really good-looking. Gorgeous blue eyes. I think he's got Italian heritage. Ned suggested that you might want to go on a date with him."

I stared at her, doing my best to remember that she only had my best interests at heart. I'd never even met Ned. Yet apparently the two of them had been having a heart-to-heart over her poor single son. Only that same poor, single son was perfectly happy to remain so. "No, thanks. I'm fine as I am."

My mother sighed sadly, patting my hand. "It's been such a long time since..." She stopped before she said his name again. "Well, you know. I just want to see you happy... that's all."

I leaned forward, putting every iota of sincerity I could manage into my expression. "I know, Mum. But I'm fine. Honestly, I am."

She sighed again; this one was even longer. "So there's no one?"

Dark hair, hazel eyes, and perfect lips curled up into a mocking smirk flashed into my head. I pushed the image away and shook my head. "No, not at the moment."

* * * *

I paused at the entrance to the pub. I'd figured a pint before bed on my way home wouldn't hurt, but whether it was my mother's voice or a certain Russian one, I found myself wanting to prove them both wrong. It wasn't like I *needed* alcohol. I could go one night without a drink. Neither of them knew what they were talking about. I turned and walked in the opposite direction, nodding a greeting to a regular who was just on their way in.

Back at home, I lay on the sofa and closed my eyes. I knew what I'd see. It was the same thing I'd been seeing ever since I'd left his hotel room two days ago. Valentin. It was also the last time I'd caught so much as a glimpse of him. He'd missed rehearsals for the last two days. I'd even considered whether he could be avoiding me, but I doubted that I had made that much of an impact on him, whereas I couldn't seem to get him out of my head. All I could think about was the taste of his skin, the way he'd thrown his head back as he rode my cock, the way he'd looked with his eyes closed when I'd been able to study him without him realizing.

I was bombarded by images from the moment I woke up to the moment I went to sleep: the curve of his ass, the perfection of the lips I wasn't allowed to kiss, the moment he'd stood naked in front of me at the hotel, the robe at his feet, the pointed chin, the patrician nose, the curve of his neck. It was ridiculous. This didn't happen to me. I'd been happy for years to lurch from one quick fuck to the next, never looking back, never thinking about the man

74

I'd had sex with again. So I didn't understand what was going on. What was so different about Valentin that I couldn't simply accept that he didn't want to see me again? He felt like a burr trapped under my skin, an itch that I couldn't get rid of no matter how hard I tried. Yes, he was hot. Yes, he was like no one I'd ever met before, but there were thousands of attractive and unusual men scattered throughout London. So what made him so special? I had all these feelings I wasn't used to having, and I didn't have a clue what to do about them. Even the desire to pick up other men had gone away. I'd been approached by two men, at different times, the night Valentin had rung, both making it perfectly clear that they'd be up for some no-strings fun. I'd waved both of them away, unable to muster the interest. Yet the moment Valentin had called I'd run halfway across London like a man who was at his beck and call.

Despite the way he'd treated me — twice, I knew without a shadow of a doubt that given half a chance, I'd go back for more. If Valentin Bychkov was a disease, then I was well and truly infected — with no cure in sight.

* * * *

My heart thudded as he took his place center stage. After three days of not seeing him, my eyes devoured him hungrily. He looked just as gorgeous and untouchable as ever. The irony of thinking that, after I'd fucked him twice, wasn't lost on me. He was the only man I'd ever met who could switch from totally unapproachable to naked or half-naked and offering himself up, at the drop of a hat. He was dressed in white today: white ballet tights, the same scraps of material adorning his throat as ever, just in a different color. I couldn't help feeling that black suited him more. He took his opening stance, his arms held out to the side, and I waited for him to start dancing.

One of the assistants in the sound booth coughed. *Fuck!* He was waiting for the music. Which wasn't going to happen unless I took my head out of my ass and started it. I fumbled with the controls, noting the theater director's frown as he looked over, no doubt wondering what was taking so long.

The first few notes filled the auditorium, and I watched Valentin dance. Even though I'd seen the routine numerous times, I never got bored of watching. There was something different about him today though. Not being an expert, I couldn't pinpoint what it was. Was it linked in some way to his absence for the last couple of days? Was he ill? Despite my preoccupation, I avoided any further mistakes, and Valentin had already turned to leave the stage, almost before the last note had faded.

The rest of the day passed slowly. Even Glenn seemed less flirty than usual. Either it had finally dawned on him that I wasn't interested, or someone had warned him off. The prime candidate for the latter had to be Noel. If so, I'd have to think of some way of thanking him.

As the last to leave, I killed the lights in the sound booth before heading toward the exit at the end of the auditorium, fighting the urge to visit a certain person's dressing room to see if he was there. When had I turned into such a masochist? When had being belittled and made to feel worthless become an acceptable price for amazing sex? And that was the crux of the matter. It *was* amazing sex. It wasn't just the fact that Valentin had an amazing body and knew exactly how to use it. Our bodies just seemed attuned to each other. We fitted together as if we were two puzzle pieces made entirely for that reason. He might be a shit afterward, but his body didn't lie. I was pretty sure that he hadn't been faking any of his reactions. Nobody was that good an actor. And he probably thought I hadn't noticed the way he'd responded when I'd wrested control from him back in the hotel room, but I had. He wasn't used to it, but he'd gone along with it. To me that spoke volumes about the fact that there was something else going on behind what he wanted the world to see. It was intriguing, and it made me wonder what else there was to discover about him. I wanted to know the man behind the mystery. And if I was wrong about him, well, maybe then, I'd be able to brush my little obsession under the carpet and return to the way life used to be. But I wasn't there yet.

Lost in thought, I almost walked into the man barring my way. My head whipped up—and there was a long way to go—given how much taller he was. It was one of Valentin's bodyguards. I didn't know which one. I'd heard their names mentioned in conversation, but I hadn't exactly gone out of my way to be able to tell them apart. I took a quick glance around, relieved to see that the other one wasn't there. One of them was bad enough to have to deal with. "Excuse me."

When he made no move to step aside, I attempted to go around him. A meaty hand settled on my arm, the fingers squeezing just hard enough to make it clear that I wasn't going anywhere until he allowed it. I gave a covert glance back to the auditorium, hoping there was still someone around who might be able to intervene. There was no one. It was just me and him.

When he spoke, he spoke slowly. It was clear that his command of English wasn't that strong. "You... need... come with me."

"To where?" Was he taking me to see Valentin? A surge of happiness filled my veins at the thought of Valentin sending his bodyguard to collect me. I'd known deep down that despite the things he'd said and done that he did want to see me again. It had been written all over his face. But I'd expected him to hold out for longer than three days. My cock tingled at the thought of getting up close and personal again, and it was hard to keep the smile from my face. I guessed that explained the absence of the other bodyguard: one of them had needed to stay with Valentin.

"Dmitry has... asked for... how do you say... audience with you."

And just like that my bubble was well and truly burst, the throb of desire metamorphosizing into something akin to fear. Dmitry was the man Noel had warned me about. The one who supposedly had links to Bratva. I'd never seen him, but I'd certainly noted a tension in the theater after his arrival that hadn't been there previously, and his name had been whispered in numerous corners, all with that strange mixture of reverence and caution. I'd put it down to his financial investment, meaning that he had a great deal of sway over what happened on a day-to-day basis. But what if the rumors were true? What if, ridiculous as it might sound, he was a member, or even worse, a leader in the Russian mob? If so, then a summons from him couldn't be anything good. And why would he want to see me of all people? Did he know I'd had sex with Valentin? The bodyguards had been there so it was entirely possible. Was he going to warn me off? Tell me to stay away from him? Or something worse? I swallowed, trying to force saliva back into a suddenly dry throat. "And if I say no?"

The fingers still wrapped around my arm tightened further, and the man smiled. At least I think it was meant to be a smile, but the scar running from his temple, through one eye, and extending down as far as his lip, turned it into something much more sinister. "Not option."

He tugged on my arm, and I was forced to follow him down the corridor. "You can let go, you know." To my surprise he did. "Where are we going?"

"Dmitry's office."

He had an office? What was a Russian doing with an office in the Royal Opera House? "What does he want to see me about?" No response. I tried again. "Is Valentin there?"

Realizing he wasn't going to answer, I fell silent, concentrating on keeping up with the man's massive stride. I didn't recognize the part of the building where we were now, my heart rate increasing steadily with each and every closed door we'd passed through that now lay between me and the exit. I should have run back into the auditorium. Now, I doubted I'd be able to find the way out on my own, even if I tried. A sick dread settled in my stomach.

Then there was a door in front of us—plain, with no placard— and bodyguard number one was raising his hand to knock. A muffled voice gave an instruction to enter, and I was shepherded through the door, a firm hand in the center of my back giving no choice but to continue walking forward.

I quickly took stock of my surroundings, my shirt damp with nervous sweat. Whatever I'd expected to see, it wasn't the scene that greeted me. The room was empty save for two men. The other bodyguard was standing over by the window, his massive bulk blocking out most of the light that should have been streaming into the room. Another man, who looked to be somewhere in his early fifties, lounged in a leather chair behind a huge wooden desk, a glass of whiskey in one hand and a lit cigar in the other. This had to be the fearsome Dmitry Gruzdev. Except right now, with the smile on his face and his casual demeanor, he looked more like a kind uncle. He gestured to the chair on the other side of the desk. "Take a seat, my friend. And don't look so worried. We are here to have a chat. Nothing more."

Although his English was practically perfect, he had a much heavier accent than Valentin did. I sat in the chair he'd indicated, still too nervous to return his smile. He waved a hand at an expensive-looking crystal decanter. "Mikhail, pour the man a drink. He looks like he needs one." His eyes fastened on me, smiling blue eyes with laughter lines at the corner. "Do you drink whiskey, my friend?" I nodded, and the bodyguard who'd escorted me there poured a good measure and pushed the glass across the desk toward me. I wrapped my fingers around it. Dmitry gestured toward it impatiently. "Try it. It is very good. Single malt and twenty years old. I highly recommend it."

I obediently lifted it to my mouth and took a sip, pulling a face of appreciation that would have been the same even if I'd discovered it tasted like shit. It didn't. It was by far the best whiskey I'd ever tasted. Probably the most expensive as well. "It's very good."

Dmitry's smile grew as if he was pleased by the compliment. "I hope Mikhail was polite to you in extending my invitation?"

I rubbed at my arm, still able to feel where the man's fingers had dug in, my face obviously giving away some of what I was feeling.

Dmitry tutted, his eyes darting over to where Mikhail had joined the other bodyguard, the two men bracketing the window like bookends. "I apologize. Sometimes, they have no finesse. Unless I give them explicit instructions, they start having these" — he twirled a finger by his temple — "crazy ideas. They make me look bad."

I nodded and managed a small smile as I sought to process the fact that Dmitry was being polite and apologizing for Mikhail's actions. Did it mean that he was nowhere near as bad as people said? Or that I had to be careful about trusting what was on the surface? To say I was conflicted was an understatement. I took another sip of the whiskey, enjoying the smoothness as it slipped down my throat. "That's okay. No harm done. I'm not sure though why you need to speak to me?" Dmitry took a long drag of his cigar before answering, the room rapidly filling with the thick, acrid smoke.

"Valentin, of course. I hear you have taken quite an interest in my... charge?"

Nerves kicked in again. What if all this friendliness was nothing but an act to lull me into a false sense of security? "What do you mean?"

The hand holding the cigar waved in the direction of the bodyguards, leaving a trail of smoke behind in the air. "It is their job to share security concerns. They, of course, informed me that you were *alone* with Valentin in his dressing room."

I sat back in the chair, my brain struggling to put all the pieces together and work out what I was supposed to say. He'd only mentioned the dressing room. Did that mean he didn't know about the hotel room?

While I was still trying to think of something to say, Dmitry leaned forward in his chair. "You like him, yes?"

"Yeah... I mean, yeah, he's..."

He stubbed the cigar out into the ashtray on the corner of the desk, his eyebrows rising. "Good. You will accompany us to a party tonight."

"A party?" I failed miserably at keeping the surprise out of my voice. I'd been expecting the worst, that at the very least I was going to be threatened, and instead I was being invited to a party. "That's very kind, but—"

"I insist. Any friend of Valentin's is a friend of mine. We will drink more whiskey. We will relax, and we will have a good time. Yes?"

I couldn't stop myself from asking the question. "Will Valentin be there?"

Dmitry winked. "Of course. I would not invite you otherwise. I expect he will be pleased to see you."

I had serious doubts about whether that would be true. But strange as it was to be invited to a party by a man who was supposed to be scary but had been nothing but nice, I did want to see Valentin again. The chance to get close to him again was too good an opportunity to turn down. "I need to go home and get changed. If you let me know the address, then I'll — "

He waved his hand dismissively. "Pfftt. It is not that formal a party. Mikhail and Igor will take you there."

The twin mounds of muscle immediately moved forward to flank me on either side. Dmitry said something to them in Russian, and they both nodded. He turned his attention back to me and smiled. "I have boring business phone calls to make, so I will travel in a separate car. I will see you there, my friend." Then I was being led from the room, unable to shake the feeling that despite Dmitry's apparent niceness, I was being led to my execution rather than a party. What had he said to them in Russian? There was no point in asking them. One of them rarely spoke, and the other had already made it clear that he had no time for my questions.

* * * *

I'd never been more relieved to arrive at a public place — the venue, a basement nightclub in Camden. The journey to get there had proved excruciatingly awkward, sandwiched as I was between Tweedledee and Tweedledum with neither of them speaking or seemingly willing to offer even the slightest bit of information about where we were going or what I could expect to find when we got there.

I was made to stand on the pavement and wait while another car drew up and Dmitry got out. At some point, he'd gained a third musclebound guardian, the new addition even bulkier than my own two travel companions. Dmitry strolled past with barely a glance in our direction, talking loudly into a phone in Russian.

A hard shove in the middle of my back was the first indication that we were meant to follow. We headed down a dark set of stairs, the heavy thud of bass growing gradually louder the further we descended into the club. A bored-looking cashier waved us past without ceremony. It looked like this was a private party. We headed through a door to the main part of the club, and I stopped dead, struggling to take in what I was seeing.

There couldn't have been more than fifty people there. With a club designed to hold hundreds, it looked decidedly empty. The clientele seemed to consist of men in suits, the majority around Dmitry's age, in their late forties to early fifties. The rest were scantily clad dancers; most of them wearing nothing more than a tiny pair of shorts. Some danced on a pole or podium, their bodies moving sinuously to the music while onlookers leered. Another was draped over the lap of one of the suited men, the older man's hands roaming to places I didn't even want to think about. *What kind of party is this?* At least ninety percent of the dancers were men, but scattered here and there around the room was the occasional topless woman, going largely ignored by the suited men. The women seemed out of place as if they were there for appearance's sake only. Like someone had visited the local strip joint and gathered up a few of the women as some sort of cover story to hide what was really going on.

Dmitry's path took us straight to the bar where a line of bottles was stacked up, with the intention of people helping themselves. I gawped at the nearest dancer on a pole, his limbs gyrating and pulsing to the music as he effortlessly maneuvered himself around it. It wasn't his dance skills though that made me stare. It was the fact that I recognized him. He was one of the ballet dancers I'd watched rehearse onstage every day. How did he go from ballet dancer during the day to pole dancer at night?

"I don't understand."

Dmitry turned, his phone conversation having come to an end, dragging his gaze away from a small, blond twink writhing around a pole. *Is he gay?* Or was I imagining things? I hadn't seen him so much as glance at any of the large-breasted women yet. He pushed a glass of dark liquid into my hand that I assumed was whiskey. "What don't you understand, my friend?"

"I recognize some of these dancers. They're from the show." I'd spotted at least two more who looked familiar. "Why are they here?"

Dmitry clinked his glass against mine before taking a long swallow, his gaze shrewder than it had been back in the office. "They're partying. You think they are not allowed?"

They didn't look like they were partying. They looked like they were working. And although I wouldn't go as far as saying they looked miserable, there was a certain deadness to their eyes as if they didn't really want to be there. "No. I just—"

Dmitry's lips curved into a smile, but there was a glint in his eye that I didn't like the look of. Maybe it was the dim lighting, but he no longer had the demeanor of a kind uncle. I glanced toward the door we'd come through to find that Igor and Mikhail had stationed themselves on either side of it. It was clear that there was no leaving without Dmitry's say-so. The question was when would that be, and why had he been so adamant about me attending in the first place? Because there was no dressing it up any longer. He may have extended it as an invitation, but I'd never had any choice in the matter, simply the illusion of it.

I took a gulp of the whiskey, the need to calm my nerves winning out over the voice in my head that suggested it would be far more sensible to stay sober so that I could keep my wits about me. I scanned the room again, averting my gaze from where a man with white hair and a huge bald spot had his hand down the shorts of a dancer who looked at least forty years younger than he was. I felt sick. Was Valentin even there? Or had that been a ruse simply to get me to come without a struggle?

Given what was going on at the party, it was probably better that he wasn't. I couldn't stop myself from asking the question though. "Where's Valentin? I thought you said he would be here?"

Dmitry moved closer, his arm pressing against mine. I forced myself to remain still, despite the natural inclination to put space between us. He spoke directly into my ear, someone having turned the music up. "That is a very good question. Where is my Valentin?" He lifted his arm to point. "Ah, there he is. He has been taking some... private time."

I followed the direction of his finger to where a door at the back of the room had opened. Valentin was indeed stepping out of it, but it wasn't to him that my eyes were drawn first. It was the man with his arm around Valentin, his face nuzzled into his neck. He was younger than the majority of the party guests, but I would have still put him at mid-forties, and in my opinion, he was still too old to have his hand curled possessively around Valentin's bare biceps as if he owned him.

There were no shorts for Valentin. He was dressed as he usually was: full-length ballet tights and nothing on his top half.

As I continued to watch, he bent to whisper something in the other man's ear and then pushed him gently away. The man blew him a kiss and then walked toward the bar. I'd been so caught up in watching the scene unfold that I'd forgotten about Dmitry until his voice sounded in my ear, the silken tones bearing a menace that hadn't been present before. "Valentin is *very* popular. I am sure that *you* of all people understand why."

It was clear that *this* — whatever *this* was — was what I'd been brought to see. I refused to give Dmitry the satisfaction of responding to what he'd just said. Whatever reaction he was hoping for, I wasn't going to give it to him. Not willingly anyway.

Valentin lifted his head, and our eyes met across the room. A multitude of emotions flickered across his face in quick succession. Surprise. Fear. And then finally resignation. His eyes moved to where I knew Dmitry was, still leaning over my left shoulder, his breath hot against my cheek. I dreaded to think what expression his face held. Then Valentin schooled his face, his usual blank expression falling back into place as easily and quickly as if he'd flicked a switch. He turned away, almost as if he'd never seen me in the first place. Dmitry came closer, our faces almost touching. "Hmmm... how strange. He doesn't appear very pleased to see you after all."

My nails dug into my hands with the effort to stay still and to stay silent as Dmitry twisted the knife. He'd known Valentin would ignore me. Even so, I was still tracking him. I needed to know what he'd do next. Just because he'd been in a private room with someone didn't mean that I should be jumping to conclusions. I watched as he crossed the room, noting the effect he had on people as he passed, admiring glances sticking to him like glue. Then a man stepped into his path, his hand reaching out to cup Valentin's bare shoulder, his fingers stroking the skin. I was filled with an immediate and irrational seething rage, the urge to rush over there and pull the man's hand from his shoulder, finger by finger, burning me up inside. They talked. Valentin nodded, and then they were retracing the path that Valentin had just taken, back into the room. The door closing behind them.

Bile rose in my throat. There was no denying it now. Even if I wanted to. He might not be dressed in tiny shorts or draped over the lap of one of the men whose age was only surpassed by their bank balance, but his role was the same. I was upset, without having any right to be. He'd made no promises, offered no assurances. On the contrary, he'd done nothing but push me away, but the emotion still wouldn't go away. Reality hit. There was no hiding it anymore. Max Farley, the man who never did relationships, had hoped for something more with an exotic half-Russian dancer who couldn't care less. Except... there'd been genuine emotion on his face when he'd first seen me. I didn't know what to believe any more.

Fingers curled around the glass of whiskey I'd barely touched, plucking it from my grasp and placing it back on the bar. "I think it is time you went home, my friend. You seem... tired. Perhaps it was... inconsiderate of me to offer a party invitation. You look like you could use an early night." The words might have seemed genuine if it wasn't for the slight smirk playing on the man's lips. He knew exactly what I was feeling, and the message was clear. I'd gotten too close to Valentin for his liking, and he wanted to make sure I knew that Valentin belonged to everyone, yet no one at the same time. That what we'd shared in the dressing room had meant nothing. He didn't seem to know about the hotel room, and I hoped it stayed that way.

I nodded, forcing a smile. If we were still going to play this game of politeness and ignore the undercurrents, then I could play too. "I think you're right. Thank you for your kind invitation, but I think I've seen enough to know that this is not my sort of party." Given that I wasn't over forty, and I didn't get off on groping boys who were young enough to be my son.

I gave one last glance to the door where I'd last seen Valentin. It remained firmly shut. *What would I see if I opened it?* Valentin against the wall, just like in the dressing room, back arched while the man fucked him, or the man on a chair while Valentin rode him, like in the hotel. It didn't bear thinking about, and it made hot fingers of jealousy creep their way down my spine.

I walked toward the exit, pretending a great deal more

casualness than I was feeling and noting the hesitation in the body language of the two bodyguards as I approached. Now I'd seen what was going on, it was easy to see why they wouldn't want just anybody wandering in there off the street. The question was whether they were going to stop me from leaving, whether Dmitry was playing games, or if he truly intended to allow me to leave. I held my breath as Mikhail looked over to where I'd left Dmitry. There was a pause of what could only have been seconds but felt like much longer. Then he stepped aside. I hurried through the door.

The bored cashier was still there. She raised an eyebrow at my hasty exit. "Party not to your liking?"

I gave her no more than a fleeting glance, eager to get out of there. "Something like that." I took the stairs to ground level, two at a time, only slowing when I was back out on the street and at least a good fifty meters away. I took a moment to breathe in the fresh air, then I headed for the nearest bar.

Chapter Six

Valentin

I'd been enduring Dmitry's parties for years. They were never going to be fun. But at least in the last few years, I'd found the means to ensure that they were no more than tiresome. That certainly wouldn't have been the way I'd have described them back when they'd first started. As a naive teenager, I would have done almost anything to avoid them. Apart from giving up dancing, and unfortunately that would have been the price I'd have had to pay. Sometimes I even met the occasional decent man there, like Claude, the suave Frenchman, who'd had very different reasons for attending than most of the other clientele, and could prove to be my salvation one day if everything went to plan.

I normally spent the first hour avoiding having to spend time with anyone, choosing to sit at the bar instead and master the art of looking unapproachable. Although, I'm sure the majority would agree that I'd already mastered it. But Jeremy had been particularly insistent tonight, and I'd wanted to get my time with him over and done with. Perhaps, for one night, I'd switch things around, and get the necessary evils out of the way and *then* spend the rest of the night at the bar. Or perhaps I could even convince Dmitry to let me leave early. I turned my attention back to Jeremy as fingers inched their way slowly up my thigh. I put up with it. Even when they brushed the material-covered mound of my cock.

"Take it out! Please. I want to see."

I regarded the red-faced man in front of me with barely concealed irritation. He had one hand wrapped around his cock, furiously fisting it, as his eyes—and other hand—roved all over my body.

I gave him a disapproving look. "That's not the deal, Jeremy. You know that." I deliberately shifted my chair back, causing the hand that had been on my crotch to have no choice but to retract. It was either that or remain suspended in midair. "I let you touch, but I've always made it clear that I'm not taking my clothes off for you. What will it be? If that's not enough for you anymore, then..." I let the veiled threat hang there, knowing it would be enough.

He scooted his chair forward, his hand moving even faster on his cock. "Sorry. Sorry. It's enough. I get carried away." His hand dropped back on my thigh, the fat, sweaty fingers crawling upward again like some sort of out-of-control spider. "I'm so close. Talk dirty to me."

I fixed my gaze on the wall over his shoulder. I would, but only because it would make him come faster. Once he had, I could get

94

rid of him. "Stroke that big, fat cock. Yeah, like that. Just like that. You're so good at that. I want to see your cum so bad. I bet it's going to be a huge load."

Jeremy began to pant, his hips thrusting up to fuck his hand while his fingers continued to grope at my flaccid cock. Sweat poured off him, soaking the neck of the shirt that he still wore. "Speak Russian to me."

I lowered my voice, putting a husky tone into it. *"Budet i na nashey ulitse prazdnik."* It meant nothing. Directly translated, it meant the sun will shine on our street too, the Russian version of the English proverb, every dog has his day. Jeremy groaned, his body trembling as he reached the brink of orgasm, his hand leaving my crotch to pinch my nipple. "More. Please."

I leaned forward, running my tongue along my lips in a provocative fashion. *"Bez truda, ne vitashish i ribku iz pruda."* No pain. No gain. It amused me no end to spout meaningless rubbish and have them think that I was talking dirty in Russian. He gasped, and I moved away as cum splattered his shirt. I examined my fingernails as he cleaned himself up and sorted out his clothing.

Once he was relatively decent, I stood up, forcing a bright smile. "Ready? You don't want to miss too much of the party." I already had one hand on the door when he came up behind me, nuzzling into my neck, his tongue darting out to taste the skin, as the door swung open. I kept my shudder at bay, my gaze automatically searching the room for men I didn't recognize. Men who wouldn't be quite so easy to manipulate as the regulars I had wrapped around my little finger.

My gaze drifted over to the bar, meeting a familiar pair of eyes belonging to the last person I'd ever have expected to see there: Max. He stared right back at me, his expression making it all too clear how he felt about the scene unfolding in front of him. Shock held me immobile, Jeremy taking it as encouragement to get even closer, his groin rubbing against my thigh like some randy dog. *What is Max doing here? Had he come looking for me? But then, how had he known where to find me?* Then I registered the man right behind him with a smug smile on his face. Dmitry had brought him there. My blood ran cold. If Dmitry knew about Max, then he was in danger. I'd put him in danger. And if I showed that he meant anything to me at all, that I had any sort of attachment to him, then I'd be making things ten times worse.

I turned my head away, the imprint of Max's hurt expression ricocheting around my head as I peeled Jeremy away from my body and assured him that of course I would have time for him at the next party. I always had time for him as long as he stuck to the rules. He blew a kiss in my direction and strutted away, peacocking the fact that he'd been allowed to spend time with Valentin Bychkov. I'd managed to convince Dmitry that my attention was far more valuable if I remained exclusive to a small and select bunch of men. It meant that those men got to boast, while others who weren't on the list could only cast jealous looks in their direction.

Little did Dmitry know that those men who made it to my list had been picked because they were easy to manipulate. They were easy to string along, always hoping that they'd get more than the tiny crumbs I offered them: a touch here and a stroke there. Just enough for them to have enough hope that one day I might allow them more. And the real beauty of the plan was that none of them ever dared to complain. To do that would be to admit that the previous time they'd spent with Valentin Bychkov wasn't what they'd made it out to be. So far it had a hundred percent success rate. I dreaded the day though that two of them might compare notes and realize that they weren't the only one that I held at arm's length. On that day, I'd have an awful lot of explaining to do to Dmitry. But so far it hadn't happened.

Every now and again, I dropped someone from the list and added someone new, to give it a bit more authenticity. Dmitry was happy. The men were happy — mostly. And as for me... well, I wasn't happy exactly, but I survived without having to share my body with anyone who wasn't of my choosing. That thought immediately brought Max to mind, the last man I'd chosen to let close. Twice. I wanted to turn my head and see if he was still there. If so, was he watching me? Was there hatred burning out of his eyes? I didn't turn. I kept my gaze averted from the last place I'd seen him. It was better for him if I treated his presence as completely inconsequential.

A man blocked my way. I froze until I realized it was another of the men currently on my list. He hadn't attended the last few parties, either in London, Russia, or in France where the majority happened. Most of the men were rich enough that paying for the exclusive party *and* travel to wherever they happened to be wasn't a problem so it tended to be the same men, no matter what the country. The fact I hadn't seen this one for a good few months was therefore unusual. I'd hoped that for the sake of his wife he might have given them up. I forced a cheery note into my voice. "John! How lovely to see you! It's been a long time." John wasn't his real name. I expected that there wasn't a man in this room who wasn't going by an assumed name.

He tried for a smile, but it was overshadowed by the quiet desperation in his eyes. "Can I spend some time with you?"

In other circumstances, I might have felt sorry for some of these men. Most of them were trapped in a loveless marriage, spending each and every day pretending for whatever reason that they weren't gay and didn't lust after men young enough to be their sons or grandsons. I tilted my head to the side, pretending to give the question a great deal of consideration before finally nodding.

Then I led him back to the room I'd just left, grateful that my status had made it easy to demand privacy, unlike the other poor

98

wretches scattered around the club who had no choice but to endure being groped in public, either because they needed the money, or because they'd been told in no uncertain terms that it was a part of their dance contract. I'd long since come to the conclusion that there wasn't anything I could do to help them. They had to have known, on some level, the path they'd chosen when they threw their lot in with Dmitry Gruzdev. Or perhaps it simply made me feel better to believe that. Then there were the women who got dragged into these parties with the opposite problem to the dancers. They were left wondering why they'd been brought there at all when they were virtually ignored. Occasionally one of the men might throw them a few crumbs of attention. But on the whole, they spent their time standing around and chatting, or danced while no one watched. Their sole purpose was for Dmitry to be able to claim, when asked, that they were the service offered, rather than the young men. In the end, they were paid for doing very little so I guessed that they wouldn't complain too loudly once they recovered from their egos having been dented.

"Will you suck my cock?"

I shifted my attention back to John, pasting a look of regret on my face. "You know I can't, John. I've told you before. I can't live with the guilt. I've met your wife. How could I face her? How could I talk to her with the same lips that had been wrapped around your cock?"

He undid his trousers, pulling out a long, thin cock that was already hard. I didn't fool myself that that was all about me. No doubt, John had spent the time while he was waiting to intercept me, *playing* with one of the other boys. "But you'll give me a hand job?"

I lowered myself onto the chair. "Of course. But there's no rush. Sit down. Let's catch up before we get to that." The longer I spent with John, the more convincing it was to everyone on the outside, including Dmitry, that more than a hand job had taken place behind closed doors.

I thought about Max again, wondering if he was still out there or whether Dmitry had let him leave. At least I didn't have to worry about him coming anywhere near me again. There was no doubt in my mind that he'd give me a wide berth, exactly as Dmitry intended. The man was clever. He had more than one way of achieving a goal. I should know; I'd been on the receiving end more times than I could count. His techniques for breaking any attachments I might form, no matter how tenuous they might be, were never the most obvious. Why use threats when the truth could suffice? Or at least what Dmitry thought of as the truth.

* * * *

I stared as the name Max flashed up on the screen of my phone. It was the phone that I'd claimed was broken, and had been subsequently replaced by Mikhail. It would take Dmitry at least a few weeks to realize I was still using it, and by that time I'd have come up with some sort of story to cover it. I made no move to answer the call. It was hard to fathom any reason why Max would be calling unless he felt like he was owed some sort of explanation. If that was the case, then there was nothing I could say that was going to make him feel better. The mistake had been made when I'd invited him inside my dressing room. I'd compounded it with my weakness in picking up the phone and inviting him to my hotel room. I couldn't rewind and take back either of those mistakes. For either of us. The phone fell silent while I continued to stare at it. I waited for a few more seconds to see if he would leave a message. He didn't.

I lounged back on the bed and closed my eyes, allowing myself the luxury of remembering the way Max's body had felt against mine, inside mine. My cock gave a twitch, the first of the night despite the number of hands and pairs of eyes that had lingered there. I slid my hand down, doing no more than massaging while I contemplated whether jerking off to the memory of a man I'd fucked twice—but wouldn't or couldn't fuck again—was a good idea.

The phone buzzed. I glanced over. Max again. He was certainly persistent. Against my better judgment, I brought the phone to my ear, connecting the call but not saying anything.

"Are you alone?"

The voice in my ear was slightly slurred. No prizes for guessing where Max had spent the rest of the night. By the lack of background noise, I assumed he'd now returned home. "What answer do you want me to give to that?"

"The truth, Valentin. The truth. If you even know what that is. Stop playing games with me for once and answer the damn question."

Anger I could have coped with. But he sounded more confused than anything. Confused and sad. It made me feel things I didn't want to feel, like guilt and regret. "*Da*, I am alone."

"Are you at the hotel? Or still at the party?" He said the word party as if it left a bitter taste in his mouth. It probably did. I could only imagine what Dmitry's parties looked like to an outsider. I'd been forced to attend them for the last nine years, and I still found them largely unpalatable.

"I'm at the hotel." There was a long silence. I could hear him breathing, but he didn't speak. Maybe he had nothing left to say. "Listen, Max, it's late. Say whatever it is you called to say. Get whatever it is you need to off your chest. Or... hang up."

My demand finally seemed to bring out the anger I'd been expecting since the start of the conversation. "You're an absolute bastard!"

I ignored the sting of the words. "Probably true."

"*You* had the nerve to throw money at me for sex, when all the time... you... you're the one who..."

My fingers tightened around the phone. "Be careful what you say there, Max. You might just hurt my feelings if you're not careful." I made the words sound light, belying the underlying truth to them.

"So, you're not even going to deny it?"

I had two options. The first was to let Max believe that everything he'd seen today was true, that all his assumptions were correct. That would be the sensible thing to do. It would ensure he stayed away from me for the duration of the show, and more importantly, it would keep him safe. The second option was to defend myself. I didn't have to tell him the whole truth, just enough that he'd know that there were two sides to every story.

I opened my mouth, fully intending to lie and say I was a prostitute. I could claim that Max owed me money. That would guarantee him hanging up. But something about the fact he'd bothered to call made me hesitate. He'd seen me with two men tonight, both old enough to be my father, neither of them attractive enough that anyone could ever believe they were genuine relationships. Yet Max was still willing to listen to an alternative explanation. What was it about this man? I kept showing him my absolute worst, and he kept searching for the best. Did that make him stupid? Did it make him an optimist? Or did it mean that somewhere underneath all the layers I'd concocted, he saw the real Valentin? Because no one else ever had.

I laid my head back against the pillow. "Sometimes situations are not black and white, Max. Sometimes there are shades of gray."

"What's that supposed to mean?"

What did it mean? Nothing. Apart from the fact that I couldn't quite bring myself to look as bad as I needed to, in front of a man I was beginning to realize I actually liked.

"Do you know what I think is going on here?"

I sat up again, intrigued by what he was about to say. "Go on. I'm not saying that I will confirm whether you are right, though."

"I think Dmitry is controlling you..." I winced. *Pretty close.* It would seem that Max was more than just a pretty face. "I don't think you have a choice—"

"Everyone has a choice! I'm not a victim, Max. I've never been a victim. It's just that with some choices you pay a higher price than others. That's all. I made my choice seven years ago. I could have walked away at eighteen"—I wasn't going to mention that my arm had been twisted, that walking away would have sounded the death knell for any chance of a dance career—"but I didn't. Now, I live with those choices. And they're *my* choices. No one elses. *Mine.*"

"Did you have sex with those men, tonight?"

I didn't manage to disguise my sharp intake of breath. I hadn't expected him to be so direct, and I also hadn't expected him to have enough insight to ask the question. "Define sex."

Max's sigh reverberated down the phone line. "For fuck's sake! Is there any point? You're probably going to lie to me anyway."

A wave of sadness hit. Max didn't seem to know what to believe. "I won't lie. But you have to ask the right questions."

"Did any of them fuck you?"

"*Njet*. No."

"Did you fuck any of them?"

"*Njet.*"

"But you gave them blow jobs?"

"No." I could almost feel Max's confusion. "And no, they didn't give me one either, before you ask."

"I don't understand."

I swallowed, surprising myself with what I was prepared to admit tonight. "The important thing is the illusion. The important thing is what everyone *thought* was happening, not what actually did. I told you, Max. I'm not a victim." Seconds ticked by without a response from him. "You need to stay away from me."

"Yeah, I got that message loud and clear from Dmitry tonight." There was a sound, as if he was shifting the phone from one hand to another. "I don't want to though."

I smiled, glad he couldn't see me, the admission doing something strange to the rock I had in place of a heart. "But you will? You'll do the sensible thing for both of us. You won't make this any more difficult than it is already?"

"I guess so."

Then we were both silent. I could have gone to sleep, listening to the sound of his breathing. "Max?"

"Yeah?"

"I have to go." Then I hung up and turned off my phone. I wouldn't switch that phone on again.

Chapter Seven

Max

It took a while to register that the auditorium had long since fallen silent. Since the incident culminating in the audience with Dmitry, I'd taken great pains to ensure that I left on time and always while there were still people around. Unfortunately, a few technical hitches with the equipment had warranted the need to stay behind to run a full systems check. If an engineer needed to be called in, then I'd much rather do it sooner than later, especially with rehearsals ending and the show itself starting in a few days. So far though, there didn't appear to be anything major, just a few settings that needed tweaking which was well within my capabilities to sort without external help.

A knock sounded at the open door, and I turned to find a smiling Glenn. He waved at me despite the fact we were only a foot apart. "I was on my way out, and I saw the light. I wasn't sure if you were still here or someone had left it on."

"I'm still here." I probably didn't need to state the obvious, but he seemed determined to make conversation, and it was the best I had. "I'm leaving soon. I just had a couple of things I needed to do first."

He crossed his arms and leaned against the doorjamb. "I'm on my way to a party. Wanna come?"

"A party?" My words sounded hollow. Images of the last party I attended came to mind. Only in place of the boys I'd seen, there was a young, innocent Glenn being groped by perverted old men. "One of Dmitry's?"

He frowned. "Dmitry? Why would *he* invite me to a party? He doesn't even know I exist. I said hello to him once, and he looked straight through me. I'm apparently not good enough to speak to the likes of him."

I relaxed, surprised by how relieved I felt. It seemed like somewhere along the line, Glenn and I had gotten to the point of being friends. "Good! Keep it that way. If he ever does invite you anywhere, say no. Okay?"

His frown grew deeper. "Okay." He shifted slightly. "So, do you wanna come or not?" A flush appeared on his cheekbones. "Oh, and I'm not inviting you to try and get off with you, if that's what you're worried about." He looked away, his cheeks going even redder. "I probably shouldn't admit this, but I had a bit of a thing for you when you first started working here." He waved a hand. "I think it's the whole dark and brooding thing you've got going on."

He paused, and I felt like I had to fill the gap with something.

"Did you? I hadn't noticed." It seemed nicer to lie rather than state that he'd made it plainly obvious. The only way it could have been any clearer was if he'd come up and announced it to my face.

He shrugged as if he wasn't quite buying my story. "Anyway, you don't have to worry... I'm past that now. Everyone can see you've only got eyes for one man around here, and it's certainly not me."

My head shot up, my heart starting to pound. "What do you mean?"

Glenn grinned. "When he dances, you get this dreamy look on your face. I don't blame you. He is hot." His face twisted as if something had left a bad taste in his mouth. "So arrogant though."

"He's not really. He's—" I stopped, realizing I'd fallen right into Glenn's trap by jumping straight to Valentin's defense. I shook my head, trying to cover my tracks as best I could. "Not that I know him."

"Most of the dancers are going to the party, so he'll probably be there as well." Glenn winked. "Just in case that changes your mind. The party's at Jason's house. It's only a few streets away, so I was planning on walking. It'd be nice to have someone to talk to on the way, and I thought you might want to socialize with us for a change."

I'd barely listened to the majority of what he'd said, my brain refusing to gravitate beyond the fact that Valentin might be at the party. *Would he?* But then, even if he was, I wasn't going to receive an enthusiastic welcome from him. I'd agreed to stay away from him. Only I hadn't expected it to be so damn difficult. He was underneath my skin. I'd told him what he wanted to hear, but I hadn't really meant it. Not for one minute. The fact he'd been honest on the phone — or I assumed he had — had only made me want him more. He was the only person I'd had sex with for the last few weeks, and the only person I wanted to. It was suddenly hard to picture myself going back to one-night stands. I didn't know what that meant. I was trying not to think about it.

Realizing Glenn was still waiting for an answer, I affected a casual shrug. "I'm not doing anything else tonight, so I suppose there's no harm in checking out the party. You know, seeing as it's so close." I flicked off the lights in the booth and gave the equipment one last cursory scan to check I hadn't left anything on that could cause a fire hazard. "Lead the way."

Glenn barely stopped talking all the way there. Now that he'd given up on trying to impress me, it seemed as if he was no longer tongue-tied. I found out more about him than I'd ever wanted to, including the occupations of his parents and the fact he had a cat called Harry. It therefore came as a great relief when we finally stood in front of an intercom, waiting for someone to respond and let us in. Three flights of stairs later and we were knocking on the door of an apartment. The door swung open, and a guy I recognized from the theater but had never said two words to appeared in the doorway.

He stood back, seemingly not bothered that Glenn had turned up with an uninvited guest. I followed them both into the living room. Unless there were more people scattered around the apartment, the party guests seemed to consist of seven people, not including Jason, Glenn, and myself, who brought the total to ten. The only thing I was interested in though as I scanned the room was whether one of those seven was Valentin. My heart leaped as I spotted him. He stood in the corner of the room on his own, with no sign of the bodyguards, who were normally less than two steps away. Our gazes clashed, a huge smile crossing my face, even as his remained inscrutable.

He levered himself away from the wall and headed in our direction, swiping a bottle of beer from the table on the way. He was wearing ripped jeans and a thin sleeveless T-shirt. Weirdly, it was the first time I'd seen him dressed in anything other than ballet tights. His feet were still bare though, and he was still fully made up, his customary blue eyeshadow matching the blue of the shirt.

I watched him walk toward me, enjoying the way he moved, all grace and poise. He halted in front of me, his withering glance encompassing Jason and Glenn until they took the hint and moved away. At that point, his scrutiny moved onto me. "Don't smile at me, Max."

My smile grew wider. "I can't help it. Something about you makes me smile."

He shook his head, just the tiniest movement as if he could barely spare the effort it took. "I thought we'd agreed that you were going to stay away from me."

I shrugged. "I came to a party that you happen to be at. It's not like I'm stalking you."

He turned to scan the room, and I followed his gaze. Nobody was remotely interested in what we were doing or saying, so if that's what he was worried about, he had no need. The room was heavy with smoke. It seemed as if Valentin wasn't the only dancer with a nicotine habit. His head was still turned away, and I wanted his attention back on me. "Where're Mikhail and Igor? I don't see them anywhere."

"I gave them the slip."

I laughed at the phrasing. "The slip. That's a weird way of putting it. They're your bodyguards. They're not..." The words died in my throat as another piece of the puzzle clicked into place. "Except they're not, are they? They follow you around to keep an eye on you and report back to Dmitry." He didn't answer, but the truth was there in his eyes and in the fact that he didn't bother to deny it. He held the beer bottle out, and I took it from him. "You tell me that I have an alcohol problem, and then you offer me beer. That seems a bit of a contradiction."

Hazel eyes lingered on my face. There was something about

112

having Valentin Bychkov's full attention that felt like nothing else in the world. Everyone else had ceased to exist. There was only the two of us. He lifted his chin, and I waited for the put-down that was on the way. I was beginning to work out his tells: the haughty expression that came before he unleashed words designed to make people stay away from him. "I said you had an alcohol problem. I didn't say I *cared* about it. Drink yourself to death if you want." He was already moving away before I could respond.

I took a seat on an otherwise empty sofa, my eyes still fixed on Valentin as he retreated to the same corner. He lit a cigarette and steadfastly refused to look my way. A couple of weeks ago, I would have taken it for the snub it was meant to be, but I was beginning to see through it. All of it. It was an act, and if he hadn't wanted me to realize that, he should never have made the mistake of being honest about his actions at Dmitry's party. He'd given himself away, proved that he was far cleverer than even I — or Dmitry — could ever have imagined. I wondered if he regretted it. Whether he wished that he could take those precious pearls of honesty back. Instead, he was going to pretend that it had never happened, obliterate that moment of weakness from his memory banks, and assume I'd fall in line.

A vaguely familiar dancer came through the door from what I assumed had to be the kitchen. Valentin reached out, tapping him on the elbow and motioning for him to come closer. He leaned in, speaking directly into his ear. I frowned when the dancer's head immediately turned to the side, his gaze finding mine as I watched the pair. No prizes for guessing what the topic of conversation was. The question was why. What was Valentin up to? What was he saying about me?

I didn't have to wait too long to find out. The dancer nodded as if agreeing to something Valentin had suggested. With a small smile on his face, he came and joined me on the sofa. I still hadn't taken my eyes away from Valentin, intent on trying to work out what was going on behind that stony facade. Only when it would have been incredibly rude not to, did I manage to drag my gaze away and pay attention to my new sofa mate instead. He was dark-haired with huge gray eyes, reminding me somewhat of a pixie. I remembered him now. He was an understudy to one of the principal dancers, which explained why I hadn't seen him enough to have recognized him straight away. I had no idea what his name was though or even what letter it began with. "Hi."

He moved closer, his thigh touching mine. "*Privetik.*"

I nodded, assuming that had to be Russian for hello. "Do you speak English?"

He shook his head, shuffling even closer, his hand settling on my thigh, and a smile playing on his lips. I glanced over at Valentin, the reason he'd sent him over to me suddenly clicking into place. Hazel eyes studied me, his face purposefully blank.

114

And then a hand on my cheek was turning my head away from Valentin and toward him at the same time as his other hand slid inside my shirt. Russian pixie lips met mine, his tongue immediately seeking entrance. He clambered onto my lap and straddled me, all without breaking contact. Worried he'd overbalance in his overexuberance, my hands moved to grasp his hips. He moved sinuously against me, his already stiffening cock rubbing against my abdomen. I kissed him back. It seemed rude not to. But I felt nothing. I was going through the motions while my brain struggled to work out what Valentin was getting out of it. Did he like to watch? Was that it? If so, he should have just said so. It wasn't as if I'd never had a threesome before.

I'd automatically closed my eyes when we'd started kissing. Even while our tongues dueled and my hands smoothed over the pixie's back whose name I still didn't know, I opened them, needing to see Valentin's reaction to the show he'd instigated. Where he'd stood, there was nothing but an empty space.

I wrenched my lips away from my eager partner, his words of protest lost on someone who didn't speak Russian. I pushed him off my lap, hoping he understood enough English to recognize an apology when he heard one. After all, it wasn't his fault that he'd gotten caught up in whatever it was that was happening between Valentin and me.

Glenn floated into my field of vision. I clambered to my feet and grabbed his arm. "Which way did Valentin go? He was here a minute ago."

He shook his head, and I walked away before the rapidly growing smile on his face could turn into a full-on "I told you so" expression. The Russian pixie stared at me balefully as I left the room and went in search of Valentin. Nobody made any move to stop me as I flung open any door I came across. I'd already checked the kitchen, bathroom, and one bedroom with no success, finding more party guests scattered around the apartment. Could he have left? I was down to the last two doors, and the first turned out to be a cupboard. I pushed the last one open, finding another bedroom and breathing a sigh of relief when I spotted the lone figure by the window.

I let the door close behind me and, for some reason, locked it. Maybe I was trying to slow any possible escape attempt from Valentin. He had to have heard me come in, but he didn't offer any acknowledgment. He may as well have been a statue. "What was that?"

He twisted around slightly. "What was what?"

"You, throwing one of your friends at me?" I crossed the room to stand in front of him, his gaze finally meeting mine while my own unwittingly strayed to his lips. Those were the lips I wanted to kiss. The ones I dreamed about. The ones that were completely unattainable.

One eyebrow arched. "Hardly throwing, Max. He likes you. I

thought it would be good for both of you. He doesn't speak English, but I thought there were other ways you could communicate. He didn't exactly need a lot of encouragement. I told him you looked lonely and that I thought you would appreciate some company. The rest was his idea."

I crossed my arms and attempted to stare him down. He didn't so much as flinch. "And that's what you normally do when someone gets too close to you, is it? You throw some distraction their way?" His chin lifted, and I got in there first. "Oh no, you don't. Know this, *Valentin*" — I made sure to put extra emphasis on his name — "whatever cruel, cutting comment you're about to come out with will *not* make me leave this room. You've already told me to kill myself with alcohol, which" — I held my arms out to the side — "has clearly had zero effect because I didn't run away from the party, crying. So you can say whatever you want. It won't make me leave because I see you now. I see who you really are behind that mask you wear."

His mouth closed without so much as a sound escaping.

I smiled. "Oh my God! I've managed to silence the mighty Valentin. No cutting comments. No mockery. Nothing. Whatever will we talk about now?" His lips twitched. It was just the tiniest of micro-expressions, but I still saw it. "And he might even smile." I reached out, grasping the nape of his neck and tugging him closer, our eyes locked together. "I don't want some random

117

dancer whose name I don't even know. I want you."

"Andrei."

"What?"

Valentin reached up, his fingers curling around my wrist as he used the grip to pull my fingers from his neck. "The random dancer, as you so casually called him, is Andrei. He's a very nice boy."

I stepped closer, my breath feathering over his face as we reached the point where our bodies were almost touching. "I don't want a boy. I want a man."

He shook his head. "If Dmitry finds out—"

"He's not here. You said you gave your..." I couldn't think of a suitable word to describe them, now that I knew their true purpose in Valentin's life, so I left it hanging. "No one knows you're here, right?" I slid my arms around his waist, the skin of his neck warm against my lips, his pulse beating rapidly beneath the surface.

His hands came up to grasp my biceps. "They'll come looking. If they find us together—"

"I locked the door."

I felt his exhalation against my cheek. I gave him time to think, not wanting to rush him into making a decision, our bodies plastered together. His voice sounded husky in my ear. "One last time, maybe."

"One last time." The words were an echo of his, but even I was surprised by the note of longing in it. "Can I kiss you?"

"No."

"Why not?" He made a halfhearted attempt to pull away, but I didn't allow it, holding his body still against mine and enjoying the warmth leaching out of it.

He sighed. "You ask too many questions. Do you want to talk, or do you want to fuck?"

Both. I didn't say that though. It wasn't what he wanted to hear. I inclined my head toward the bed, hoping whoever's room this was wouldn't mind. "We should do it on the bed. We've only ever managed a wall, a chair, and the floor."

He pulled back enough to look me in the face, the familiar smirk appearing. "You're so vanilla, Max Farley. I give you a bit of excitement in your life, and you yearn for a bed. To be like everyone else in the world. Where's your sense of adventure?"

I shoved him, enjoying the shock on his face as he tumbled backward onto the bed, looking less graceful than I'd ever seen him before, his limbs sprawling in all directions. I pulled my wallet out of my pocket, extracted the three condoms, and dropped them on the bed next to him.

His head turned to the side, giving them a cursory glance. "I knew you carried three. Am I meant to make a choice?"

"No." I crawled onto the bed, running my hands along the jean-clad thighs before pushing them apart and insinuating myself between them. "We're going to use all three."

He laughed. "Oh, Max! I call you vanilla, and you think you have to prove your manhood."

I ignored him, reaching down and tugging his T-shirt over his head before lowering my mouth to his collarbone. I might not be able to kiss him on the lips, but it was way overdue that I finally got to kiss and touch the rest of his body. Twice he'd manipulated me into a quick fuck and nothing more. This time, he was going to learn that I wasn't so easily swayed. "Not proving anything. I'm going to enjoy myself. And while I'm enjoying myself, you will too. That's a promise."

I felt a light touch on the back of my head as if he'd reached for my hair and then thought better of it. I licked and sucked my way over his chest, my teeth grazing a nipple and my tongue darting out to taste it.

This time his fingers did tangle in my hair. He tugged my head away from his chest so that I had no choice but to look up into his face, at least if I didn't want to lose a chunk of hair. "If we're doing this, we need to be quick. Before Mikhail and Igor discover where I am."

I propped myself up on one elbow, unable to hide my smile. He was *so* predictable. "You'd like that, wouldn't you? If I just flipped you over and fucked you. Then you can imagine that I've gotten what I wanted, and you can get rid of me." Hazel eyes slid away from mine. My smile grew wider as he made no effort to try and deny it. I definitely had him worked out. "You're very quiet tonight." This time I got a glare. I didn't care. I was too busy stripping the lower half of his body until he lay naked on the bed.

It took mere seconds for me to add my clothes to the pile I'd created next to the bed. I eased myself back into the space between his thighs, lifting the taut muscles of his calves and draping them over my thighs to bring our bodies closer together. I risked a glance at Valentin's face, his silence beginning to give me second thoughts about the way I was handling him, only to find his gaze centered on my erect cock. "What's Russian for cock?"

He rolled his eyes but answered anyway. "*Khui.*"

"Do you like my *khui*?"

"It's acceptable."

"Acceptable!" I tried to mimic the exact way he'd said the word.

He slid his hands behind his head, his face showing clear disgust. "Your Russian accent is appalling."

I grinned. "I'll work on it."

"Please do."

I let my gaze travel slowly down his body from the bulging muscles of his arms to the beauty of his hard cock resting on the taut abdomen. "I know I've said this before, but you truly have an amazing body."

"You should put your acceptable *khui* inside it."

"Not yet." I tamped down on the dizzying wave of lust and

desire that made me want to do exactly that. I wanted to take him fast and hard. But we'd been there, done that. Twice. I wanted something different. I wanted to try and break through that steely facade he affected, even if it was only for a moment. I wanted a glimpse of the real Valentin. Something that would convince me once and for all that there was more between us than he let on. I realized he was watching my expression closely, his eyes narrowed as if he too was trying to work something out. I doubted though whether it was the same thing. "What?"

He cocked his head to the side. "You know why you *think* you want a relationship with me, don't you?"

I went still. "I never said I wanted a relationship with you." *Was that what I wanted?* I'd had one relationship in my life, many years before. And to say it had ended badly would have been a gross understatement. I'd vowed never to go there again. It wasn't worth it. Yet there was no denying the fact that I couldn't get enough of the gorgeous Russian man naked in front of me. I never saw the same guy twice, but there we were about to have sex for the third time. And I knew that despite saying it was the last time, I'd want more. I'd always want more when it came to Valentin.

"But you do."

I let my fingers dance across the skin of his torso, tracing the bumps and hollows and mapping them as I tried to decide on the best answer. "Let's say for the sake of argument that you were right." Even saying it, made me feel strangely light-headed.

"What's this amazing theory of yours?"

Valentin propped himself up and reached for a condom packet. He tore it open with his teeth and rolled it down onto my cock, knowing that I was so intent on waiting for the answer to my question that I wouldn't protest. Yet again, he was managing to make things move much faster than I wanted them to.

"Valentin?" He passed across the packet of lube and waited until I'd smoothed a generous amount down the length of my cock. "Tell me."

He lay back again, shuffling down the bed until he could position his legs over my thighs again and tipped his hips up invitingly. "I'll tell you when you're inside me."

My hands automatically moved to his hips, all my good intentions about foreplay going right out of the window. There was nothing left except the desire to do exactly as he asked, at the same time as getting an answer to the question.

I pulled him further onto my lap, the lubed head of my cock notching perfectly against his hole. I pushed forward, watching his teeth bite into his lip as he fought to accept me. There was a momentary hesitation, then a clear effort on his part to relax, and then in one long, smooth slide, we were joined. I slid my hands up his chest, my fingers stroking his nipples as both of us breathed raggedly. "Tell me now."

He smirked. "Your subconscious allows you to *believe* you want a relationship with me because you know it's not possible. If you actually thought for one minute it was, you'd be going into panic mode. I probably wouldn't see you for dust."

My fingers trembled on his thighs. *Was he right?* Did I only want him so much because I couldn't have him? If he'd turned to me on that first day in the dressing room and asked me out on a date rather than mocking me, would I have lost interest? Would I have turned him down? There was a twisted truth to what he was saying, but I was having real trouble picturing it. Did that mean he was wrong?

"Poor Max."

My eyes flicked back to his. All the time I'd been trying to think it through, he'd been watching. "You drive me absolutely crazy."

"I know." There was no apology in his eyes, no regret for sending my head into a spin. Was this another one of his games, or was he simply trying to prove to me that everything I felt for him wasn't real?

I closed my eyes, trying to clear my head and trying to ignore the throbbing of my cock as it reminded me that it was buried to the hilt in Valentin's tight ass. All of our previous meetings flashed through my mind, snippets of conversations, the expression Valentin had worn when he'd first noticed me at Dmitry's party, the phone conversation where he'd been honest, and suddenly it all became clear. I opened my eyes and smiled. "You're wrong! *You* want to believe that so that when you tell me *yet again* that there's no future for us, you can believe that there never was anyway. You're trying to make *yourself* feel better for pushing me away."

Valentin's face registered surprise, and I knew I'd hit the nail on the head. He wasn't used to someone seeing through his manipulations. He opened his mouth to say something, and I laid a finger over his lips. "Not now. After. We'll talk more after." I came down on top of him, plastering our chests together and fastening my lips on any part of his skin I could reach while my hips began to move in earnest.

He'd set out to convince me that he meant nothing to me, and it had backfired. Instead he'd done the opposite. I, Max Farley, the man who didn't do relationships, was falling for a cold, enigmatic Russian ballet dancer who was an expert at giving the impression that he didn't give a fuck. Well, he could take that not giving a fuck, and he could moan for me like he actually did. That became my sole aim for the next few moments. Each gasp, each moan, each time he dug his fingers into my skin or gasped out my name became one more piece of evidence that he felt exactly the same way I did. He couldn't be cold when his skin burned so hot beneath my touch.

I sat back on my heels, dragging his boneless body on top of me and sliding back in, in one smooth stroke, my hands gripping the muscles in his back. We'd fucked like this on the chair. But this was nothing like that time. In the hotel room, he'd still been in charge, any real emotions hidden behind that cool facade of his. Here, with him flushed and moaning, his gasps loud in my ear, and his body moving against mine without perfect synchronicity—just wild and hungry and desperate—I felt as if I was meeting the real Valentin for the first time.

I was on the verge of coming, but I fought it, wanting to hold on to the moment for that bit longer, knowing that once we were done, he'd retreat to the cool, calm persona that was his defense against the world. He bit my shoulder as he came, the brief spark of pain triggering a headlong rush into my orgasm. For a moment, we clung together, his head resting on my shoulder. It was more intimacy than I'd had with anyone since I was seventeen, and I loved it. I breathed in the scent of his hair, memorized the feel of his skin against mine, dreamed of a scenario where I could have this all the time.

Then he was climbing off and reaching for a cigarette in the pocket of his jeans. By the time he'd lit it and leaned back against the headboard, smoking it, it was like looking at a completely different person. I got rid of the condom, sparing a thought for how the inhabitant of the room would feel about someone using their bed for sex and leaving the evidence behind in their bin. I stretched out beside Valentin on the bed, both of us still naked. "I know you like me."

He flinched. "It doesn't matter whether I do or not."

126

"Dmitry?"

He nodded but didn't say more.

"He really controls your life to the point where you can't be with someone? Maybe if you talked to him... tried to explain."

"It's complicated. You wouldn't understand."

I bit down on the frustration I was feeling, knowing that it would only serve to push him further away. "Then make me understand. Are you saying you're not even allowed to have sex with someone of your choosing?"

"I can have sex."

"So what's the problem?"

He examined the cigarette, turning it around and around as if there was something particularly interesting about it. "Just not with the same person. Dmitry doesn't like me to have... attachments."

Dmitry this. Dmitry that! I was beginning to be sick of the sound of the man's name. Valentin was a person, not a possession. It made no sense that he could control a person's life to the extent that he apparently was. I shifted my body to face Valentin, but he continued to stare straight ahead. "Okay. Let's say for the sake of argument that we ignore Dmitry. I mean... what's he going to do to me..." I let out a sound halfway between a snort and a laugh. "...kill me?"

Valentin's head turned slowly my way, the truth written all

over his face. I stared at him, suddenly bereft of saliva, my heart rate almost doubling. I thought about the man I'd met, the way he'd plied me with expensive whiskey, called me his friend, and apologized for the heavy-handedness of his hired thugs. Then I thought about the fact that he held parties where rich, old men groped and presumably did a lot more to young men. "Really?"

Valentin took a long drag of his cigarette. "Do not underestimate how dangerous he can be."

We both froze as voices sounded directly outside the bedroom door. They grew louder before fading again, and we both relaxed when we realized it was just someone walking by.

Valentin smiled, but it carried a great deal of sadness. "That feeling. That moment of panic you had there, Max. Remember that. Because if that had been Dmitry, I wouldn't have been able to protect you. And three times with the same person is way beyond what Dmitry would ever class as being acceptable."

"Three times? But he doesn't know about the hotel room, does he?"

Valentin leaned his head back against the headboard, the cigarette almost down to the filter. "He knows. He wouldn't have invited you to the party based on the dressing room alone."

"How? There was only the two of us there."

He stubbed the cigarette out in the ashtray by the bed, his shoulders lifting into a shrug. "He may have already been suspicious of the fact that I told him to take Igor with him when

128

he was only intending to take Mikhail. He probably talked to the concierge or asked to see the CCTV. He is nothing but thorough."

I thought about what he'd said. "So why invite me there? If you knew how risky it was?"

He turned, shifting himself to sit cross-legged. "I was weak. It was an error of judgment."

A bolt of satisfaction shot through me. "Because you like me?"

One corner of his mouth quirked up. "I like your cock."

I wasn't going to let him get away with that. What we had was more than sex. "Would it kill you to admit that this thing between us is mutual?"

"It doesn't matter." He rested his chin on his hand. "Think of it this way. Even if we could be... together." He faltered on the word as if it was difficult to say. "After the show, I will be going back to Russia. Are you coming to Russia, Max? Are you leaving your family and friends behind... for me?"

"Is that an invitation?"

His expression was nothing but weary at the fact I was making light of it. "And then I will be off to whichever country I am required to go to. My life is dancing. A... relationship is not in the cards for me, whether that is dictated by Dmitry"—he shrugged—"or circumstance."

The words hurt. Not just because they were delivered in his usual blunt fashion but also because I could recognize the truth in them. While he was performing, he'd need to travel all over the world. "You really meant it when you said this was the last time?"

He nodded. "It has to be. More for your sake than mine. Dmitry will disapprove. He will be angry with me, but he won't hurt me. Nothing lasting anyway. I am too valuable to him. But you..."

"I'm nothing to him."

"Exactly."

I planted a hand on his chest, pushing him back until he lay flat on the bed again. I moved over him, fitting our bodies together and watching the way his face warred between the desire to let me do what I wanted and to push me off in order to back up his words. His cock stirred beneath my thigh, and I smiled smugly at the knowledge that he wanted me again so soon. I still needed more, though. "Tell me that it's not just about sex. Tell me that you like me."

"Max..." There was a heavy dose of warning in his voice.

"I need to know. If this is going to be the last time, then I need to know that I'm not crazy. That it's not all been one-sided." I slid my hand between our bodies, pressing it against the place where his heart lay. "Give me that at least."

His eyes closed, and I could almost picture the argument going on inside his head. I kept my hand where it was, feeling the reassuring thud of his heart beneath my palm.

His eyelids flickered open, and for a moment, I was blinded by the raw emotion I saw there. Emotion he'd never shown me before, and I'd probably never get to see again. He smiled. Not one of his mocking smiles, but an honest-to-God genuine one. "I *like* you, Max. I don't know why, but I do. You're almost as fucked up as I am. Maybe that's it. Like attracts like. Happy now?"

I nuzzled into his neck, a profound mixture of happiness and sadness rushing through me, the certainty that we could really have been something. I pushed the thought out of my head. I still had him in my arms. There'd be time later to dwell on what could have been. I shifted so that our cocks aligned, my hips starting a slow grind to push them together, my fingers trailing through the slight stickiness of cum on his abdomen from his last orgasm. "There're two more condoms. It doesn't end until we've used both. Then you can walk away. Deal?"

I expected him to protest. I expected Dmitry's name to appear. I expected him to tell me — yet again — that there were a hundred reasons why we couldn't and shouldn't take any more risks. But it was Valentin. So he did the one thing I didn't anticipate; he simply said, "Deal."

I reached for condom number two, my cock already more than eager to be back inside him.

Chapter Eight

Valentin

I pursued Yakov down the corridor, the rehearsal schedule that had been delivered only moments before still clutched in my hand. "There must be some mistake."

Yakov turned with an inquisitive look on his face, so I sought to explain, switching to Russian so that there was less chance of what I had to say being misconstrued. "It says I am to rehearse all four dances today. I cannot do four. It's out of the question."

His brow furrowed. "The show begins next week, and you have still not done a full run-through."

"Yes, I know... but..." Although Yakov had been informed that I was on partial medical leave, I knew that he was less clear on the reasons for it. Dmitry had claimed that it wasn't fair to let the man worry, to put extra strain on him when he was already trying to put a show together. Therefore, as far as I knew, he'd been led to believe that I'd been suffering from some sort of lingering virus, that my reasons for cutting back on dancing were down to lack of stamina while I was still recovering. There was nothing I could say without admitting that Dmitry had lied to him.

"Is there a problem?" I turned my head to see the familiar figure of Dmitry bearing down on us, a look of consternation on his face. The silent shadows of Mikhail and Igor moved to either side of the corridor to let him through. He looked first to Yakov and then to me when no answer from the theater manager was forthcoming. I waved the piece of paper. "I'm down to rehearse four dances today."

Dmitry shrugged. "Then you will do four dances." He leaned conspiratorially toward Yakov. "Dancers, they are so difficult to handle. I do not know how you stand to be around so many all the time. I have my hands full with just the one."

I walked away as they both started to laugh, hoping that the door to my dressing room would be sufficient to drown them out. I'd wait there for the call to go onstage. I shut the door and leaned my head back against the wall, turning my ankle in slow circles and trying to ignore the jolt of discomfort caused by the movement. I guessed that it was make-or-break time. My ankle either would withstand four dances, or it wouldn't, and the latter didn't bear thinking about.

* * * *

I crossed to the center of the stage for the third time. I'd gotten through the first two dances with very little pain due to the high-strength painkilling injections, but it was starting to wear off. Either that or the stress and strain of dancing the previous two had bled through the effects of the opiates. The first two had been solos, whereas this was a group dance. Once I got through it, there was only one more. Then I'd be able to retreat to my dressing room and deal with the aftereffects of the pain.

I glanced in the direction of the sound booth, half expecting to see a pair of blue eyes looking back at me, but Max's head was down. Three days had gone by since the party, and he'd kept his word to the point where there had been no contact. At least I assumed he'd kept his word. He could have called, but I hadn't turned the phone back on. There was too much temptation in being able to pick it up and talk to him. It should have made me happy that he was doing exactly what I'd asked him to do. Instead it left a huge, gaping hole I wasn't used to feeling. I should never have been stupid enough to admit that I felt something for him. It felt as if that knowledge was out there now, taunting me and reminding me of what I couldn't have. It was silly because despite the relatively small amount of time we'd spent together, it was still far longer than I'd spent with any one person before, and I suspected it was the same with Max. In many ways we were like two peas in a pod. After the party, we'd not only used all the remaining condoms, just as Max had demanded, but lingered in the apartment until the early hours of the morning, talking. Not about anything meaningful, more about countries, and food, and films; things that meant nothing, yet meant everything when it came to learning about the other person. I'd been surprised at how enjoyable I found it, given I wasn't one for small talk. But in retrospect, it had been yet another mistake. I couldn't seem to stop myself from making them when it came to Max.

Then I'd had to weather the subsequent storm from Dmitry, demanding to know where I'd been, and why Igor and Mikhail weren't with me. I'd told him the truth. Or at least a version of it, claiming that for once I'd wanted to spend time at a party without supervision. I'd just left out the key fact that Max had been there too. As long as Dmitry didn't decide to dig any further, it would be fine. I didn't think he would. I doubted that his arrogance would ever let him believe that Max would have had the courage to come anywhere near me after his veiled threats.

"Starting places."

I followed Yakov's instruction, holding my arms aloft and waiting for the first strains of the music to begin. I shifted my balance slightly, almost stumbling as a sharp stab of pain traveled all the way up from my ankle to my thigh. A cold sweat broke out on my forehead, and for the first time, I gave serious thought to whether I could get through the dance. I considered bringing a stop to it, simply walking off the stage and refusing to do it. But then I would have to face Dmitry's wrath, and then what would

135

happen next week when I no longer had a choice? It was better to get on with it and reassure myself that four dances were in fact possible. Painful. But possible.

The music started, and I let it filter through me, concentrating on my form with each leap and twist. My arms needed to be in a certain position; an inch out and it would look wrong. My neck had to be in perfect alignment with the rest of my body. My breathing had to be regulated in order to take enough oxygen in without it affecting my movements. There were hundreds of things I needed to consider. I may have made it look easy, but it wasn't. It was years of practice. Years of learning exactly what worked and what didn't. Years of working through any small error until I could eradicate it completely. And I wasn't perfect. I still had things I needed to work on. Small margins that would make me an even better dancer.

I was two-thirds of the way through the dance when I landed and something felt wrong. There was a moment where I thought I'd imagined it and everything was going to be all right, but then it was closely followed by a rush of such excruciating agony, the likes of which I'd never felt before. Then my whole body crumpled, my ankle unable to hold its weight, and I hit the floor, my cheek rebounding off the wooden stage. I lay there stunned, watching the other four dancers continue the steps that I should have been doing. It seemed to take ages until the music slowly died away and all movement around me ceased.

It seemed strange that none of the other dancers offered any help. I might not have been popular due to my penchant for keeping to myself, but I wasn't hated enough for them to let me lie there like a collapsed and broken doll. The reason for their lack of interference soon became clear as a shadow loomed over me, and I looked up into Dmitry's face. I'd seen him wearing a number of expressions over the years, but I'd never seen him look as furious as he did at that moment. He liked to play the harmless, urbane gentleman too much to let such crass emotions leak through. In public at least. I was so good at hiding mine because I'd learned from the master. Therefore, the fact he was making absolutely no attempt to hide his anger did not bode well. He spat the words, "Get up," at me in Russian.

Ignoring the pain, I tried to do what he'd asked. I really did. But there was no way I could put even the slightest bit of weight on that ankle. I forced myself almost to a kneeling position before collapsing again, tears of frustration leaking down my face. "I can't. I'm sorry. It's..." I gestured at my ankle. It was already beginning to swell. I didn't need a doctor to tell me that whatever I'd done was serious. There was no way I was going to be capable of dancing in the show. "My ankle. It's not right. I need a doctor." I waited for Dmitry to pull his phone out of his pocket and call someone, but all he did was continue to stare at me.

"I'm sorry, Dmitry." I was sorry, but not because I'd spoiled his

137

plans. I was sorry that I'd ever let him talk me into dancing in the first place when I'd felt... no, when I'd known that my ankle was getting worse by the day. Now my whole dance career was most likely in jeopardy, and the man who had steered it, molded it, controlled it, didn't have so much as a grain of empathy to spare for me. More tears spilled down my face. I dashed them away, ashamed to be so weak in front of him. Maybe, though, it would be the thing that got through to him, that wiped the fury from his face and got him seeing me as a human being rather than a commodity. "I don't know what you want me to say."

He leaned closer, his voice ominously low. "You have ruined all my plans with your carelessness." Then he switched to English, projecting his voice so that the whole theater would hear and understand. "What use is a dancer who cannot dance? I will tell you. *It* is of no use! *You* are of no use!" His next words went out to the whole theater, the majority of onlookers standing around in stunned silence. "Let him crawl. It will teach him some humility. He will need it, now he is no longer a star." Then he walked away, leaving me in a heap on the stage. Nobody so much as twitched. You'd have thought the theater was empty. I understood their quandary. No one was willing to go against Dmitry's wishes. No one dared to paint a target on their back. Two of the dancers on the stage had attended his parties. They knew how he operated. They'd seen at least some of what lay beneath the smart suits and the friendly demeanor.

138

I twisted my head to the side, contemplating the stairs I would need to crawl down in order to get to my dressing room. It would be a long, slow, painful process with every movement jarring my ankle. I psyched myself up to begin, trying to eradicate the pride and superiority that I wore as a defense mechanism. That's what Dmitry wanted. In his head, I'd hurt him, so he was going to hurt me in return. It was the way he'd always been: an eye for an eye and a tooth for a tooth.

Then strong arms wrapped around me, a thumb reaching out to wipe the tears from my face. I turned my head, mystified as to the identity of my savior. Max's face swam into view, his grim expression changing to a smile when our eyes met. He tugged, trying to get me to rise to my feet. Or one foot anyway. I made a weak and feeble attempt to push him away. "Don't help me!"

He pulled harder. "Shut up! I'm not leaving you like this. Valentin Bychkov is not crawling anywhere." Then we were both on our feet, the majority of my weight resting on Max as I kept my injured foot from touching the floor. With me hopping, we made our slow way across the stage with Max somehow managing to maneuver both of us down the stairs to the auditorium. I kept waiting for someone to step in and enforce Dmitry's decree by urging Max to leave me be, but there was only an eerie silence as people watched, but made no move to do anything more. Even Mikhail and Igor—who I'd spotted near the exit—said nothing.

We paused for a moment at the foot of the stairs, neither of us seeming to have a clue what to do next.

"Can I do anything?"

My head turned toward the voice, but he wasn't talking to me. He was talking to Max. It was the same boy who'd brought him to the party. Gary? George? No, Glenn. That was his name.

Max gathered me more tightly against him, the heat from his body soaking into my bare chest. "Can you call a cab? I'm taking him to the hospital."

Tempting as it was to soak up his mental strength, I forced myself to protest. "Max, don't! I'll be fine." I pointed to the closest chair. "Just... help me get there... and then go."

Glenn paused with his finger poised on the call button, looking back and forth between us as he tried to work out which one of us he was supposed to listen to.

Max shook his head, gesturing at Glenn and ignoring me completely. "Make the call."

Glenn nodded and lifted the phone to his ear, speaking a few words into it before hanging up. "They'll be outside in five minutes. Do you need anything else?" This time the question was aimed at both of us, and I wondered what I'd done to deserve the help of a boy I'd never even spoken to and probably looked straight through on more than one occasion. Yet out of everyone, he was the one prepared to go out on a limb and help. Not the dancers I considered friends. Not the theater manager, who seemed to be trying to melt into the background. I didn't blame them though. I knew they were scared of Dmitry, but it made me wonder why Glenn wasn't. Naïvety maybe. Or maybe he was just that damn nice. I hoped he didn't live to regret it.

I didn't get a chance to thank him before Max was half pulling, half pushing me toward the exit where Igor and Mikhail stood. We paused in front of them, Max's body almost vibrating with tension beneath my hands. I spoke to them in Russian. "Are you going to stop us from leaving?"

To my surprise, it was Igor, who answered. "Dmitry has made it clear that you are of no more use to him. Therefore, until he says differently, you are no longer our responsibility." I nodded. They weren't being kind; they were simply stating a fact. They stepped aside, and by the time we'd made our slow, faltering way to the street, the cab was already waiting. Max helped me into the back of it before climbing in himself and directing the driver to take us to St Thomas' Hospital.

I grabbed his arm to get his attention. "I have a doctor here. Dr. Chambers. I don't need to go to the hospital."

Max's look was scathing. "And an absolutely fantastic job he's obviously been doing. Or am I meant to believe that this injury was something that happened today?"

I shook my head. There was no point in denying it. The secret was well and truly out. "No. I've been struggling with it for a while, but Dmitry, he..." I sat back, a mixture of exhaustion and pain making it so I lacked the strength to explain. I guessed that Max could read between the lines anyway. He already knew how much control Dmitry exerted over my life, so it wasn't a huge leap for him to realize that he'd also control where and when I danced. I closed my eyes, reliving the moment where Max had swooped to my rescue like a knight in shining armor. It was stupid. It was reckless beyond belief, but it was by far the sweetest thing that anyone had ever done for me. If he hadn't already admitted to having feelings for me, it would have been obvious from that action alone. I didn't know what I'd done to deserve it. But without him, I'd probably still be trying to crawl my way to my dressing room.

By the time I opened my eyes again, we were already outside the hospital. Max helped me out of the cab with the same careful gentleness he'd employed to help me into it, even pausing to remove his jacket and drape it around my shoulders when it dawned on him that I was bare-chested and shivering in the cold London chill. "You're sweet."

He pulled my arm around his shoulder, steadying me with an arm around my waist and managing to pay the cabbie at the same time. "You must be in an awful lot of pain."

I took a few hops forward. "Why?"

"You said something nice. I wasn't sure Valentin Bychkov was capable of such a feat."

"Yet, you're still helping me. What does that say about you?"

He hitched me closer as his grip started to slip. "That I'm a complete and utter masochist. I'd already worked that one out."

Our arrival at Accident and Emergency forestalled any possible response I might have given to Max's statement. He sat me down in a plastic chair, next to a man bleeding profusely from a cut on his temple. I couldn't say I'd had any experience of mixing with the general public in a British hospital. Dmitry had always paid for private medical care. Looking around at the smorgasbord of sick and injured, I couldn't quite decide whether the prospect was horrifying or fascinating.

Chapter Nine

Max

I glanced back to where I'd left Valentin, checking he was still there. He was. Not that he could get far if he tried to escape when he couldn't even walk. My mind went back to the moment he'd collapsed onstage. I hadn't seen it—having decided after the party that if I couldn't have him, I would only watch him dance when it was absolutely crucial to doing my job properly. But I'd heard the stunned silence that had descended on the theater, lifting my head to find the horrifying image of a prone Valentin lying on the stage.

I'd watched Dmitry stroll to the stage, his slow amble completely at odds with the anger on his face, as if Valentin's collapse was a personal affront to him. I didn't know what the Russian words he'd spoken were, but the cold tone they'd been delivered in had left no doubt that they were less than friendly. I'd continued to watch as Valentin had made a valiant attempt to get to his feet, only to fall again, agony etched across his face. I'd scanned the theater, waiting for someone to go to his aid, but no one had moved. Some had even left. Even the theater director had edged his way to the back of the auditorium, the furthest he could get from the stage without actually leaving.

Dmitry's final cruel words, delivered in English for maximum impact, had rung in my ears, and I'd known that anyone who might have been in two minds about helping, now wouldn't. They'd be too scared to bring the attention of Dmitry crashing down on them. For a few horrifying seconds, I'd actually considered following their lead. All I had to do was stay in the sound booth and look away. After all, it wasn't as if Valentin would thank me for rushing to his aid. In fact, he'd probably be furious. But my legs had already been moving toward the stage. Halfway there, I'd been brought to a premature halt when someone had grabbed my arm. Expecting to find a muscle-bound goon, I'd been surprised to discover that of all people it was Noel, his face a picture of concern. "Max! Leave him." I had no idea what he knew, whether the rumor mill after the party had filled him in on the fact that I'd ignored all his previous warnings or whether he was simply acting on instinct, but to be honest, I didn't care. Valentin needed me. Any repercussions could wait. So I'd shrugged Noel off and climbed onto the stage.

"Fill these in, please."

The request from the receptionist, together with the fact she was holding out a clipboard of forms that needed completing in order to get medical treatment, brought me crashing back to the here and now. I took them from her outstretched hand, offering a smile, and returned to where I'd left Valentin. The pain etched on his face hit me anew. I was used to seeing him looking haughty and superior, acting like nothing and no one could hurt him, so seeing him brought to his knees — literally — caused an overwhelming mixture of feelings that I wasn't quite ready to process.

I sat next to him and handed over the forms. "You need to fill these in. Then I'll take them back to the receptionist. I don't know how long we're going to have to wait for treatment. It depends on how many emergency cases come in."

He took the pen from my hand and started to fill it in, his handwriting a messy scribble. "And after a doctor has seen me. What then?"

"What do you mean?"

He gestured down at himself, a reminder that we'd left the theater without collecting so much as a shirt or shoes. "I can't go back to the hotel where Dmitry is. I need to... give him time to calm down. I don't have money for another hotel." His expression darkened, and he looked uncomfortable. "Can you lend me money? I hate to ask. Just for one night. It doesn't have to be anywhere fancy." He forced a smile. "I can slum it for one night. I'll work out a way to pay you back."

I stared at him aghast. "You think I'm going to dump you in some shitty hotel and leave you? You're coming home with me."

146

He reared back as if my announcement had carried actual physical weight, and I braced myself for the argument that I knew was on its way. "You can't do that."

I sighed. "I can. And I am. And don't."

"Don't what?"

"Don't sharpen your knives and say something deliberately hurtful in order to try and convince me to get rid of you." I could tell from his expression that that was exactly what he'd been planning to do. I smiled smugly. "You're so predictable."

"Not to most people."

The admission made my smile grow wider. I leaned in, kissing his cheek, not giving a damn who might be watching. "Now, finish filling that form in, or we're not going to get out of here before midnight."

"Max?"

"Yeah?" I waited, wondering whether I was going to receive even more insight into the man who sat next to me.

"I need a cigarette."

I let out a laugh. "I'll get you one. I'll even hold you up while you smoke it. *After* you've filled in the form."

* * * *

The wait to see a doctor had taken nearly three hours. Once

inside the examining room, the doctor had gotten Valentin to lie on his stomach while he examined the injured side from his calf down to the ankle. I sat on a plastic chair at Valentin's side while the doctor carried out a thorough examination, pressing on the muscle in various places and asking how much it hurt. Satisfied he'd seen enough, the doctor instructed him to sit up. Valentin gingerly maneuvered himself to a seated position, his legs dangling over the edge of the examination table.

"You've partially torn your Achilles tendon. I'm guessing from the extent of the inflammation that this has been an ongoing medical issue and that you were probably warned that there was a risk of this happening if you continued to dance on it."

Valentin nodded, a look of resignation on his face that was hard to swallow. If he wasn't going to stick up for himself, then I was. "It's not his fault. He was pressured into continuing to dance." I didn't know that for sure. I hadn't even known about the injury before today. But given everything else he'd told me about Dmitry, and everything I'd experienced when it came to him, it wasn't a huge leap to assume that sitting out the show had never been an option.

The doctor's face maintained a professional blankness. "I see. Well, whatever the circumstances, you now have an injury that's going to require extensive rehabilitation and *may* still require surgery. We need to do an MRI before I can say for certain. If the tear is not too severe, then there's a chance we can get full range of motion back without surgery. Tendons do heal on their own, but it's going to take a long period of rest and then physiotherapy."

"So he'll dance again?" It probably wasn't the wisest thing to blurt out the question like that, particularly given the way Valentin's fingers reflexively dug into his thighs.

The doctor looked up from the note he was making. "We'll know more after the MRI, but if I'm right about it being a partial tear, then there's no reason why he shouldn't as long as he's careful from this point on."

The relief on Valentin's face was palpable. "I will. I don't care what anyone else says anymore. I won't dance until my ankle is a hundred percent better."

The doctor nodded. "Stay here. Someone will be down to take you for an MRI soon, and then we'll have a chat about pain relief. One of the nurses will sort you out with crutches and a walking boot." He frowned at Valentin's bare feet. "Just the one I'm afraid. You'll have to come up with your own footwear arrangements for the other."

* * * *

The shower turned on, and I stood for a moment, listening for any signs of difficulty. Valentin had assured me that he didn't need my help, that even on one leg, he was quite capable of taking a shower on his own.

At least the MRI had brought good news: the doctor announcing that the injury was indeed a partial tear and *should* heal without surgical intervention. A loud bang from the ceiling above caused me to rush to the bottom of the stairs. "Valentin? Are you okay?"

His voice sounded muffled, due to the closed bathroom door between us. "I'm fine. No need to panic. One of my crutches fell. That's all. You can stand down." He sounded amused by the fact I was so worried, but it was hard to get that image of him lying helpless on the stage out of my head. I returned to the kitchen, getting a beer out of the fridge before settling down at the kitchen table to wait.

Alone, the enormity of my actions started to sink in. I'd gone against a dangerous man's wishes. He'd wanted to see Valentin humiliated, and I'd stopped that from happening. The question was, what did that mean for me? There was no doubt in my mind that Dmitry would find out. He might not have stuck around to witness it, but there'd been plenty of people left in the auditorium to let him know, not least the two hired goons, whose job it was to report to Dmitry about all things Valentin related.

But then, he'd made it clear that he didn't care about Valentin, that he was of no more use to him. So did that mean he'd let him go? If that was the case, then maybe he wouldn't care one way or another? I could only hope. I jumped as my phone rang, my mind immediately leaping to the assumption I was about to be faced with an irate Dmitry on the other end. If Valentin had managed to get hold of my number, then it stood to reason that a man with all the connections Dmitry had could get it too. Did I answer it? Did I let it go to voicemail? I reached out, bracing myself for the screen to show an unknown number. Instead, it said Noel. I breathed a sigh of relief but didn't bother to take the call. He could wait a bit longer for an explanation. He might be a friend, but I didn't owe him anything.

The shower turned off, and then a few minutes later, there was the awkward scraping and bumping sound of Valentin maneuvering himself down the stairs one by one. I tamped down the urge to offer help again and watched the kitchen doorway, waiting for him to appear. When he did, I almost did a double take. I'd only ever seen him in full makeup and with his hair teased to perfection. Face scrubbed and with his hair still wet, lying flat against his head, he looked like a completely different person: younger and less hard-faced. He left his crutches by the door and hopped the last couple of steps to join me at the table.

He grimaced when he picked up on my scrutiny. "Sorry. You'll have to put up with me looking ugly. Unless you've got makeup I can borrow?"

I shook my head, slow to pick up on what he'd said. "You're not ugly without makeup. Far from it. Don't say that."

He shrugged. "Dmitry hated the way I looked without it. He—"

"I'm not Dmitry."

He reached across the table, curling a hand around the beer bottle. I thought he was going to take a drink, but instead he turned it around to where there was a gap in the label, pulling it closer to see how much beer was left in the bottle. "He must have done a real number on you... this man who you drink to forget."

I went still, my fingernails digging into my palms, the words far too close to the truth. "I don't know what you mean."

He smiled. "Yes, you do. You know exactly what I mean. The man who you never talk about, the man who made you vow never to have a relationship again." His gaze fastened on mine. "The man who broke your heart."

I snatched the beer out of his hand, downing the last few drops and immediately getting up for another, my heart pounding far too fast.

"What was his name?"

I spun around. "This is the thanks I get for helping you? I get hounded." My words sounded way too accusatory, not to mention defensive. I waited for him to bite back. At least then we could have an argument, and I could storm out of the room and avoid the subject. He simply arched an eyebrow and patted the seat I'd recently vacated. He waited until I was seated again, his voice much quieter than it had been before. "Have you ever spoken about him to anyone?"

The familiar mixture of feelings flooded my body: guilt, self-loathing, teenage devastation, and a good dose of shame. I shook my head. It was easier than speaking.

"Was he anything like me?"

My head jerked up, and I couldn't help the laugh that escaped. "Like you? I've never met *anyone* else like you."

Valentin traced invisible patterns on the tabletop with his fingertips. "Good! I was worried your interest in me was about chasing the memory of something you lost."

"It's not." I felt as if I should say more, but I was still reeling from how easily he'd been able to psychoanalyze me, and I was also struggling to come to terms with the fact that there was a tiny part of me—buried deep down inside—that wondered how I'd feel if I did tell him. Would it be like lancing a boil? Would all the bad memories finally seep out of me and disappear? Or would remembering bring everything back into sharp focus after so many years of pushing it down that I'd at least managed to give it fuzzy edges?

"If you're not going to talk to me about anything meaningful, we should play a game."

"A game?" I studied his face, trying to see through the words. He looked much better than he had earlier, the sick exhaustion of pain having given way to something lighter. "What sort of game?"

His lip quirked at the corner. "A game of choice."

"Okay... I think."

He laughed. "Don't look so worried. I think you'll find that you win either way. I'm just intrigued to find out what you'll go for." He held his hand out, palm up, his fingers retracting into a clear instruction to hand something over. "Your beer."

I grudgingly handed it over to him, my eyes never leaving his face.

He placed it on the table in front of him, leaning forward on his elbows so that his face came much closer. "Here's the choice. What would you rather have a taste of?" He gave the bottle a poke. "This beer, or" —he dragged out the pause— "my lips? You can only choose one."

I rocked back in my chair, staring at him as if he'd grown two heads. "Are you saying I can kiss you if I get rid of the beer?"

He cocked his head to one side, and I waited for him to say that he was joking or that he just wanted to see how I'd react. He said neither, his tongue darting out to moisten his lips. "I guess that's exactly what I'm saying."

I snatched up the beer bottle, noting the immediate disappointment on his face. That was until I got up and poured it down the sink. "Do I need to pour the rest of them down there as well?"

"Would you?"

"Yes." My answer was instantaneous, but even if I'd had longer to think about it, it would have remained the same.

154

He rested his chin on his hand, looking thoughtful. "Well, that's interesting, isn't it?"

I retook my seat at the table, reaching out to draw him even closer, my hand tangling in his hair, the strands unusually soft beneath my fingertips without the usual hairspray. I tugged him forward, our lips only inches away. "Is it?"

He shrugged. I kept expecting him to pull away. How many times had I asked him point-blank if I could kiss him, and the answer had always been no. What had changed? I sought for the right question to ask, the question which would check for consent without changing his mind. But words were jumbled in my head. There was only Valentin and Valentin's lips. Everything else had ceased to exist. Dmitry himself could have walked in, and I doubted that I'd have even registered his presence.

"*Ty che, blyad*, Max! What the fuck! Would it help if I said that the offer is only open for about five more seconds?"

I smiled and closed the remaining space between us, starting a gentle exploration at one corner of his mouth with just the slightest pressure. It was the complete opposite to the way sex was between the two of us, but this seemed infinitely more precious. It was strange, but I knew that Valentin offering his lips meant far more than the day he'd stood in his dressing room, pulled down his ballet tights, and offered his ass.

My hand moved from his hair to his cheek, tilting his head to

155

one side as I deepened the kiss. His lips parted, and I took the open invitation without a moment's hesitation, my tongue dipping inside to meet his own. I'd already known I was falling for him, but it was funny that one kiss could make that so much clearer. He was a craving. He was a need. And now I'd tasted those lips, there was no way I was letting him go. When he finally brought an end to it, our lips separating and my hand falling from his face as he sat back in his chair, I protested, not caring how desperate I came across. I stared at him, noting the lidded eyes and the flushed cheeks. My cold Russian was definitely heating up.

"What was his name?"

I closed my eyes and concentrated on breathing, and for the first time ever, I wanted to talk about it. I wanted to tell someone, or more specifically, I wanted to tell Valentin. When I opened them again, Valentin hadn't moved, his hazel eyes expressing nothing but empathy and a willingness to listen to whatever I had to say. "James. James Wentworth. He was my... teacher at school." I didn't get any more reaction than the slight lift of an eyebrow. "He was fifteen years older than me."

"How old were you when it started?"

Valentin had an unerring knack of getting right to the heart of a situation. I had no idea how he did it. It was as if he could read minds. I shifted restlessly. "Do you want a cup of tea?" I didn't want one myself, but if I was going to talk about things I'd kept locked up inside me for years, then it seemed as if it would be far easier if I busied myself with doing something else.

Valentin nodded, and I climbed to my feet, filling the kettle with water, and turning my back to him. "Milk and sugar?"

"Yes. Both. One sugar."

I got two mugs out of the cupboard, my fingers itching to reach for a beer instead, but the kiss still lingered on my lips, and I'd made my choice. For a moment, there was nothing but the sound of the kettle boiling. I clenched my fists on the countertop, watching the steam as it rose from the kettle. "As far as I know, people think it started when I was sixteen. It was a huge scandal. He lost his job because, although I was legally old enough, I was still a student, and he was still my teacher."

"What did he teach?"

I frowned. Of all the questions I'd expected him to ask, that wasn't one of them. "Does it matter?"

"Humor me."

I opened the drawer and pulled out a teaspoon, reaching for the sugar. "History. I thought he was the best teacher in the world. He made everything so interesting, and he always had time for me. He made me feel"—my voice cracked, and I felt like the biggest idiot in the world. I tried to cover it by busying myself with spooning sugar into both cups—"special." I got the milk out of the fridge. "And our relationship, it wasn't nothing. I mean... I

157

moved in with him. For a year. That's not nothing." The silence behind me was deafening. "And then he left. He just upped and left one day, and I was left with an apartment I couldn't pay for."

"Where did he go?"

"I don't know." I poured hot water into the cups. "He left a note, but it didn't really say anything, and I never saw or heard from him again. I was at college. There was no way I could have stayed on at school after everything that had happened. I had to move back in with my mum. She couldn't understand what had gone wrong between us. She'd had to weather the scandal. She'd had to listen to all the bad things that people had said about her son when he moved in with a man almost old enough to be his father. So I'd always told her everything was perfect between us, even when it wasn't. All couples fight though, right? I kept telling her how we were meant to be together. She wanted to know why he'd left, and I couldn't tell her because I didn't know myself... and it was all such a huge mess."

"Except you did know why he'd left, didn't you, Max?"

I swung around to face him. "I just told you I didn't."

Cool hazel eyes held mine until I was the first to look away. "Why did he leave, Max?"

"I..." I'd never said the words aloud before. The truth made me feel stupid. It made me feel naïve. It reminded me of how much of a liar I'd been when even my own mother hadn't seen the truth. I'd been that good at hiding things. No sixteen-year-old should ever have been that good at keeping secrets. Secrets I'd kept until this very day. I lifted my head and looked him straight in the eye. "I'd gotten too old." My mouth twisted, nausea bubbling in my stomach. "I was no longer to his tastes. He hadn't touched me for three months before he left."

Valentin held out his hand, and I automatically headed toward him, the tea forgotten. He took my hand and squeezed it reassuringly, his thumb stroking the back of it. "Tell me the rest. Get it all out. Once and for all. Everything, Max."

I did. The words came out in a rush, the stopper finally released from the bottle after so many years. "I was fifteen when it started. At first, it was just special attention. You know, asking me to stay behind after class, telling me how intelligent I was, how good at history I was, asking me if I needed help with homework. Then there were slight touches, nothing that could be construed as too inappropriate if I'd protested, just a brush here and a touch there. I was flattered. He was a handsome man, and he knew so much about the world, and he really seemed to get me. I started having dreams about him, about the two of us together. In the end, it was me that kissed him first. I initiated it. I started the ball rolling."

The hand wrapped around mine squeezed harder, but then Valentin started shaking his head violently. "No, you didn't. You know what he was doing. Say it."

159

I took a shuddering breath. "He was grooming me."

"Why?"

"Because he was a..."

"Go on."

I shook my head, the familiar feelings of recrimination and self-loathing coursing through my body.

"Say it, Max. He was a what?"

"He was a"—I wiped my face with my free hand, surprised to feel the wetness of tears—"pedophile."

"Correct."

"But I was still stupid to be taken in by him. I should have seen through him, or I should have told someone what was going on. I lied for him. When the shit hit the fan because we were caught together, he got me to say that nothing had happened until I was sixteen, and I did that. For him. Because I loved him."

Valentin yanked my hand toward him, the rest of my body following so we were face-to-face, an intense expression on his face. "Now, listen to me. You were fifteen. He knew what he was doing. You did nothing wrong. Not when you kissed him. Not when you had sex with him. Not when you moved in with him, and not when you lied for him. It was all him. And if you loved him, well, that wasn't stupid either because that was exactly what he intended to happen. You. Weren't. At. Fault. So stop feeling guilty. Stop feeling stupid, and for God's sake, stop drowning yourself in alcohol so you don't have to think about it."

I studied him, trying to work out what it was that I was feeling. Then it hit me. I felt raw, but I felt cleansed somehow because I knew he was right. How could the adolescent be the one at fault? I should have spoken to someone years ago. I just hadn't met anyone pushy enough who refused to let me get away with not talking about it. "Thank you."

He sat back in the chair with a sigh and crossed his arms over his chest. "I'll bill you for the therapy later."

Chapter Ten

Valentin

He may have said thank you, but I wasn't wholly convinced that Max meant it. Not yet, anyway. He would be grateful once he finally learned to let go of the guilt and began to heal. Ever since the first moment I'd met him, it had been obvious that he was carrying around a lot of baggage. Given his relationship history, or lack of, it had been obvious that there had to be a man at the center of it. The rest I'd pieced together during our conversation from his body language and the things he wouldn't say. Then it had simply been a case of asking the right questions in order to get him to open up.

He sat staring into space, a slight furrow on his brow. I'd expected a demand that I return the favor and talk about my own past, but it hadn't happened yet. He was too busy processing. What he needed was a distraction, a reminder that the present was always far more interesting than the past. "Let's go to bed."

The frown grew deeper. "Bed?"

"You have one, right? I'm assuming that you don't hang from the rafters like some overgrown bat?" At least that comment elicited a faint smile. I struggled to my feet. Even with the special boot provided by the hospital, I was loath to put weight on my ankle, the memory of what happened onstage all too vivid in my mind. I reached for the crutches, wedging them firmly beneath my armpits. Max hadn't moved an inch, his gaze still fixed on the surface of the table. "Bring condoms."

"Condoms?"

He needed to be shocked out of the state he'd fallen into, not treated with kid gloves. I gave him my best Valentin Bychkov withering glance. "This echoing thing is getting a bit tiresome, Max. On your feet. Condoms. Make yourself useful and fuck me."

He stood, leaning on the kitchen table as if he needed it for support. "But your ankle?"

I took a few steps. I was getting better on the crutches. Once I thought of it as being like a dance and had everything coordinated in the right order, it was much easier. The doctor had said that I would only need to use them for the first few days, just until I was confident enough that the protective boot would do its job. "I don't fuck with my ankle. I think we'll manage." I continued to the stairs. "Don't worry, I'll find your bedroom on my own. I didn't want a tour or anything." Truth be told, I'd already taken one before having a shower. The contents of Max's closets didn't reveal anything about the man that I didn't already know.

I began to make my slow way up the stairs, Max hovering

behind me. "I could carry you. That might be easier." His tone said "and quicker," but he had more sense than to voice it aloud.

The offer made me smile. Not that Max could see it when I had my back to him. It was tempting, but old habits of independence were hard to shake off. "I can manage."

"I know you can, but..."

I stopped for a breather halfway up the stairs, turning slightly and waiting for Max to finish his sentence. It never came. There was only a shrug. It took another few minutes, and I was sweating by the time I'd managed it, but I finally reached the top of the stairs. I took another quick breather before I attempted the last few steps to his bedroom. Using the tip of one crutch to push open the door, I pretended to view the room as if it was the first time. It was your typical bachelor's bedroom, bare apart from a huge bed, a TV, and necessary storage for clothes. I sank onto the bed, letting my crutches fall noisily to the floor, and eyed the expanse of the bed. "How many men have slept here? Apart from you?"

Instead of joining me on the bed, he leaned against a chest of drawers. "I bet you already know the answer to that, don't you?"

I held up my hand, shaping my thumb and forefinger into a rough circle and arching my eyebrow in a question.

He nodded, his gaze flitting away as if he was embarrassed to admit to it. "Are you sure you wouldn't rather sleep on the sofa?" His mouth twitched as he realized what he'd said. "Hang on. What am I saying? You'd be more likely to tell *me* to sleep there,

164

while you have the bed."

I pulled my borrowed T-shirt over my head, stretching my arms back to show off the muscles in my chest. "That's true. But guess what. I'm feeling generous, so I'm going to let you share."

He crossed his arms over his chest. "I can't believe how calm you're being."

"About what?"

"About everything. About what Dmitry did to you. About your ankle. Aren't you worried?"

I removed the medical boot, staring down at my swollen ankle, the anti-inflammatories and the ice pack having brought the swelling down slightly, but it still looked angry and red. I laid my hand against it, the skin feeling warm to the touch, and I thought carefully about what Max expected to hear. Then I scrapped that and told the truth. We'd come too far for me to hide behind half-truths. "Of course I'm worried. More than worried. I'm... scared." I swallowed, trying to fight down the panic threatening to claw its way up my throat. "But panicking won't make it heal any quicker, so it's a waste of energy... and the doctor said it will heal, even without surgery, so I should dance again." I didn't like the way the last sentence sounded in my head, so I hurried to correct it. "No! I *will* dance again! Not for a while. But eventually. And"—I smiled—"when I do, I will be glorious."

Gaze fixed on me, Max advanced toward the bed, a hunger in

his eyes, the likes of which I'd never seen before. He pushed me back and then straddled my hips, bare hands sliding across my chest. "You will be. I have no doubt." Seconds went by as we stared deep into each other's eyes. When I'd told Max to fuck me in the dressing room, I'd thought that's all it would be. A selfish moment of pleasure I'd grabbed for myself numerous times before with men whose names and faces I couldn't recall. But this thing between us kept growing bigger and bigger. I imagined the icy film around my heart slowly beginning to melt. Scared he'd be able to read the intensity of my feelings in my expression, I tapped him on the chest. "Clothes off." He reluctantly climbed off and started to strip while I did the same. "I love the fact you do what I tell you."

He paused with his trousers halfway down his thighs. "A diva like you needs to believe that."

I threw my head back and laughed. "Oh, I'm a diva, am I?" Careful not to jolt my ankle, I wormed my way backward on the bed until my head touched the pillow. "Come here, and I'll show you how much of a diva I can be in bed."

Naked, Max crawled across the bed until we both lay on our sides, facing each other, his stare considering. Slowly, he reached out, his hand barely skimming my shoulder before moving to my neck. "What are the chances of you allowing me to take it slowly?"

I moved my neck, trapping his hand against my shoulder and rendering it immobile. "How slow is slow?"

He shuffled closer so that our bodies touched, my cock giving a twitch of appreciation at the contact. "I just thought, what with your newfound love of kissing that we could throw in a bit more foreplay than we have before."

"I don't love kissing. I was prepared to endure it in order to wean you away from the beer."

"That's very charitable of you." Max dipped his head, his lips barely brushing mine. When I instinctively moved forward to reinitiate the contact, he laughed. "Say please."

"Fuck off."

"Diva."

I planted a hand in the middle of his chest, intending to push him onto his back and make it clear who was boss. The jolt of pain from my ankle reminded me that it wasn't a good idea. I rolled over onto my back. "As I'm incapacitated, I guess that just this once you can do whatever you want."

Max didn't need asking twice. I watched through lidded eyes as he knelt at my feet. He dragged a pillow across, kissing the swollen skin of my injured ankle before propping it carefully on the pillow. It was an incredibly sweet gesture that brought a lump to my throat. I was suddenly glad that past circumstances meant that for the past however many years, he hadn't been with anyone for more than one night. Even though he wasn't, it made him feel like mine and mine only. He moved across to the other leg, kissing his way up my calf and smiling when I instinctively attempted to jerk away when his lips located the sensitive skin of the back of my knee. He continued up my thigh, bypassing the swollen part of my anatomy that most wanted attention from his lips to move to my chest instead. I made a feeble attempt to push his head back down to where I wanted it. "Suck my cock."

He licked at one nipple before moving to the other. "Not yet."

"Max?"

My plea went unheard, and I resigned myself to the fact that he was going to drive me crazy first. I wasn't used to this. I was used to getting from A to Z in record time, where intensity of pleasure drove the possibility of other feelings out of my head. But here, with lips exploring every inch of my body and my poor neglected cock getting no more attention than the occasional graze of his torso when he shifted position, there was no choice but to feel. I turned my head to the side, fastening my attention on the chest of drawers and following the pattern of the wood. A firm hand gripped my chin, forcing my head back to him and I found myself looking up at Max as he loomed over me. "Stay with me."

"I can't. It's..."

He lowered his body over mine, our bodies fitting together like they were made for each other. "I know. I feel the same. But we can either fight it or give in."

"I don't know if I can."

He kissed his way along my jaw, each touch of his lips causing a pinprick of sensation. "You can. You just need to make that leap." He grabbed hold of my wrist, lifting my hand off the bed and placing it on his lower back. When I made no move to do anything else with it, he slid it slowly down until my hand cupped his ass. "Touch me."

Then his lips were on mine, and his tongue was in my mouth. It was nothing like the kiss had been in the kitchen. There we'd been fully dressed, learning each other's mouths, learning the way we moved and what we liked. Here, with that knowledge safely tucked away and our naked bodies pressed together, we went straight to inferno level. It had been a mistake to bargain with him, to use his weakness as an excuse to prove to him that there were things in life he wanted more than alcohol. But, my God, what a mistake! I kissed him back feverishly, needing it more than I did oxygen, my fingers digging into the taut muscle of his ass.

Of its own accord, my other hand lifted from where it had been clasped in the sheets. It mirrored the one already on his ass, and just like that, the dam broke, and I gave in, refusing to hold myself back anymore. We writhed together, mouths fused, hands exploring, both of us needing to be closer, even though we were already glued together. I wrenched my mouth away from Max's. "I need your cock."

For once, he didn't argue. There was a fumble of ripping foil, a squish of lube, and then Max was braced over me, a hand pinning only one thigh back. I was touched that when I could barely think of anything but getting him inside me, he was still considerate enough to remember my ankle. There was a burning pressure as he pushed forward and then the delicious feeling of fullness. I slid my hands back down to his ass, controlling the speed and depth of his thrusts as I captured his mouth again, only breaking apart when one of us needed to take a shuddering breath.

Max mumbled something against my cheek, but I was too far gone to register what it was. I cried out as he pegged my prostate, managing to squeeze a hand between our bodies to give my cock a few strokes. That's all it took to come, my body lighting up as he continued to thrust, his groans loud in my ear as he thrust deep and filled the condom.

Satiated lips found mine, and I kissed him back. It was as if now that we'd started, we couldn't stop. These kisses were slow though. Lazy. They were the kisses of two satisfied men, thanking the other one for getting them to that point.

Max finally rolled off, throwing the condom into a wastepaper basket by the side of the bed. I could feel his eyes on me as he propped himself up on one elbow. "How's your ankle?"

I flexed my foot, slowly but carefully, reaching down to extract the pillow beneath it and hand it back to Max. "It's fine."

Still his gaze bored into me. I gave him a searching look, at the same time as I reached for a tissue to clean myself up. "What?"

His lips quirked. "This is the point where you normally walk off or try and get rid of me. I'm waiting for the cool mask to snap into place."

He had a point. "Well... I can't walk. And it's your house, so the first two are out of the question, and as for the mask" — I rolled my head to the side so I could see him, my eyes narrowed — "I don't know what you mean."

He laughed and pulled the duvet over both of our bodies before draping himself around me, his body heat burning into my skin. "Right. Got it. No mask. You're naturally emotionless and cold three seconds after an orgasm."

"Three?" I turned slightly, my head resting on his chest. "You're being rather generous there."

"I'm a generous man."

I knew he meant it as a joke, but when I thought about everything he'd done for me that day, it was hard to dispute. He'd gone against Dmitry, he'd sat with me for hours in a hospital, he'd held me up literally as well as figuratively, and then he'd brought me back to his house. The generosity wasn't in doubt. The question was why. It went way beyond just developing feelings. "Are you falling in love with me?"

There was the tiniest hitch in his breathing, but no hesitation apart from that. "Yes. Does that scare you?"

"Does it scare *you*?"

"Do you have to answer a question with a question?"

171

"Do you?"

His chest shook as he laughed. Then it subsided suddenly. "After James, I didn't think I'd ever have feelings for anyone again. Maybe it helps that you pretend you don't have any. Which is also why you're about to change the subject."

I considered his words and then did it anyway. Love was a concept that I was going to need a lot longer to wrap my head around. "You know you can't turn up for work tomorrow, right? You have to stay away from there. Stay away from Dmitry."

He nodded, his chin moving against the top of my head. "I'm not stupid. I'd worked that out. I guess that means though that you'll have me all to yourself tomorrow."

"Great!" The word laden with sarcasm might have been convincing if it weren't for the smile I couldn't quite manage to hold back.

Max shifted slightly. "Will you tell me about him? About your history? I'd like to know."

My smile died. "Who? Dmitry?"

"Yes."

I closed my eyes. And there was the question I'd expected earlier, raising its ugly head. "Sure. But not tonight. Later. I'll tell you anything you want to know."

Chapter Eleven

Max

I dropped my keys on the table, the clatter sounding loudly in the empty hallway. "Valentin?" No answer. My senses immediately went to red alert, nightmare scenarios jostling in my head for the position of most likely from Valentin leaving to Dmitry having found him and dragged him away from there.

We'd spent three days holed up together. The only person I'd spoken to in that time was Yakov. I'd called him at the theater and made up some bullshit excuse to cover not returning to work. The fact he'd accepted it so readily told me that he knew the real reason, that we were both going through the motions for courtesy's sake. At least I was freelance, with an otherwise good reputation. Leaving without notice shouldn't cause any problems long-term. After all, I'd stepped in at the last moment as a replacement anyway. Noel had called constantly, but so far, I'd ignored him. It was probably a blessing that we'd left the theater without any of Valentin's possessions, including his phone, or I dreaded to think what sort of calls he might be getting.

Today was the first day I'd left the house, and I'd only been gone for ten minutes. *Could someone have been watching? Ready to spring into action the moment I'd left Valentin alone?* I took a step forward, fear, a living, breathing creature sitting on my chest. I repeated his name but louder this time. "Valentin?"

He appeared in the doorway of the living room with a frown on his face. "Why are you shouting? I'm not deaf."

He'd stopped using the crutches around the house, the boot doing a good enough job of protecting his ankle from being put under too much strain as long as he didn't try to do too much. Relief made my tone terser than it needed to be. "Then answer the first time."

He hobbled past me toward the kitchen, his only response the slight lift of one eyebrow. I followed, aiming my words at the back of his head. "Sorry. I was worried when you didn't answer."

He crossed his arms and looked decidedly unimpressed. "You're the one who insisted on going out, even though I told you it wasn't a good idea. And you're worried about me?"

I held up the carton of milk. "You don't drink tea without milk. I have to keep the diva in the style that he's accustomed to."

He tilted his head before gesturing down at himself, clad as he was in borrowed sweatpants and an old T-shirt. There'd been no other option, other than him living in the ballet tights he'd left the theater in. "Really? Well, you're sadly lacking in that department, then."

I moved forward, depositing the milk on the table before wrapping my arms around him and nuzzling his neck. His neck, which sported a number of red marks where I'd gotten carried away in the heat of passion. I'd apologized after the first one, and then when he hadn't seemed remotely bothered — and I suspected he was actually quite pleased — I'd added to them. I kissed over each of the marks before moving to his lips. He responded for a moment before pulling his head away. "You are obsessed with kissing."

I smiled against his lips. "No. Just with you."

We both startled as my phone started to ring. I scanned the kitchen, locating it over on the kitchen counter. Valentin grabbed my arm. "Don't answer it."

"I don't even know who it is. It might be my mum." He refused to let go, so I ended up dragging him with me. I held the screen up so he could see. "It's Noel. He keeps calling and leaving messages. I'm going to have to answer it eventually. He's entitled to some sort of explanation." Valentin looked less than convinced, and I realized that the bubble we'd co-existed in for the last few days where nothing mattered apart from sex, banter, and more sex had had to come to an end at some point. We still hadn't talked about Dmitry, and that conversation was probably well overdue, the anxious look on Valentin's face showing more clearly than words ever could that I needed to know exactly what I was dealing with. It was one thing to know the basics, but I needed to get my head out of the sand and know the full story.

I pressed the button before the call could go to voicemail, Valentin still glued to my side. "Hey, Noel. If you're going to shout at me, can we pretend that you've already done that part and skip past it?"

"Max?"

I frowned at the phone, wrapping my arm around Valentin's waist so that he could lean against me and take some of the weight off of his ankle. "Who else would be answering my phone?"

"Can we meet tomorrow? I need to talk to you. We could grab a coffee at that place around the corner from the theater?"

Valentin was close enough that even without the phone on speaker, he could hear both parts of the conversation. He started shaking his head. I gave him a squeeze to show that I understood what he was trying to communicate. "Can't we just talk on the phone?"

"No." There was a long pause. "I need to... see you. It's important. I really need your help with something."

This didn't sound like the usual Noel. He could be intense, but he wasn't usually this bad. "Are you all right, mate? You sound stressed."

Valentin leaned up to whisper in my ear, his breath hot against

176

my face. "Tell him no."

I covered the receiver with my hand. "I can't. He's an old friend. We've known each other for years. Something's going on with him. I can tell."

Fingers dug into my arm. "You can't go near the theater. It's too risky."

He had a point there. I racked my brain for an alternative. I could invite him to the house, but then what about Valentin. I could hardly make him hide in the bedroom while Noel was there. If I said no to Noel, then there was a chance that he might drop around uninvited anyway. Therefore, it was better to bite the bullet and get the meeting over and done with so that he could moan about my hasty exit from the theater, and get whatever else was bothering him off his chest. But I needed the meeting to be on my own terms.

I pulled the phone back to my ear. "Listen, I'm really busy tomorrow, so I'm not going to have time to get over to Covent Garden and back. Can you come here? There's that little place on the corner of the High Street. Do you remember? The one that does all the fancy cakes?"

"Yeah, I remember. I'll meet you there at twelve."

I was halfway through agreeing when the click in my ear signaled that he'd hung up. I pulled a face at the phone.

"You can't go."

I maneuvered Valentin in my arms to face me. I'd finally gotten used to seeing him without makeup. He was still gorgeous. He was just gorgeous in a more natural way that made him look a damn sight more approachable, even when he was doing his best haughty Russian act like he was now. "What's the alternative, I never leave the house again?" I gestured at the milk. "Besides, the café's not much farther than the shop was. I'll be fine. And it's only Noel. He probably wants to borrow money, or he's had a row with his girlfriend or something. He said it was important and I don't want him coming here to the house. Not with you here."

"Max, I am concerned."

I gathered him close, pressing his body against mine and burying my nose in his hair. Three days ago, he probably would have pushed me away, but my icy Russian was slowly thawing. "I know, and it's sweet, but lovely as your concern is—and don't get me wrong, it *is* lovely—I have to go out at some point. I have to see my mum in two days anyway, and it's not like I cannot bother to work forever. I have savings, but they'll run out eventually."

Valentin's sigh reverberated against my shoulder. "I need to tell you about Dmitry. Then perhaps you will change your mind."

I pulled a face at the mention of the man's name. "Let's eat first. I have a feeling that whatever you're going to tell me will ruin my appetite." Valentin didn't bother to dispute the fact. He gave a terse nod and stared grimly back at me.

* * * *

Valentin leaned back against the headboard of the bed, a lit cigarette clasped between his long fingers. I'd seated myself in a chair next to the bed, wanting to give him a bit of space. I wasn't overly happy with him smoking in the bedroom, but I suspected he needed the comfort of the nicotine to be able to tell the story he was about to. He exhaled, a plume of smoke rising into the air. "Where do you want me to start?"

He'd told me so little it was hard to know. All I knew was that Dmitry *might* have connections to Bratva and was a dangerous man, and technically it wasn't Valentin who had told me that, it was Noel. Valentin had just confirmed it. "Wherever you need to."

He thought about it for a moment. "The very beginning, I guess. I grew up in Kasimov in Russia, a small town on the banks of the river Volga. It is very picturesque, but there is not a lot there. A chocolate factory, a fishing net factory, houses. It is not a rich place. There is very little in the way of opportunities if you come from a place like that." He cupped his hand under the cigarette, suddenly becoming aware of how precarious the long line of ash had become.

Instead of an ashtray, I gestured toward the mug on the nightstand. He tapped his cigarette on the side, the ash falling into the cold remnants of tea. I waited for him to start talking again.

He frowned. "Actually, I probably have to go back farther than that, explain how my English mother ended up in Kasimov. She was a dancer, a ballerina." A small smile flitted across his lips. "That's why she was in Russia, to learn from the best. She was only nineteen. She was on the precipice of having the world at her feet."

"What happened?"

His mouth twisted. "Love happened. My father, or should I say the man that would become my father, saw her dance. He hung around by the stage door for hours afterward, just for the chance of being able to introduce himself to the woman that had already captured his heart." He tapped his cigarette against the side of the mug again. "They went for coffee. They talked all night. By the morning, they were already in love. My mother had... obligations. She was only meant to be in Russia for a few short weeks and my father, well, my father had connections which were less than savory."

"Bratva?"

He nodded. "An English dancer was far from an acceptable choice in their eyes."

I could join the dots and see where the story was going to go next. "So they ran away?"

Valentin smiled, but it carried a lot of sadness. "They chose love over duty. But it left them with nothing. Hence, how we ended up in Kasimov: my father working in a fishing net factory and my mother doing people's laundry. She was already pregnant by that time, but they hid it. They were married, and when I arrived earlier than expected, they lied and kept up the charade that I was premature."

"Why didn't they both come to England? Surely, they could have had a better life over here?"

Valentin stubbed out the cigarette and immediately lit another. "I think they tried, but immigration laws made it difficult. They ran the risk of ending up separated, and I assume that my father was concerned that his passport would gain unwelcome attention at an airport. Bratva is nothing but thorough. Don't get me wrong, Max, my childhood was happy. When my mother wasn't doing laundry, she taught me to dance. I used to perform for all the children in the town."

Although it was a fascinating insight into a young Valentin, impatience still got the better of me. "Where does Dmitry come into this?"

"We'll get to that. All in good time, Max. All in good time."

"Sorry." I gave him my best guilty expression.

"They managed to hide away for years. But I guess it was always inevitable that their whereabouts would be discovered eventually. Bratva doesn't let things go. So one day, we had visitors. I'll never forget the look on my father's face when they turned up at the door. Four men, all in suits — charming on the outside, but their eyes said something completely different. He knew the game was up. I was fifteen at the time. I was sent to my room out of the way, so I have no idea what was said in that conversation. I asked, but they wouldn't tell me. A week later, my parents were both dead, killed in a tragic car accident when the brakes failed."

I rocked back in my seat, taking a moment to process what he'd said before I risked saying something stupid. The question had to be asked though. There was no ignoring it. "You think there was a connection?"

Cool hazel eyes met mine, his fingers tightening around the cigarette. "It was one hell of a coincidence if not, wasn't it?"

I leaned forward. "What do you *think* was said in that conversation that you didn't hear?"

Valentin thought for a moment. Although, I found it hard to believe that he hadn't considered it at least a hundred times before, given what he'd told me. "I think they were given an ultimatum. And I assume that my parents told them what they could do with that ultimatum. My father had gone too far to let himself be sucked back into that life. We may not have had much, but he was happy nonetheless. We all were."

"Then what happened?"

The second cigarette joined the remnants of the first. Valentin's fingers twitched as if he were fighting the urge to light another. "I was too young to live on my own. I would have gone to an orphanage. For a year at least until I was sixteen. There would have been no dancing. My life from that moment would have been finding a factory job and working many hours to make ends meet. And even then, it would have been barely. Then Dmitry showed up and made me an offer. He said that it was not fair that I should be punished for the actions of my parents, that I deserved to be embraced into the bosom of the family that I'd never been given a chance to get to know."

"And you told him yes?"

Valentin's face took on an expression as if I'd insulted him. "Not exactly. Am I an easy person, Max? Or would you call me stubborn?"

I smiled. "Definitely stubborn."

"I told him no. I told him that I'd rather live on the streets. That I had no intention of becoming involved with an organization such as Bratva."

"And he accepted that?"

Valentin lost the battle and lit a third cigarette. "He made a counter offer. He told me that he was prepared to personally take me under his wing. Separate from the organization. That he would provide the best dance lessons that money could buy, and give me everything else that I needed in order to be a success, and in exchange, I would give him a large percentage of my earnings and *make myself useful*."

"The parties?"

Valentin nodded. "Although I didn't know what he meant at the time. I was only fifteen. My only kiss was with a boy I went to school with. It was difficult to be gay in a small village in Russia. The parties didn't start until I was sixteen."

My blood ran cold at the thought of a sixteen-year-old Valentin being forced to entertain a string of middle-aged men. He may have learned to pull the wool over Dmitry's eyes since, but I suspected that had come much later. No sixteen-year-old virgin was capable of that. But I knew from our phone conversation that he didn't like to be thought of as a victim so I didn't broach the subject of what those early years must have been like for him.

There was another unanswered question though. Something I'd been considering ever since I realized the control Dmitry exerted over Valentin. Sometimes not knowing the truth was easier, but shying away from it wasn't fair on Valentin. And I had a feeling that this was the one and only time that he would be this forthcoming. I stumbled over the words. "And what about... Dmitry? Did he... is he? Christ! I don't know how to ask this."

"Did he touch me?"

I gave a jerky nod, hardly daring to breathe, my eyes fixed on Valentin as he stared into the distance without speaking. Finally, he shook his head. "No. Not in that way. I thought he would. I spent many nights lying in bed in his mansion, waiting for the day that I would have to accept that that was the way it was going to be. But he was never interested in me in that way."

"But he is gay?"

Valentin's scrutiny settled on me. "What makes you say that?"

"I saw the way he was looking at someone at his party, a cute blond guy. He seemed to be checking him out. Are you saying he's not?"

Valentin's mouth twisted. "Not openly. I'm guessing his organization wouldn't like it. I've never seen him do more than look at the parties. But I figured that his willingness to throw the parties in the first place — much as he might try and pretend that they cater to all sorts — means that he shares his preferences with the clientele. I guess I was just never small and blond enough for him. Lucky for me."

"Those men. They must be horrible."

Valentin thought for a minute. "Not all of them. Some are lonely. Some are trapped in a marriage that they should never have gotten into, and some of them just wouldn't get anywhere near the boys at the party without paying for it."

He sounded as if he almost felt sorry for them. But then I guessed that after years of attending the parties, he'd had to find his peace with them somehow. I was still confused about Dmitry though. "If he's never been interested in you in that way, I don't get why he's so determined to..."

"Control me? Even though I would not join Bratva?"

I nodded.

Valentin cocked his head to the side. "I have thought about the same thing numerous times. The best explanation that I can come up with is this..." He stubbed the cigarette out and I moved the packet farther away from him before he could reach for a fourth. He raised an eyebrow but didn't protest. "He has a car back in Russia. I do not know what brand it is. Cars are not my thing, but it is one of a kind. He doesn't drive it. He won't sell it. It just sits there, and it is his, and everyone knows that it is his and they cannot have it. I am like that car, a one-of-a-kind possession."

A smile hovered on his lips, and I wondered what he could possibly find amusing about the fact he'd basically admitted that Dmitry owned him. "But he's let you go now."

His gaze swung toward me. "Has he?"

My brow furrowed. "He told you that in front of everyone. He said you were of no use to him anymore."

Valentin sighed. "Dmitry is a volatile man. He says one thing, and then an hour later, he says something different entirely. Which means me being here puts you in danger."

"I don't care!" It was true. I didn't. In my eyes, the risk was worth it. "And don't go saying something stupid like you'll leave. You're staying. And that's not up for debate." I reached across, grabbing his hand and refusing to let go, even when he looked at me like I was forcing an act of depravity on him. "And you'll bloody hold my hand as well."

"Is this another thing you're obsessed with?"

I pushed him over, making room so that I could join him on the bed. "I told you. I'm obsessed with you. That means your hands, your lips, your" — I struggled to recall the right word — "*Khu il?*"

He shot a disgusted look my way. "*Khui.*"

I grinned, glad that I could lighten the mood somewhat after Valentin baring his soul. Talking about his parents couldn't have been easy. "Sorry. My Russian teacher is severely lacking."

He rounded on me. "Darling, I am not severely lacking in anything."

I tilted my chin. "Kiss me then. Prove it."

He affected a bored look. "Must I?"

I slid my hand down, smoothing it over his crotch, ready to back off at a moment's notice if it was too soon after such a harrowing conversation. He parted his thighs, giving me better access, and initiated the kiss.

Chapter Twelve

Valentin

"Come and look at this." I angled Max's laptop toward him and waited until he'd obediently ambled over before pressing play. The YouTube video started, and the version of me on screen began to dance. It was one of my best performances from just before the problem with my ankle had started. I'd danced my heart out, knowing that it was my audition for the starring role in London. Dmitry may have had a lot of financial pull, but I'd still had to back it up with a performance to match.

Max's hand shot out, and he pressed pause. "Let me check what I'm expected to do here. I'm meant to watch this and tell you how beautiful your dancing is and how talented you are. Do you require me to get my cock out and jack off while I'm watching as well?"

I laughed. I couldn't remember there being anyone since my parents who'd been able to make me laugh as much as Max did. "The first two definitely. A diva requires adoration. The latter won't be necessary." I affected a slight look of confusion. "Unless

188

that's what you were used to doing in the sound booth. I always thought it was drool on the glass. Now I'm not so sure."

Max made a halfhearted swat at my head which I avoided easily. The mood had lightened considerably since I'd told him about my past and where Dmitry fit into it. Which was stupid really. He should have been throwing me out onto the street and putting as much distance between the two of us as he possibly could. But I guessed there was something about a mutual baring of souls that brought two people closer together, particularly when neither was used to doing it. I'd had no one to tell, and Max, well, he'd been hiding under the misapprehension of it being his fault. "Just say if you do not want to watch it."

Max rolled his eyes and pressed play again. While he watched the video, I watched him, noting the flush on his cheeks. "Does it turn you on when I dance?"

He didn't take his eyes away from the screen. "You know it does. Even from the first time I saw you onstage, I wanted you."

I hooked my good leg around his calf and used it to pull him closer. My seated position brought his crotch into perfect alignment with my mouth. I paused the video so that his gaze returned to me and then deliberately licked my lips. I hadn't blown him since the hotel room. I was looking forward to getting reacquainted with the taste of his cock. His hand dropped to my hair, and he groaned. "You know I have to go out. I have to meet

189

Noel."

I traced the line of his cock through his trousers. "Or you could forget all about that, and come in my mouth instead."

The firm length under my hand gave a decided twitch. I stroked it harder. I wanted to blow him, but even more than that, I didn't want him to leave. Everything was good between us. Him leaving meant a chance that the status quo could be disrupted in some way. I moved my hand to his zipper, getting it halfway down before his hand grabbed my wrist. "Val, stop trying to manipulate me into not meeting Noel."

I stared at him aghast. Not because he'd accused me of trying to manipulate him, that part was true, but because he'd shortened my name. "What did you call me? Val! I am not a middle-aged woman with four children who works in a supermarket."

Max's lips twitched with amusement as he pulled his zipper back up, my hand falling from his crotch. "I do apologize for my overfamiliarity there, Mr. Bychkov. I have a horrible habit of mistaking someone's hand on my cock as breaking through the intimacy barriers." He leaned forward and dropped a kiss on my lips, taking away any opportunity to respond. "When I get back, you can blow me to your heart's content, and I will most definitely come in your mouth if that's what you want."

I gave it one last try as he grabbed his jacket. "Stay."

He turned back, a look of regret on his face. "I'm only going to be gone about half an hour. An hour at most, depending on what it is that Noel needs to talk about, and it's just down the road. Lock the door after I've gone, and if anyone knocks, don't answer it. It won't be anyone important anyway. If it makes you feel better, draw the curtains so it looks as if there's no one in. And don't worry about me. I'll be fine."

It was pointless arguing with him. He was right about the fact that we couldn't stay locked up together forever, but I would have been more than happy to put it off for one more day. I reminded myself that he'd left the previous day and had come back completely unscathed. "Bring me cigarettes."

Max pulled a face. "Sure. Because I love kissing an ashtray."

I folded my arms. "Don't kiss me then." He knew I was only joking. Once that dam had broken, it had broken spectacularly.

"Or"—Max lifted a finger, his eyes crinkling as he smiled—"I find something to offer you instead of the cigarettes. It worked for you with the beer."

It had. He hadn't touched a drop since, but I suspected that was more about the fact that I'd been constantly distracting him than anything else. That, and probably the relief of finally getting things off his chest. "Your ass maybe."

His eyebrows shot into his hairline. "Oh! You never said... you didn't... I didn't know."

I let him flounder around for a good thirty seconds. "You never asked."

I sauntered over to him — or as much as I could saunter when one of my feet was encased in a huge, spongy boot — never taking my eyes away from his face.

"Do you... Max?"

He swallowed. "Do I what?"

"Bottom?"

His tongue darted out to moisten his bottom lip. "Not since..."

I nodded, not needing him to say the name out loud. "About time we changed that then."

"Okay." He backed toward the front door, almost falling over a table in his inability to look where he was going. He let himself out, my laughter no doubt still ringing in his ears.

And then I was alone.

I spent a few minutes wandering aimlessly from room to room, picking things up and then putting them down again. I paused by the bedroom window, but there was nothing out of the ordinary to be seen: no strange cars, nobody watching the house. Nothing.

I found myself back in front of the laptop, starting the video up from where it had left off. But without being able to watch the lustful expression on Max's face, it was

depressing, a reminder of what I couldn't do and wouldn't be able to do again for the foreseeable future. I clicked on the cross in the corner to close down YouTube and checked my watch. Max had only been gone for ten minutes. Going by what he'd said earlier, he would only just have reached the café where he was meeting his friend.

Even if it was a short conversation, there was no way he'd be back for at least another thirty minutes. My hand hovered over the mouse, the temptation to do something I'd wanted to do ever since Max had told me about his past growing stronger. I wanted to Google search his sleaze of an ex-boyfriend, had even managed to get his surname out of Max for that exact reason, but with Max always around, there hadn't been the chance to put the plan into action. I had a sneaking suspicion of what I might find, but there was only one way to find out.

I typed in his name, hoping I'd spelled it right and pressed search. I skimmed through lots of useless information: people with the same name who obviously weren't him, and then my eyes were drawn toward a news story from a few years ago. *"Tutor jailed for six years for molesting fifteen-year-old boy."*

Knowing I'd been right didn't make it any easier to stomach and gave me one hell of a quandary. If I told Max, would it make it easier? Make him feel less of an idiot for being taken in by him? Or would it only make it worse? Would he wallow in guilt, knowing that if he'd spoken up, he might have been able to stop the pattern from reoccurring? I chewed on the dilemma, trying to grapple with the unusual situation of actually caring.

It was incredible to think that what should have been a quick fuck against the wall in my dressing room had blossomed into so much more, in the space of a few weeks. For the first time ever, I could picture a future where I wasn't alone. Where I'd have someone to share the good times with as well as the bad. Where I'd have someone on my side, fighting in my corner.

It couldn't happen though, right? Unless...

I closed my eyes and pictured Dmitry's face, the way he'd looked at me as I lay on that stage, the disgust in his face at the pathetic sight I'd become. He'd certainly given every impression that he never wanted to see me again. What if he'd actually meant what he'd said? What if he no longer had the remotest interest in me? That would mean I was free.

A surge of optimism hit. It had been four days since I'd collapsed onstage, and there'd been nothing. I knew Dmitry. I knew that had he wanted to, he could have snapped his fingers and gotten hold of Max's address in the space of a few seconds. So there were only three possible explanations. He didn't think that I was with Max. That seemed unlikely, especially given the fact that Max hadn't returned to the theater. It didn't take a genius to work out that that wasn't a coincidence. The second was that he didn't care, and I wished with all my heart for that to be the case. Or... the third was that he was simply biding his time and expecting me to crawl back to him.

My heart sank. The latter sounded like the Dmitry I knew. But he wasn't a patient man. How long would he actually wait for that scenario to happen without taking action? And what form would that action take?

Chapter Thirteen

Max

It took a few seconds to spot Noel as I surveyed the café. It wasn't that the place was huge. Far from it. It was just that he'd tucked himself away in the farthest corner of it. I grabbed a coffee before joining him at the table, his head shooting up and his hand knocking over the salt shaker, the lid flying off. He swore as he didn't manage to right it in time and a cascade of salt poured out onto the table. I grinned at his failed attempts to clean it up with a napkin. "A bit jumpy, mate, aren't you?"

He gave up on the pile of salt, settling for throwing a napkin over the mess to hide it. "Why would I be jumpy? I'm not jumpy."

I held my hands up in the universal gesture of surrender. "Whoa! Don't jump down my throat. It was only an observation. Nothing more. I'll retract it if it bothers you that much."

Noel ran a hand through his hair. "Sorry. I'm just... it doesn't matter. It's been a stressful few days. What with you disappearing and leaving us without a sound engineer just before the show and other stuff at the theater?"

"I didn't disappear. I rang Yakov and told him my reasons for leaving. I decided that circumstances meant that it was better I didn't go back."

"I got you that job."

I sighed. "I know and I'm grateful. I really am. It was just that, you know, things happened that I never expected to."

Noel's look turned accusatory. "You mean like screwing the star dancer? I told you to stay away from him. I told you that going anywhere near him would cause nothing but trouble."

I took a sip of my coffee while I fought to keep my temper under control. I needed to remember that Noel knew absolutely nothing about Valentin's circumstances. He only saw the rich, privileged dancer who had the world at his feet. Therefore, there was absolutely no point getting riled on his behalf.

"He must be pretty good in bed, that's all I can say... for *you* of all people to get sucked into this."

I gave him a steely stare. "You're overstepping, Noel. You've managed to insult both me *and* Valentin all in one breath. I thought we were friends."

"Sorry. I'm struggling to understand what's going on here. Where is he anyway? Is he with you?"

I sat back in my seat, not liking the direction the conversation was taking. I'd assumed that there was something amiss in Noel's personal life. But all he seemed to want to talk about were my actions and Valentin's whereabouts. "Why?"

He shrugged. "Just curious. Everyone at the theater saw him leave with you, and then no one seems to know where he is. There's been a lot of gossip." He smiled but seemed unable to look me in the eye, his gaze hovering somewhere over my right shoulder. "It doesn't seem like too much of a stretch to assume that he's with you or that you know where he is."

Alarm bells started to ring. I glanced around the café, checking for anyone in the vicinity who looked suspicious or seemed to be eavesdropping. But the only two people close to us was a mum with her young daughter, and she looked far too stressed to be carrying out any kind of covert surveillance. Besides, I doubted that even Bratva stooped to that level of subterfuge. But something didn't add up. When you put Noel's jumpiness together with the questions he was asking, it definitely added up to a conclusion I didn't like.

I looked Noel straight in the eye and lied. I didn't take pleasure in it, but it felt necessary. "I took Valentin to the hospital. Where he went after that, I have no idea. He's probably got friends in London. You know... other dancers." I affected a shrug. "Hopefully, he's okay."

"Really?"

"Yes, really. Anyway... you said you needed to talk to me about something important. What is it? Money problems? Girlfriend trouble? Is Laurie giving you grief again?"

When Noel only stared at me blankly, I knew I wasn't being paranoid. I'd been stupid to come, and I'd been even more stupid to leave Valentin alone in the house. I drained my coffee before getting to my feet. "Nice seeing you, Noel. But I've got to get back. I've just remembered something I need to do."

I was halfway to the door when he called my name. I turned back, surprised by the conflicted expression he wore. "What?"

He shook his head. "Nothing. I'll see you soon."

I hurried out onto the street, terrible thoughts going through my head, making me pause for a moment and take stock of my surroundings, in particular the parked cars outside the café. But there was nothing out of the ordinary. I turned and headed for home, wondering whether I should get Valentin his cigarettes or not. I smiled as I imagined the diva strop he'd probably pull if I arrived home empty-handed. Chances were, he'd send me straight back out again. But I wanted to get there and see with my own eyes that nothing had happened to him.

I was still smiling when a car with blacked-out windows pulled up alongside me and two men I'd never seen before climbed out. One of the men inclined his head toward the back of the car where the door still stood ajar. "Get in the car." No Russian accent this time, a Cockney one instead. But that didn't mean anything. He must have been able to tell from my face that I was giving serious consideration to running because he shifted his jacket to one side, just enough for me to be able to catch a glimpse of the gun he carried. "Don't make a scene."

Sheer panic caused my brain to go into meltdown. If I got in the car, then I was allowing myself to be trapped in there with them, completely at their mercy. But if I didn't, then what would they do? They wouldn't shoot me in broad daylight, out on the street where anyone could see. Surely. But then, was I really prepared to test that theory?

I was stuck between a rock and a hard place with no viable solution. Despite at least one of them not being Russian, they were obviously Dmitry's men. But where was he? And where were Igor and Mikhail? For all their bulk, at least they'd appeared to have a reasonable streak. Like when they'd stepped aside to let Valentin and me leave the theater. The vibe I was getting from these two was much more calculated and malicious.

I looked around, hoping for some sort of salvation. Maybe a police car parked close by or someone taking an interest in what was happening. There was nothing and nobody; I was on my own. One of the men leaned in close enough to speak directly into my ear. "I'm losing patience. Get in the car." He gripped my elbow, steering me inexorably toward it. I struggled, wishing I'd made the decision to run when I'd still had the chance, my feet dragging along the pavement. But he was stronger, his fingers bruising my arm as I was shoved headfirst into the back of the car, the leather seat squeaking as I sprawled across it. I just had time for the random thought to cross my mind that they wouldn't want to get blood on the expensive upholstery before the door was slammed shut behind me.

The driver had his hands resting on the steering wheel, the engine still running.

I stared at the back of his head, trying to place if he was someone I'd seen before or yet another unknown element. It was hard to tell though from the limited view I had. It could have been the same man who'd driven me to the club in Camden, or it could have been someone else entirely. Dmitry's network of men at his disposal was beginning to seem never-ending. One of the thugs joined me in the back seat, while the other climbed in beside the driver. "Where are we going?"

The one in the front twisted his head around, giving me no more than a cursory glance. "You'll see."

That wasn't exactly comforting. The farther the car took me from home, the more my sense of disquiet grew. I'd told Valentin I'd be no longer than an hour. I wondered what conclusion he'd come to when that time passed and there was still no sign of me. That was always assuming that Valentin was safe and well. In an effort not to think about him, I concentrated on trying to work out where I was being taken. We weren't heading toward Central London, so it wasn't the theater. From what I could tell, the destination seemed to be somewhere in East London.

It was another twenty minutes before the car turned off, slowing to a halt outside a wrought-iron gate. Thug number one climbed out of the car to open it, and the car rolled through, with the gate shutting firmly behind it. It wasn't locked, but it would still provide a major obstacle to any escape attempt. We stopped and the car door next to me was wrenched open. "Get out."

I took a look at my surroundings as I followed the order. The place appeared to be an abandoned scrapyard with piles of twisted, rusty metal dotted here and there. It was also deserted, with not a soul in sight. My mind automatically recalled the gun that one of them carried. *Were they going to kill me? Is that what they'd been ordered to do?* If so, it was hard to see any way out. My legs started to shake, and I thought about all the people I hadn't been able to say goodbye to — my mum, my friends, and then of course there was Valentin. Would he know what had happened? If he did, he'd blame himself. But it wasn't like he hadn't tried to warn me. Several times. He'd point-blank told me to stay away from him. More than once. I was the one who had ignored him. I wished more than anything that I'd had a chance to tell him that.

Thug number two gave me a shove in the middle of the back. "Walk."

I moved in the direction he'd indicated, my legs shaking so badly they were barely capable of holding me up. We seemed to be heading toward a Portakabin that I hadn't noticed before. When we were within a few feet, the door opened, and Dmitry stepped out, followed closely by Igor and Mikhail. Now I was outnumbered by five to one. Not that I'd have been able to overpower even one of them. They were taller, broader, and packing more muscle than I could ever have dreamed of, and that was before you took the gun into consideration.

Dmitry was dressed in his usual expensive, designer suit, a lit cigar clasped between his finger and thumb. I stumbled at the sight of him and received another shove in the back for my hesitation. We halted in front of Dmitry, and despite the cold sweat trickling down my back, I tried to force myself to look him in the face and not show fear.

His lips curled into a smile. "We meet again, my friend."

It would probably have been better to stay silent, but if they were going to kill me anyway, then what was the point? I might as well go down fighting and hang on to a modicum of self-respect. "I'm not your friend."

Dmitry laughed as if I'd said something hilarious. "Oh, he has found his backbone at last. It is about time, but it will not do you any good." His glance flicked to the two heavies who had escorted me there. "Did he give you any trouble?"

It was thug number one who answered. "He was reluctant. Apart from that, no."

"Reluctant!" Dmitry's smile grew wider as if the concept amused him further. "Surely not." His gaze flicked back to my face. "You must have been expecting to hear from me? After all, you have something of mine."

My mind was a jumble. Would denial help? Would claiming that I didn't know where Valentin was, the same as I had with Noel, have any effect whatsoever? The realization that Noel had been tasked with getting me out of the house hit like a sledgehammer. He had to have been. It was too much of a coincidence: the car happening to follow me on my way back home. Did that mean that they didn't know where I lived? It seemed unlikely, but then why drag me all the way out here? Why not just turn up at the house? But then Dmitry liked to play games, didn't he?

Dmitry watched the play of emotions cross my face with a smirk. "I'm talking about Valentin. Just in case you're too stupid to make that connection. You took him, and I generously let you hang on to him for a few days, but now it is time to give him back." He rolled his shoulders as if he were trying to ease out some stiffness. "And of course pay the price for taking him in the first place."

"He's not a possession! You don't own him." Even though I knew it was a terrible idea to antagonize him, I couldn't keep the anger out of my voice.

Dmitry chuckled. "Did you hear that?" He glanced at Igor and Mikhail, and they took the cue to add their own laughter to his. "Valentin does not belong to me." He leaned forward, pushing his face close to mine. It took every bit of strength and willpower I had not to take a step back and put space between myself and this odious man. "I have looked after Valentin since he was fifteen. He is like a son to me. I have fed him. I have clothed him. I have hired the best dance instructors the world has to offer for him. I have invested in shows so that he could achieve his dream. I have put him up in the best hotels, I have paid for first-class flights. I have protected him. I have—"

"You've pimped him out to your friends... and you..." My heart gave a jolt. I'd almost accused him of murdering Valentin's parents.

His eyes narrowed. "I've what?"

I shook my head. "Nothing." Even if it were true, Valentin would hardly thank me for breaking his confidence. There was nothing to be gained from mentioning it and everything to lose.

Dmitry gave a nod to Igor and Mikhail, and I didn't have to wait long to find out what instruction it conveyed as they moved forward and grabbed an arm each. Even knowing it was pointless, I still struggled, but their hands held on tightly, the grip unrelenting "Anatoly, Steve. Do the honors, please."

I didn't have long to contemplate thug one and two's names before a fist drove into my stomach. It was like being hit by a truck. I'd been punched before, but never like that. Unable to breathe, I crumpled straight to the ground, too intent on the struggle to take in oxygen to have any chance of avoiding the fists and feet that rained down on me.

I had no idea how many of them were delivering the beating. It felt like all four, but it could have been two. I doubted that Dmitry ever got his hands dirty. As a particularly vicious kick landed in my abdomen, I made an effort to curl up into a fetal position. It worked, somewhat. There were fewer blows landing on my midsection, but unfortunately it left my face more vulnerable. As a result, a kick rebounded off of my cheekbone.

I had no idea how long the beating lasted. It felt like hours, but in reality was probably only minutes. Just when I'd resigned myself to the fact that they were going to beat me to death, it stopped. I turned my head to the side and coughed, a splatter of blood hitting the ground in front of me. It hurt to breathe. It hurt to move. It hurt to do anything. I kept my eyes tightly closed, praying for the sound of footsteps walking away.

There was a rustle of material and the familiar sound of Dmitry's voice far closer than it should have been. "Open your eyes, Mr. Farley. So that I know you are listening to me extremely carefully. I have some very important things to say."

I made an attempt to open them. I really did, but one was completely swollen shut. And the one I could open provided nothing more than a blurry picture. The outline of Dmitry crouched next to me finally swam into focus. He waved a hand in front of my face, smiling when I followed the movement. "Good.

The first thing is that I would not suggest that you contact the police. My organization has contacts in a number of places. It would be" — he shrugged — "a huge waste of time. Theirs and yours. Are you with me so far, Mr. Farley?"

I spent a few seconds contemplating which response was likely to be the less painful, a nod or speaking. In the end, I went for the nod. It was the barest of movements, but it seemed enough to satisfy the cheerful monster in front of me.

"Excellent! I am so glad that we are in agreement. I knew we would be on the same page once you had a chance to think about it. The next thing... and it's very important that you remember the wording exactly, is the message you need to pass on to Valentin for me. Are you clear on that?"

Another nod.

"Tell Valentin that I expect him to return home tomorrow morning, where he will grovel for my forgiveness. Tell him that if that does not happen, then the next time we meet, my men will not treat you with the same care and respect that they have today." He leaned closer. "Some of the parts that he likes about you may even be missing. Do you understand me, Mr. Farley?"

I managed another nod, a bolt of nausea shooting through me.

He cocked his head to one side. "So, we're almost done here. I need you to repeat the message back to me, as I'd hate for there to be any more misunderstandings."

I opened my mouth, only to have to spit another mouthful of blood. Luckily, I avoided Dmitry's shoes. "Home... tomorrow morning... grovel... or you'll cut pieces off of me." I turned my face to the side and emptied the contents of my stomach, the action causing even more pain as my bruised abdomen was forced to contract.

Dmitry chuckled before rising to his feet. "That'll have to do I suppose." His feet, the only part I could now see, moved a few steps away. "Take him home. I fear that if we leave him here, he won't get any farther than the yard, and I need my message to be passed on. He's more delicate than he looks."

The next instructions were delivered in Russian. They could have been about me or they could have been about arranging where they were going to meet later for a nice glass of wine to celebrate a job well done. I had no way of knowing. My arms were suddenly yanked up, and I was pulled to my feet and half dragged, half carried to the same car we'd arrived in. I was unceremoniously dumped in the back seat, my body lurching over to one side, my face squashed into the seat. So much for my theory about them not wanting to get blood on the upholstery. It was a blessing that nobody tried to join me in the back seat as I wasn't sure I could have sat up, even if I'd tried. The car set off, each jolt of the vehicle sending a new wave of pain shooting through my body.

I managed to convince one arm to move, using the fingers of

one hand to probe at my midsection, concerned that my ribs might be broken. It hurt, but there was nothing that felt any worse than severe bruising. I closed the one eye that was open, putting all my energy into keeping my body as still as possible and weathering the rest of the bumps.

"You still alive back there?"

"Fuck off!"

It wasn't the cleverest of responses. I doubted he would have gotten into trouble had he ordered the driver to stop so he could get a few more hits in. But he simply chuckled as if I'd made a joke.

Another ten minutes passed by before the car slowed to a stop. I managed to heave myself up onto my elbows enough that I could see out of the window. My front door lay a tantalizing distance away.

"Out you get, sunshine. I'm not helping this time."

"I don't need your help." The words would have been a lot more convincing if I could have said them without slurring. I fumbled for the catch on the door, finally managing to get a good enough grip on the handle to force it open. It took even more effort to maneuver my body out of the car until I was out on the sidewalk, my body upright, but swaying precariously.

I would have leaned against the car if it weren't for the fact that it had driven off almost immediately. I turned toward the door, contemplating the number of steps it would take to get there. My garden path had suddenly become Mount Everest. I took a step and then another, hoping my neighbors weren't looking out of their windows at that precise moment. I didn't need the added complication of one of them calling the police. Despite the pain, that thought alone was enough to get me to speed up. The door finally in front of me, I leaned against the wall, trying to reach into my pocket in order to extract the key that would get me inside. I'd just managed to wrap my fingers around it when the door flew open.

I attempted to smile at Valentin, but my face wouldn't cooperate. The look on his face was far from a smile. It could only be described as sheer, unadulterated horror. "It's not as bad as it looks."

"Fuck!" He stepped forward, reaching for me in an effort to take my weight so he could help me inside.

I batted him away. "Don't! Your ankle."

He acquiesced but followed me closely as I used the support of the wall to make my slow way into the kitchen. I made it to a chair and sat down, wondering whether lying down would have been a better option. Valentin hovered in the doorway for a moment before coming in, his face twisted with remorse. "I'm so sorry, Max."

I held up a hand. "Don't! Don't you dare apologize for this. *You* didn't do it."

"But I—"

"You warned me. More than once. I was the one who chose to ignore it. Therefore, if it's anyone's fault, it's mine."

Valentin came and stood next to me. He took a deep breath. "We should try and get you cleaned up. Do you have a medical kit or something?"

I put a hand to my face, regretting it when my fingers came away red with blood. "Bathroom."

He nodded and backed out of the room, and I was left alone to contemplate the afternoon's events. There were a lot of things that didn't add up. They'd dropped me off at the house. No one had asked for my address. Therefore, they'd known all along where I lived. So why hadn't they come here in the first place? What was with the unnecessary trip to the other side of London? But then I supposed they could hardly have delivered the beating they had in the middle of the High Street.

My phone began to vibrate in my pocket. I pulled it out, noting the crack now running through the middle of the screen, and looked at the caller display. Noel. Oh, this should be interesting. I clicked the answer button, my voice sounding none too friendly. "What?"

He exhaled so loudly I could hear it on the other end of the phone. "Oh, thank God! I was worried you were..."

"Dead?"

"Something like that."

"So you did set me up?"

"I had no choice!" His voice sounded desperate. "They threatened my family, Max. What was I supposed to do? What would you have done?"

I shook my head. It was an impossible question to answer. I might have dragged him into this simply by virtue of being friends with him, but that didn't change the fact that he'd betrayed me. He'd used our bond as friends to get me out of the house and into the clutches of men who could have killed me for all he knew. I could see the situation he'd been put in. But surely, he could have found some way of warning me. He could have slipped a note into my pocket, or sent a text while we were in the café. If he had, he might have given me a fighting chance, rather than sending me out there like a lamb to the slaughter. Yet he'd said nothing. "It's done now."

"I'm sorry. I truly am. I couldn't think of any way out of it besides doing what they asked. They said they just wanted to talk to you. I'm guessing they did a bit more than that. Are you all right?"

I stared at my fingers, still stained with blood. "Not really. But I will be."

"Fuck! Do you need anything? I could come around. I could... I don't know."

"I don't need your help. You've done enough." I didn't have it in me, right at that moment, to make him feel better.

Valentin walked back into the room, clutching the majority of the medical supplies I owned as well as a washcloth and towel. He placed them on the table before walking over to boil the kettle. "Listen, Noel, I've got to go. We'll speak later."

I hung up before he could say goodbye and turned my attention to Valentin.

I studied him. I knew him well enough to know when he was rattled. He was trying to hide it, but the truth was there in the set of his shoulders and jaw. "A cup of tea would be nice."

He offered a weak smile. "Can you drink it?"

It was a valid question. I moved my chin experimentally, unable to hold back the wince caused by the movement. "I think there're some straws in the cupboard."

Valentin nodded before pulling out a mug and adding sugar. The message from Dmitry burned in my chest. It was the last thing I wanted to say, but he needed to know. Seconds ticked by as he finished making the tea, depositing it in front of me with a straw. It was only when he came over with a bowl of water and the washcloth and started dabbing at my face that the dam broke. "I need to tell you what Dmitry said."

His face was purposefully blank. "Tell me."

"He said..." I jerked my head away as Valentin pressed a little too hard. "Ow! You need to work on your nursing skills."

213

"I'm not a nurse." He dipped the washcloth in the water, the water slowly turning red.

I dreaded to think what I was going to see when I finally mustered the courage to look in a mirror. "Are you trying to stop me from telling you what he said?"

Valentin's hand froze in midair. "Probably. But putting it off will not change it. Besides, I'm sure I could probably guess. When does he expect me back? Tonight? Tomorrow?"

"Tomorrow morning. He expects you to grovel."

Valentin dabbed at a patch of dried blood, his mouth twisting into a grimace. "Of course he does. I would expect nothing less from Dmitry. And what did he say would happen to you if I didn't crawl my way back to him tomorrow morning?"

I didn't want to say the words. It made it all too real and put a pressure on Valentin that made me want to vomit. Valentin pulled back, his gaze boring into mine. I looked him straight in the eye and lied. "I'll be fine."

He shook his head. "Yes, you will. Because I will go back to Dmitry. I will grovel spectacularly, and then he will leave you alone."

I grabbed his wrist, stilling his hand and forcing his eyes back on me. I put every ounce of conviction into my face that I could. "You can't go back to him. Not after telling me that you think he killed your parents. You don't know what he's capable of. You need to get away from him. We'll..." I'd been going to say that

214

we'd go to the police, but then I remembered Dmitry's words, the way he'd stated that he had connections in high places. I cast about for another solution. Another way where we could find a way out and be together. It was hard to believe that Valentin could be so calm when I felt like someone was slowly carving my heart out with a rusty spoon, piece by piece. "There must be something we can do. We could run away. Go to another country. Hide."

Valentin's answering smile was full of regret as he placed the now red-stained washcloth back on the table. "That's a nice idea, Max. But there's nowhere far enough to hide from Dmitry's reach, I'm afraid. I'll go back to him. He'll strut around for a while, spewing words of hate and blaming me for everything, but eventually he'll calm down and forgive me. I just need to stroke his ego enough. And you... *you* will stop letting your past ruin your future. You'll find some nice men to date, and you'll find one who means more to you, who you want to have a relationship with. You'll take him home to meet your mum. You'll buy a house together and get a cat and argue over whose turn it is to do the dishes."

I wanted to cry. I knew what he was trying to do, but I couldn't picture anyone else filling that role except him. I wanted to live with *him*. I wanted to argue with *him*. *He* was the one who had unwittingly chipped away at the barriers I'd erected. *He* was the

215

one who I'd confided in about my past. If I hadn't met him, I would have probably taken those secrets to my grave. "I don't want to date other guys. I only want you!"

Valentin gestured that I should take off my shirt, my words seeming to bounce off his hardened exterior. Was he really that blasé about returning to his old life? Or was he

simply that good at putting on an act? I lifted my arms as he peeled the shirt from them. I looked down, unsurprised to see that my chest was a mottled mess of red, purple, and blue. Valentin cursed in Russian. At least I assumed it was a curse going by the way he said it. He sighed. "I was hoping that your face had taken the brunt of it." He probed at my abdomen, slowly moving up over my ribs while watching my face closely for the reaction. "I don't think anything's broken or you'd be in even more pain than you are. Do you want to go to the hospital?"

"What would I tell them?"

Valentin inhaled deeply and closed his eyes before opening them again. "I don't know. But if you need to go there..."

I shifted slightly. It was sore. There was no getting away from that, but now the shock had worn off, I wasn't in agony. Nobody could take multiple kicks to the chest, abdomen, and face and come away unscathed. I reached out and grabbed Valentin's hand, winding our fingers together. I half expected him to pull away, but he didn't. He wouldn't look at me though. It was as if he was already distancing himself. I was back to staring at the cold

Russian of a few days ago. I let go of his hand, and he turned away.

Chapter Fourteen

Valentin

When Max had been gone for an hour, I'd been able to shrug it off. He was meeting a friend. Friends often got talking and lost track of time. After an hour and a half though, dark thoughts had started to creep in. By the two-hour mark, I was climbing the walls, only capable of pacing restlessly from room to room, which wasn't easy to do when walking was a problem.

At the slam of a car door, I'd rushed downstairs, instinct telling me that it was connected to Max. My earlier optimism had disintegrated at the first sight of his face. He didn't need to tell me what had happened. I already knew. It was obvious. I'd broken Dmitry's rules. I'd dared to dream of a life that wasn't dictated by him, and this was my payment, and poor Max had been caught in the middle. I hadn't needed to hear Max's message from Dmitry. I'd already known at that point that I would be returning to Dmitry. Only the news that it would be the next day and not immediately came as a surprise. Maybe Dmitry thought it would hurt more, or maybe it was something as simple as him having business to contend with that evening. I didn't know. All I knew was that at least it gave me a chance to look after Max, the same way he'd done for me with my ankle. I'd patched him up as best I could, and then I'd slowly started the process of rebuilding the barriers that had no longer seemed necessary between the two of us. One of us needed to stay strong, and Max was in no physical shape for it to be him.

Max's pleas about the two of us running away hadn't fallen on deaf ears. I wanted it. More than anything. And maybe if it was a year from now it might have been possible. I'd been working on something, a plan of sorts, in case things ever got to the point with Dmitry where I felt I couldn't go on. Unbeknownst to him, I'd met a contact at one of Dmitry's parties. He'd maneuvered his way onto my list and eventually come clean about his reasons for being there. I'd found myself confiding in him. When he'd admitted to searching for someone, I'd given him as much information as I could. In return, he'd helped me to hatch a plan. But that plan wasn't ready to implement yet. It was missing something crucial that I hadn't been able to get hold of.

Once I'd managed to get Max undressed and, if not comfortable in bed, at least settled, I had every intention of sleeping on the couch. It would be the best thing for both of us and make tomorrow's impending separation much easier. I turned to pick up the spare blanket, hoping to get out of the room before

Max realized my intention.

"Stay!"

I froze, my fingers tightening reflexively in the folds of the blanket. I responded without looking at him. "It's better if I don't. It will only drag things out."

Max's voice sounded slightly slurred. "Please. Just until I fall asleep." I'd given him some of my painkillers, and they seemed to have done the trick. At least they'd alleviated the pain enough for him to make it up the stairs and into a hot shower. They'd also made him drowsy, so I supposed it wouldn't hurt to stay for a few minutes. That's probably all it would take for him to slip into a drugged sleep. I let go of the blanket and spun around, finding Max's bleary gaze locked on me. "Okay.
Only until you fall asleep though." I removed the protective boot but left the rest of my clothes on as I eased myself under the covers, my gaze fixed on the ceiling.

"What will happen to you... after tomorrow?"

I contemplated Max's question. It was only natural for him to need some reassurance now that he knew exactly who Dmitry was. "I'll be sent back to Russia. Dmitry has an estate with lots of people there to keep an eye on me. He still has an investment in the show, so I expect he will stay for a while, which is good for me." I looked sideways, forcing a smile. "It means that I will get some time without him, which is always good."

"And then what?"

I had a feeling he'd see straight through any lie I told, so I told the truth. "Until I can dance again, there'll be parties. Other ways he can extract his pound of flesh from me." Max looked like he wanted to throw up. "It's fine, Max. I'm used to it. This has been a nice holiday, but that's all it ever was and all it was ever going to be." There was no way I was going to share those moments with Max where I'd led myself to believe that Dmitry had moved on. In retrospect, they'd been nothing but a fantasy, a fairy tale that had no place in the life I'd chosen.

"You can't let him force you to dance until you're properly healed."

The old Valentin would have snapped at him. He would have hidden his worries about the subject behind a studied wall of indifference. But even though I was intent on putting distance between me and Max, he wouldn't have been convinced by it. "I know. I'll think of something. I'll have some time when I'm back in Russia to come up with some sort of plan that will convince him. He's not going to ruin my dance career."

A hand crept over the sheet, fastening around mine and giving it a reassuring squeeze. I squeezed back. For a moment, there was only silence until Max broke it.

"I can't believe that tomorrow we're going to have to..."

I held his hand tighter, tears pricking my eyes. I blinked

rapidly until it passed. Valentin Bychkov never cried. I'd spent years actively avoiding anything that could make me happy because I'd always known it would be ripped away from me. It was my own fault for breaking my own rules. By the time I'd composed myself enough to speak, Max was already asleep.

Even though I knew it was a bad idea, I stayed, lying next to him and listening to the sound of his steady breathing until I couldn't stay awake any longer.

* * * *

Max wasn't handling things well. He'd ignored everything I'd put in front of him, the toast and tea completely untouched. I wished I could put it down to his physical state, his face already turning a distinctive shade of purply blue, but I knew it was more to do with the impending separation. The only thing I could do was pretend I hadn't noticed. If I admitted I was hurting too, it would make it worse. In many ways, it would have been better if he'd left me lying on that stage. We wouldn't have spent days getting an insight into the way things could have been. I put a false note of cheeriness into my voice. "Where's a place near here where I can buy makeup?"

Max lifted his head from where he'd been studying the cold tea. "Makeup?"

"*Da*! Dmitry doesn't like to see me without it" — I lifted one shoulder in a shrug — "and I'm meant to be worming my way back into his good books, so I figured I'd stop off on the way and get some."

"Dmitry's a fucking idiot!"

Despite the turmoil going on inside me, that comment still managed to raise a smile. "Maybe so. But that's not helpful, Max." His mouth turned down at the corners, and he looked even more miserable. As soon as I was out of that door, he was probably going to get stinking drunk, and all my good work was going to be in vain. "Is there someone you can call to come over here? Until your mobility is better?"

He'd gone back to staring at the tea. "My mum. But she'll want to know what happened."

I spun his phone toward him on the table. "Call her now. And tell her the truth. Tell her you got yourself mixed up in something you shouldn't have, but that everything's going to be all right now."

He stared at the phone but made no move to pick it up. "There's a pharmacy around the corner." At my confused stare, he elaborated. "It sells makeup."

"Thanks." I needed to get out of there. This was doing neither of us any good. "I hate to ask, but I don't have any money... for a cab or for the makeup. Could I possibly borrow some?"

Max gestured toward his wallet in the center of the table. "Take as much as you need."

I hesitated with my hand halfway toward it. "I doubt I will be able to pay you back."

He looked hurt that I'd even suggested it. "It doesn't matter."

I opened it and took a few notes out, enough to cover the cab fare and hopefully buy makeup as well. I didn't need anything expensive, just enough to convince Dmitry that I'd made an effort.

Max watched with a haunted expression as I used his phone to dial for a cab, asking for it to come as soon as it could and repeating the words "five minutes" when they were relayed to me. A feeling had started up in my chest. A feeling I'd never had before. It was an unpleasant sensation, a tightness as if something was being constricted, and all I knew was that it got worse the longer I looked at Max. I needed air. I needed to be outside. I didn't care that the cab wasn't there yet. I'd walk to meet it if that's what it took, but I couldn't stay a moment longer. I dropped a kiss on Max's lips, the temptation to feel them one last time against my own winning out over common sense. Then I limped toward the door. I was wearing Max's clothes, clutching Max's money, but it felt as if I was leaving every part of him behind. I took one last look at him, muttered something about him taking care of himself, and then I hobbled away as fast as my injured ankle could carry me.

* * * *

I'd done the best I could with the makeup, the dim light in the cab, in combination with the small hand mirror I'd purchased, not exactly lending itself to making myself beautiful. But it would have to do. I stood for a moment outside the hotel, attempting to gather my thoughts. The feeling in my chest hadn't gone away. I'd been wrong in believing it would fade once Max was out of my sight. If anything, it had only gotten worse.

I took a deep breath, forcing every bit of weakness, every bit of softness I'd allowed to creep into my life over the last few days out of me. I had to be harder. I had to be stronger before I faced Dmitry. He might own me, but he'd never been able to push me down completely, and he never would. I walked into the hotel.

I hadn't been absent long enough for anyone at the reception desk to think to question me, or maybe Dmitry had already told them to expect me. Whatever the reason, I was able to walk straight past them to the elevator with no more than a nod on both sides. The time it took to travel the few floors was excruciating. There was always a chance that Dmitry wouldn't be there. He could be at the theater. In that case, I would have time to get a new room key from the reception and get changed into clothes Dmitry would find more agreeable, as well as redo my makeup. That hope was dashed as soon as the elevator door opened to reveal Igor leaning casually against the wall opposite.

I didn't attempt to hide the loathing in my eyes. Max hadn't been sure whether Mikhail and Igor had participated in his beating, but they'd both been there. Therefore, in my mind, they were complicit, no matter how ridiculous that reasoning might be. They were paid by Dmitry. They did whatever he told them to do. They always had, and they always would. It was a simple fact of life. "Is he here?"

Igor nodded, gesturing along the corridor toward Dmitry's suite and making a rare attempt to speak English. "You want me... tell him... you are arrived?"

I shook my head. "No. I'll tell him myself." I squared my shoulders and limped toward the door at the end of the corridor. This was a man I'd been dealing with for the last ten years, but it didn't get any easier. I knocked once and then let myself in without waiting for a response. Both Dmitry and Mikhail were bent over the desk, examining some sort of paperwork. They both straightened at my entrance, Mikhail staring at me blankly while Dmitry's expression was colder and more calculated. "Well, well, look who it is. The prodigal son returns to his rightful place."

I stood tall and straight, lifting my chin and refusing to show weakness in front of him. "Dmitry, it is good to see you."

He came out from behind the desk and walked toward me, an exaggerated frown on his face. "Is it? Because..." He paused for dramatic effect. "You have been gone so long. I kept waiting for the day you would come to your senses and return to where you belonged, and it never came. Instead, I had"—he waved a hand in the air—"to concoct an elaborate plan to send a message to you."

He clutched his hand to his chest. "A distasteful message that it pained me to send. Such a messy business. And completely unnecessary."

I bit the inside of my cheek until I could taste blood with the effort of not reacting to Max's beating being termed a messy business and Dmitry's pretense that he hadn't thoroughly enjoyed every minute. "You said you didn't want to see me again. I was giving you a chance to calm down."

Dmitry's gaze flicked disparagingly down my body, taking in the sweatpants, baggy T-shirt, and the trainer I wore on my good foot. "And you have come back looking like a homeless person?"

"I had no clothes. I had to borrow some."

His gaze moved to the protective boot on my foot, his nostrils flaring. "How long?"

"The doctors said months. They said—"

"We will consult more doctors. We will get a second opinion."

I turned my gaze to Mikhail. I don't know why. It wasn't as if I expected to get any help from that quarter. I was just the mouthy dancer he'd been tasked with shadowing for the last year. There was a strange expression on his face though, one I wasn't used to seeing. But as soon as he noticed my attention was on him, he masked it.

Dmitry was still talking. "I don't see much groveling. I assume your... what word shall we use to describe him... I guess casual

fuck does not work as you were cohabiting with him for days."
His hand shot out, turning my head to one side, his eyes
narrowing as he studied my neck. I knew exactly what he was
looking at: the marks Max had left there during our passionate
lovemaking. Max liked to leave marks, and I'd discovered that, in
perfect synchronicity, I liked to be marked. "I see you were quite
the whore for him."

I snapped. There was no one in the world who knew the right
words to enrage me quite as quickly as Dmitry did. After all, he'd
been practicing it for years. "Better to be a whore for him than for
you!"

Dmitry's hand flew out so quickly that there was no chance of
avoiding it, the back catching me full across the mouth and the
ring on his finger splitting my lip. I staggered back with the force
of the blow, tasting blood. Despite my precarious balance, I
somehow managed to stay on my feet. It was rare that he stooped
to physical violence, but then I was usually more careful not to
drive him to that point. Hand cupped over my face, attempting to
stem the flow of blood, I sought to regain some control over the
situation, letting the lies spill off my tongue. "I'm sorry, Dmitry.
That was a truly awful thing for me to say! I didn't mean it. Please
forgive me." I was pleased with the amount of desperation I'd
managed to squeeze into my voice. I needed to convince him I
was sincere, in order to undo some of the damage I'd caused by
accusing him of treating me like a whore. "I know you've only

ever had my best interests at heart. I really believed you were done with me. You looked so disappointed when I fell onstage." I managed to squeeze a tear out, knowing how pleased Dmitry would be at forcing the rare show of emotion out of me. "I know how hard you've worked to give me that opportunity in the show, so I can only guess how devastating it must have been for you to realize that all of your... no, *our* plans had been ruined."

His face, while not softening completely, had at least lost some of its hard edge, so I carried on, scenting a victory of sorts. "Forgive me, please! I *hate* it when we fight. Max gave me a place to go. Nothing more." A sharp pang pierced my heart as I uttered those words. It felt like the biggest betrayal ever, even bigger than walking out on him that morning had. "He meant nothing." It was a good job my hand was still clasped over my face, or he would have seen my lip quiver.

Dmitry turned away, flexing his hand as if he was concerned that the contact with my face might have caused an injury. He shook his head. "Go! Igor has a key for your room. Put more suitable clothes on, and we will talk later about what you can do to make it up to me."

I didn't need to be asked twice, turning around and limping back through the door and down the corridor. I stopped in front of Igor and held out my hand. "Key."

For a few seconds, curious eyes attempted to peer beneath my hand to discover what it was that I was hiding, and then he held out the keycard. I snatched it from him, swiping it against the door immediately and letting myself into the room, the door closing behind me. I stood for a moment and scanned the room. I'd thought that Dmitry in his fury might have gotten rid of all of my things, but everything was exactly as I'd left it.

It felt wrong when I was a completely different person. Five days—that's all the time it had been, but it might as well have been a lifetime. The urge to simply sink to the floor and cry was strong, but I forced myself to walk over to the dressing table. I sat down and took my hand away from my face and stared at my reflection. The bruised and bloody face staring back at me wore a haunted expression that was eerily reminiscent of the way Max had looked that morning. I picked up a wet wipe and began to remove the blood. Then I would take off the cheap makeup and ill-fitting clothes and begin the task of making myself into something stronger.

Chapter Fifteen

Max

I'd spent five days with Valentin, and it was only three since he'd left. It was funny how the five days had sped by in a flash, yet the last three may as well have been months. My body was slowly healing. I still looked as if I'd gone ten rounds in the ring with a professional boxer, but at least my movement was much improved and I'd managed on my own, only calling my mum to make up an excuse why I'd had to miss dinner with her. That was, if managing was classed as lying in bed until midday, spending most of the day huddled on the sofa, living on toast and soup.

Noel kept calling, at least three times a day. I assumed it was fueled by guilt, but I ignored him anyway. I understood why he'd done what he did. But forgiving him for his actions was going to take considerably longer. Everything was still too raw for me to even be able to contemplate it.

Most of all, I thought about Valentin. I recalled every moment we'd spent together from our initial meeting on the street to the look on his face when he'd left. I remembered all his expressions:

the way his lips quirked, the way he smelled. I remembered how
it felt to hold him, to go to sleep next to him with the knowledge
of waking up and finding him still there. I remembered his
sarcastic wit. I remembered the way he'd slowly revealed more
and more aspects of himself the longer we'd spent together. What
killed me most of all though was not knowing where he was. Was
he still in London? Or was he already thousands of miles away,
back in Russia?

Yesterday, I'd spent an hour staring at a bottle of whiskey that
I'd found tucked in the back of a cupboard. But every time I
reached out to pour a glass, I'd see Valentin's face in my mind,
bluntly stating that I had an alcohol problem, or giving me the
choice between kissing him or having a beer. In the end, I'd
poured it down the sink. He'd gone back to live with a sadistic son
of a bitch so that I'd stay safe. The least I could do in return was
stay sober.

I boiled the kettle to make a cup of tea, contemplating how
long it would be before I could think about finding another job.
There was no way I could walk into anywhere at the moment with
my face looking the way it did, so I'd been forced to take a
sabbatical until it settled down. Either that or I needed to learn
how to cover it with makeup. Makeup of course made me think of
Valentin again. Anger built at the memory of him feeling that he
had to wear it before he could return to Dmitry. As if he somehow
wasn't good enough without it.

I unscrewed the canister where I kept the teabags, swearing loudly when I realized it was empty. That meant either I went without, or I ventured outside for the first time since the beating to go to the supermarket. Adrenaline kicked in at the thought of having to step outside my front door.

I leaned against the kitchen counter, my heart attempting to jump out of my chest, as I tried to convince myself that I was being ridiculous. Dmitry had zero interest in me now. He had his prized possession back. I'd done what he'd said, and I'd passed the message on. And like Dmitry had always known he would, Valentin had run straight back to him to keep me safe. I took a deep breath, almost ready to laugh at myself for my irrational panic.

There I was, thinking about going back to work, and I couldn't even step outside my door to walk ten minutes to the local supermarket. I stood tall and sucked in another lungful of air. There was no way I was going to allow Dmitry to keep me a prisoner in my home. He'd already taken enough from me, including the man I loved. I grabbed my wallet and keys, pausing by the mirror in the hallway to inspect my face: one side was a mass of yellow and purple, interspersed with grazes that had now scabbed over, while the other had escaped virtually unscathed, apart from a black eye. I must have been lying on that side while Dmitry's goons beat me. I forced myself out the door before I could change my mind.

Ten minutes later, I grabbed a basket in the supermarket, figuring that while I was here, I may as well stock up on a few things. At least then I'd be able to hide away for a few more days. I wound my way around the shelves, throwing in a few things such as bread and milk and ignoring the curious stares directed my way. I could hardly blame them. I'd probably have done the same in their position. It was only natural to speculate about the origin of someone's bruises. Especially when they were as extensive as mine were.

The line to pay was blessedly short. I averted my eyes from the display of cigarettes behind the counter, attempting to push even more memories of Valentin out of my head: the way he looked when he smoked, the way he'd tasted when I kissed him after he'd had a cigarette. I'd made a fuss, pretended to hate it, told him he tasted like an ashtray, but in truth, I hadn't minded at all. It was all part and parcel of him.

I was only five minutes from home when I caught the movement behind me: two men, both dressed in smart-looking suits, one speaking into a phone. It was the suits and their build that made me look twice. They were different men, but you could have put them in a lineup with Igor, Mikhail, and the two from the other day, and they wouldn't have looked out of place. I quickened my pace, the shopping bag full of groceries banging against my thigh.

I turned a corner, pretending to look back at something else as I tried to gauge whether they were actually following me or if it was my paranoia taking over. They were still behind me, and they were closer. And worse still, their eyes were fixed on me.

There was no doubt in my mind that Dmitry, for whatever reason, had sent someone to finish the job. I rounded another corner and broke into a run, my bruised body protesting the motion loudly. I had two options: head straight for home and leave myself in plain sight, with the risk of another car drawing up next to me, or try and hide somewhere in the hope that they would lose me. I didn't want to be bundled into another car so I ducked down an alleyway before they rounded the corner. If I was lucky, they'd walk straight past, or assume I'd run to someone's house. I ran past bags of rubbish and a startled ginger cat, my gaze darting from left to right as I desperately searched for a good hiding place.

In the middle of the alley, backing onto a restaurant, were two industrial-sized bins. I eyed the back of the restaurant speculatively, my brain racing to try and come up with the best possible solution. The door was closed though and quite possibly locked, given that I didn't think the restaurant opened until the evening. I settled for slipping between the bins, wedging myself between one of them and the wall, my nostrils burning with the pungent smell of rotting food. I stayed as still as I could, praying that the men who had been following me would keep walking. But then what? I already knew that Dmitry had my address. I'd need to go and stay somewhere else. My mum's house was no good. I couldn't risk bringing trouble to her front door. A hotel, maybe? I fumbled for my phone in my pocket before realizing that in my preoccupation to give myself a pep talk before I'd left the house, I'd left it sitting on the kitchen table. Who would I call anyway? I couldn't call the police. Dmitry had made sure I was fully aware of that fact. Who else was there? I could hardly drag friends and family into it. Maybe I could leave London? How far could Dmitry's connections in this country possibly stretch? I had a sneaking suspicion that I knew the answer to that one, and it certainly wasn't going to provide any reassurance.

Then there were voices coming closer, voices with a distinct Russian accent. I loved Valentin's, but I'd quickly learned to associate all others with pain and fear. I leaned my head back against the wall, desperately trying to control my breathing and keeping the bag of groceries from brushing the wall so that the rustle didn't give me away. Sweat soaked through my clothes as the footsteps came closer. I wished I knew what they were saying. An "I don't think he came down here" or "this is a waste of time" would have meant a lot to me right then, but there was only a language that I couldn't understand a word of. I closed my eyes. The footsteps came to a halt, and the voices paused. Were they going away? Had they given up?

When I dared to open my eyes, one of the men stood directly in front of me, less than five feet away. He tilted his head to the side, a mocking smile playing on his lips. "Well, hello there."

My heart did a somersault, and the shopping bag slipped from my suddenly nerveless fingers, spilling its contents, the carton of milk bursting on impact with the ground, creating a pool of white liquid. I should have gone home. I could have gotten there before them and barricaded myself in. At least at home, there would have been neighbors who might have seen or heard something. I'd put myself in a deserted alley with no one around. I was an idiot, and soon, I was probably going to be a dead idiot.

The man in my eyeline reached into his inside pocket and pulled out a gun. He waved it in a clear gesture that I should come out. Was it good, that he wasn't going to shoot me where I stood, or was I desperately searching for positives that weren't there? On trembling legs, I did as he asked, his accomplice coming into sight as soon as I stepped away from the bin. I looked between them. "How's Valentin? Is he okay?"

The man farthest away, currently unarmed, shrugged. "No idea. I've never met him."

I swallowed with difficulty, given the lack of saliva. "What happens now?"

The man in front of me pulled something else from his jacket. It was a long metal cylinder. He looked down as he began to screw

237

it onto the end of the gun. "Do you know what this is?"

I shook my head, even though his head was still down and he couldn't see. I suspected it was a rhetorical question anyway.

He raised his head, a wide smile on his face. But his eyes were the deadest I'd ever seen. There was no negotiating with this man. He had the look of a stone-cold killer. "It's a silencer. It will mean that no one can hear the shot."

"W-why? I'm nobody. I'm nothing. And I did what Dmitry asked me to do."

The second man walked toward me, stopping on my right-hand side. He looked bored, his face demonstrating nothing more than he wanted to get this over and done with so that he could get on with doing something far more interesting. He said something in Russian and then laughed, his foul breath wafting in my face.

I shook my head again. "I don't understand."

The man with the gun sighed. "He said that you should probably have thought about that before you went against Dmitry. Now you're a loose end that he wants tying up. We would have come to your home, but" — he shrugged — "forensic evidence is so much more preserved in the house. All those fibers. All those blood spatters on perfectly clean walls." He surveyed the alley, my gaze automatically following as he scanned the bins, the rubbish-strewn floor, and the moss-covered brickwork of the surrounding walls.

The words *loose end* reverberated in my skull. I wondered if that was the case, or this was more about my rebellion of going against his wishes when I'd helped Valentin off the stage. I'd done nothing except fall in love with the wrong man, but even standing looking down the barrel of the gun and facing impending death, I couldn't bring myself to regret it. Valentin and I had had something special, and it might have only been for a few short days, but that didn't make it any less real. I just hoped that he'd find happiness at some point in the future. I raised my chin and looked the man holding the gun straight in the eye.

Unfortunately, my newfound fortitude lasted only a few seconds as a fist was planted in my already bruised abdomen. I went straight down, the pain so excruciating I didn't even register the rivulets of milk soaking into my clothes. Like some sick sort of action replay of a few days ago, a boot thudded into my chest. Only this time, I heard something crack. But then what did a broken rib matter when I was going to die anyway? More kicks followed, the fact that they were already landing on bruised skin surpassing the pain of the first beating. It lasted less time than the first, and it was only carried out by one man, but it was decidedly more vicious.

The armed man crouched next to me, his hand reaching into my pocket and extracting my wallet. "Excuse the beating and the fact that I need to take your wallet. But we need to make this look like a mugging. Another reason that we waited for you to leave

239

the house. I'm sure you understand." Then there was cold metal against my temple, and I was faced with the reality of only having seconds left on this earth. "Any last words?"

I lifted my head from the ground, giving the coldest glare I could muster. "Go to hell!"

He laughed, and his hand tightened on the gun, his finger ready to squeeze the trigger. Would it hurt? Or would the world simply be there one minute and cease to exist the next? I guessed I was about to find out. Shame that I wouldn't be able to share that knowledge with anyone.

"Hey! What's going on over there? What are you doing?"

The shout had come from the back of the restaurant. Someone must have come out to put rubbish in the bin. I waited for pain. I waited for oblivion. Neither came. Both the armed man and his companion had disappeared. The next thing I knew someone was standing over me with a phone clutched to his ear. The poor guy only looked to be about eighteen, his face ashen as he called for an ambulance. I lost consciousness before he'd finished the call.

Chapter Sixteen

Valentin

I glanced up at Mikhail, the man looking even more disagreeable than he usually did, which was saying something. He'd been even quieter than usual that morning, including back at the hotel and all through the trip to the airport. He was restless though and it was starting to get irritating. "Can't you sit down? You're making the place look untidy."

He shook his head, his gaze moving to Igor, who sat on a plastic chair to the right of mine. Something passed between the two of them that I wasn't privy to. Whatever it was, I didn't like it, but we were hardly friends so it wasn't as if I could politely enquire whether something was bothering them or even strike up a conversation. In a few hours, I would be back in Russia, the walls of Dmitry's estate becoming my prison once more, and wasn't that a happy thought. In the past, I'd had dance to keep me sane while I was there, Dmitry having had a special studio built for that purpose. But this time, I wouldn't even have that. There'd be nothing except boredom and parties.

241

And there'd be no Max. No Max ever again.

My fingers itched for a cigarette, but it would mean going outside the building. I'd smoked so much in the last few days that my voice even sounded scratchy. And I never had gotten that chance to fuck Max in exchange for giving up smoking. I'd never know what it would have been like. I could fantasize all I liked, and I had, but the truth remained that I would never know what his ass wrapped around my cock would have felt like. Maybe it was just as well. It would have added another thing to the long list of things that I would miss for the rest of my life.

"I didn't know that you had feelings."

"What?" My gaze shot to Mikhail, embarrassed that I'd let my guard down to the extent that my face had been broadcasting my emotions.

He stared at me for the longest time, and I was the first to look away. "You actually liked him?"

I forced myself to meet the steely gray eyes once again, my fingers digging into my thighs. "And you beat him up. Both of you."

I was surprised to see Mikhail look uncomfortable. "We had orders. We *all* follow Dmitry's orders. You included."

I let out a snort. "Isn't that the truth."

Mikhail stepped closer, his gaze showing an intensity I wasn't used to seeing. He glanced around the busy airport before switching to Russian. "How long have you been with Dmitry,

242

Valentin?"

My eyes narrowed at the use of my name. I was used to being addressed by both of them without it. What was his game? I played along, responding in Russian. "Ten years."

Mikhail folded his brawny arms across his chest as he digested the information. "You are sly. You are manipulative. You—"

"Wow, thanks!" I injected as much saccharine sweetness into my tone as I could. "That is *so* nice of you to say. I never had any idea that you felt like that about me."

He ignored me. "I do not understand why you have never implemented some sort of escape plan, a way to extricate yourself from Dmitry?"

My whole body went rigid. I could think of only one reason why Mikhail might have broached this subject, and it meant that all of the groveling, sweet-talking, and stroking of Dmitry's ego for the last few days had been for nothing. "He put you up to this?" Cogs started turning over and over in my head. *What did Dmitry suspect? What had I done that had led him to believe that I had secrets?*

Mikhail shook his head, the scar on his face twitching. "No. He did not. Do you have one?"

I worded my response carefully. "Even if I did, I'd have to be pretty desperate to take that risk, wouldn't I? No escape plan is foolproof."

"Do you love him?"

I didn't need to ask who he was talking about. It definitely wasn't Dmitry. The dull ache in my chest that I'd been medicating with excess nicotine for the last few days started up again. "None of your business."

Mikhail stuffed his meaty hands into his pockets. "Only if you did —"

"Don't."

My head swung around at Igor's unexpected interjection, especially given the fact that he'd remained silent up to now. Another wordless exchange passed between the two men. My heart started to race, a puddle of dread materializing somewhere in my lower gut. "Is this about Max?" Igor shook his head wearily, his face settling into an expression of annoyance. Whatever was going on, he was obviously opposed to saying anything. I wasn't going to get anywhere with him. I focused all of my attention back on Mikhail. In my haste to get answers from him, I'd dropped my guard completely, forgetting to hide my real thoughts and actions behind a carefully crafted layer of insouciance. "Is it? Because Max is safe. I went back to Dmitry to keep him safe. I'm going back to Russia so he'll stay safe. That's all I want." There was a note of desperation in my voice.

Mikhail tilted his head to the side, his craggy face expressing his surprise at my reaction. "You love him. You actually love him?"

244

There was no point in denying it after my impassioned speech. "Yes. I do." It was a shame to be telling Mikhail when I'd never admitted it to Max, but there'd never seemed to be a good time. And then it had been too late, my only option being to say it as I walked out of his life for good, which had seemed cruel and unnecessary. It was better he believed that I'd never gotten to that point.

Mikhail nodded slowly, his head lifting to stare sightlessly across the airport lounge as if he was struggling to come to some sort of decision. "Then you should probably know that Dmitry put out a hit on him last night."

The world tilted. If I wasn't already seated, I probably would have fallen. *Not Max. Anyone but him.* Snapshots of our time together flashed through my head, and I felt like I couldn't breathe. "He's dead?"

Mikhail finally sat, bringing his face onto a level with mine. "He survived. He's badly injured with numerous broken bones and a concussion. Dmitry was not happy. His men were disturbed before they could finish the job, but you know as well as I do that that won't be the end of it." He paused, the intensity back on his face. "So, I'm going to ask you again, if you have any sort of escape plan tucked away in that brain of yours?"

I forced myself to breathe slowly, processing the information that Max was alive at the moment. But if I got on the plane, he wouldn't stay that way. As soon as the opportunity arose, Dmitry would have someone finish the job and Max would be killed. For being with me. For helping me. For loving me. My eyes flicked back to Mikhail, the realization hitting that he was going out on a limb by providing this information. "Why are you helping me?"

Mikhail looked troubled. "I loved someone once." His lips turned up in the semblance of a smile. "He was everything to me. I left when I should have stayed... he asked me to stay... and when I eventually went back, it was too late and he was already dead."

"I'm sorry." And I truly was. I hadn't even known Mikhail was gay. Never mind the fact that he'd ever been capable of loving someone. In my eyes, he'd just been the pain in the ass who followed me everywhere and reported back to Dmitry. I wondered when his attitude toward me had changed. Was it when he'd witnessed my fall from grace on the stage? When he'd seen Dmitry hit me and call me a whore? Or only when he'd realized that there was something more lasting and deep between me and Max?

Mikhail straightened up, his face returning to its usual stony countenance. "So what will you do, Valentin?"

Good question. My mind clicked into overdrive, running through a number of scenarios and possible outcomes at a rapid speed. "I'd need time to put a few things into action. Time before Dmitry even knows I'm gone." My gaze searched Mikhail's face, the niggle that this could all still be part of some deliberate subterfuge on Dmitry's part to test me, to find out if I knew things I shouldn't, still refusing to go away completely. For all I knew, he was recording this conversation.

It seemed an infinite amount of time before he finally responded, each second corresponding with at least three thumps of my heart. He traced his finger along his scar. "Imagine... if we've already got on the plane. Perhaps you have been complaining about some sort of stomach upset all the way to the airport, blaming the prawns you ate last night..."

My eyebrows shot up at the fact he knew what I'd eaten. I motioned for him to continue.

"...you say you can't wait to go to the bathroom. We let you go because imagine the scandal if the rising star of ballet has a nasty accident on the plane in front of everyone. You must have somehow convinced security to let you off the plane. Maybe an allegation about being kidnapped or some other farfetched story that they believe. We do not realize until the plane has already taken off and we check the bathroom and realize it is empty that you are no longer on the plane. At that point, I would need to call Dmitry and inform him that you are missing, but of course I cannot do so until the plane has landed. Then we would be in Russia and unable to search for you."

His story held a certain amount of feasibility. It wasn't perfect, but at a stretch, it would do. "How long?"

Mikhail checked the boarding times and then his watch. "From now, including the flight time, four and a half hours."

I nodded, already starting to crunch times in my head. I could definitely work with that. "And how would you convince Dmitry that you were not involved?" They might not be friends of mine, but all three of us knew the price they would pay if Dmitry suspected that the story Mikhail had concocted was not true.

Mikhail smiled, his scar puckering. "We would tell him that you are a manipulative and cunning little shit."

It was my turn to smile. "I suspect he might be only too willing to believe that." I glanced Igor's way but addressed my question to Mikhail. "And what about him? Will he go along with it?"

"Yes."

"Why?" Mikhail had told me his reasons, but that didn't explain why Igor would be willing to go along with it, and he'd been quick enough to interject in an effort to prevent Mikhail from telling me about Max in the first place.

He simply shrugged, and I was left with the impression that although he wasn't exactly on board with the idea, he wasn't going to do anything to oppose it. Maybe Mikhail had more influence over him than I'd previously realized.

I wanted to ask more questions, but Mikhail was shoving something into my hand. I stared down at it. It was a cheap pay-as-you-go phone still in its packaging, which meant Dmitry couldn't have tampered with it. Therefore it couldn't be tracked.

Mikhail held out his other hand, and I dropped my phone into his palm. "I have a friend who I've already given this number to. He's going to send you something that may help."

I frowned. "What's he going to send?"

But Mikhail was already shaking his head, the boarding call for their flight being called out across the airport loudspeakers. "You should go." He gestured down at my ankle. "Things are going to take you longer to do due to your lack of mobility."

He had a point. I nodded, and stood up, suddenly at a loss for what to say. My glance encompassed both men, and I said the only words that came to mind, even though they were wholly inadequate in regards to what I was feeling. "Thank you. Both of you." It was ironic really because in all the time they'd shadowed me, I didn't think I'd ever said it before. Both men inclined their heads in acknowledgment, and I limped away.

I made a beeline for the nearest bathroom, fumbling the phone out of its packaging and inserting the SIM card so it was ready to go. I wondered what this so-called friend of Mikhail's was going to send, and how it was supposed to help me. Once inside, I locked myself in a cubicle before dialing a number I'd memorized. It seemed to ring for a very long time, my body twitching with nerves as I started to consider possibilities for a plan B if the man didn't answer. The problem was, I couldn't think of one. He was my one and only hope.

Finally, there was a click as the call was accepted. "Who is this?"

I exhaled, relief flooding through my veins at the sound of the man's familiar French accent. "Claude, it's Valentin."

"Valentin... this is a surprise. Is this a social call?"

"No. I need... the process we talked about..." The sound of my blood pumping in my ears was horrendously loud. "...the one we set up two years ago... it's time. I need the data I sent you, the photos... everything sent to this number as soon as possible and the arrangements made for everything else we talked about."

There was a long pause before Claude spoke again.

"Are you sure? I thought you were waiting until you had gotten more evidence. The last time we spoke, you said that what we had wasn't enough."

I gripped the phone tighter, and I thought about Max. Poor Max, beaten for the second time in a matter of days because of me. Only escaping with his life because a random fluke of luck had dictated someone happened to stumble across them at the right time. I took a deep breath. "It's going to have to be." I massaged my temple. "Something's come up which means I can't wait any longer. I'm going to have to make it work. One way or another. So, yes. Do it." I hung up.

I unlocked the cubicle door and washed my hands while I stared in the mirror, ignoring the curious glance of someone using the adjacent sink. There was a look of hope in my eyes that I wasn't used to seeing on my face. If I pulled this off, I was free. Forever. And Max would be safe. If I didn't?

Well, then we were both dead.

Chapter Seventeen

Max

The first thing I became aware of was someone holding my hand tightly. The second was that the bed felt wrong, the sheets too scratchy for it to be my bed and the smell all wrong. I struggled to open my eyes in order to work out where I was. "Valentin?" I finally convinced my eyelids to cooperate, only to close them again when the light was too bright. That wasn't right either. I never forgot to draw the curtains. On my second attempt the blurry but familiar face of my mother swam into view.

She squeezed my hand, her eyes welling with tears. "Who's Valentin?"

My gaze traveled slowly around the room, taking in the chest of drawers with a jug of water and two glasses on top of it, the curtain, half drawn around the bed, and the medical equipment next to the bed, the realization finally dawning: I was in the hospital. I'd somehow survived the second attack that was meant to kill me. But they'd try again. I knew they would. What was it they'd called me? A loose end, that was it. I tried to lift my head enough to sit up, a groan escaping from my lips at the subsequent stab of pain.

My mum placed a hand on my forehead, pushing it gently back onto the pillow. "Shh, darling. Don't try and move. You've got a pretty bad concussion. You've been unconscious for nearly fourteen hours. Do you remember them bringing you here?"

I tried to sort through the tangled mess of memories that made up my thoughts. The last thing I remembered was the alley. There was nothing after that. If I had regained consciousness at any point after that, it was completely gone. "No." I tried to swallow, but my throat was too dry. "Water?"

My mum stood, almost knocking her chair over in her haste to grant my request. "Of course. I'm sorry, dear." She half-filled one of the glasses before bringing it to my lips. I lifted my head slowly, some of the water spilling over my chin to soak the sheet, but at least I managed to get some of it to go down my throat; enough to ease the dryness anyway. "You said I had a concussion..." My mind immediately supplied the memory of a heavy boot landing on my head. "What else is wrong with me?"

She took the glass away, her lip wobbling. She looked tired. She'd obviously sat by my bedside all night. I grabbed her hand. "Hey! I'm okay. I'm not even in any pain apart from my head. I just want to know if there's anything else I should know."

She tried for a smile. "They've got you on a heavy dose of

253

morphine. You need to let them know when it starts to wear off. You've got three broken ribs, and it was touch-and-go for a while whether they would have to remove your spleen, but they managed to get the swelling down without surgery." Her hand reached out to stroke my cheek. "But they said that a lot of the bruising wasn't new, that it had been there for a few days. I told them that they must be mistaken, but they were adamant. It didn't make any sense."

I looked away while I tried to come up with a convincing story. I could claim to have been mugged. But twice in one week? There was no way anyone was going to believe that I could be that unlucky. I was temporarily saved from having to come up with an explanation as a nurse arrived at my bedside with a broad smile. "I see you're finally awake." She picked up my wrist, taking a quick pulse reading. "Any pain?"

"My head."

She nodded. "That's to be expected, given the concussion. The only reassurance I can give you is that it will wear off in time. Any double vision?"

"No."

She offered another smile. "That's a good sign. What about the rest of you?"

The questions went on for a while, my mum chipping in whenever she felt as if I needed help or was struggling to explain myself clearly. Apparently satisfied, the nurse turned to leave.

"Oh, by the way, the police are waiting to interview you. I told them that you might not be up to it until tomorrow, but if you'd rather get it over and done with, I can send them in?"

I tried to shake my head, the feeling like someone driving a knife through my brain, reminding me why it wasn't a good idea. "Tomorrow." At least by then, I might have thought of something convincing to explain the bruises from the first beating before my so-called mugging.

She nodded. "Tomorrow it is. It's probably better that you let the doctor take a look at you first anyway. Oh look, you've got a visitor!"

A visitor. It had to be someone who my mum had called. Only I couldn't think of anyone she'd call who'd rush to the hospital. We had family, but they all lived some distance away, and we weren't really that close. I couldn't imagine any of them being worried enough to make the three-hour drive required to get to London.

"Max?"

My concussion must be worse than I'd thought because for a moment there I'd imagined that the speaker spoke with a familiar accent. That beautiful mixture of English and Russian that had made me come so hard when words were whispered in my ear in the heat of passion. But of course that wasn't possible. There was no way he could be at the hospital. A shadow fell across the bed, and I looked up into familiar hazel eyes. Eyes I hadn't seen for

255

days and had thought I'd never get to see again. His lips curled into a smile as I continued to stare at him. "Are you real?"

He laughed. "*Da.* I am definitely real."

I reached out, my hand wrapping around his biceps, the flesh warm and comfortingly solid beneath my grip.

A strangled sound from the other side of the bed reminded me of my mum's presence, her mouth wide-open in shock as she stared at my hand still resting on Valentin's arm. Her confusion about who'd just waltzed into her son's room was completely understandable. "Mum, this is...Valentin. He's..." I had no idea what explanation to give besides his name.

As it was, I didn't seem to need to say any more. Her eyes grew even wider, and she stared at Valentin as if he was some sort of exotic creature. "He asked for you. When he woke up, you were the first name that came from his lips."

Valentin shifted uncomfortably, a faint blush on his neck almost hiding the marks that were still there. They were faint, but still visible, and even in my current state, I ached to make them darker again. "Really? Well, I got here as soon as I could." His face clouded over, and his gaze sought mine. "I need to talk to you, Max. Alone."

I turned my head to the side. "Mum?"

She didn't need asking twice, although she was clearly struggling to tear her eyes away from Valentin. Even as she backed toward the door, her gaze was still fixed on him. "I'll be outside."

And then it was just the two of us.

Valentin limped around to the opposite side of the bed, taking the seat my mum had recently vacated. I held my hand out, palm upward. "Hold my hand."

One eyebrow arched upward, a typical Valentin reaction at receiving such a request. It was absurdly reassuring. "Really, Max?" Despite his words, he took my hand in both of his, holding it tightly, his body hunched over so that our faces were close together.

I was giddy at seeing him again when I hadn't expected to. "I can't believe you're here. How? Why? What about Dmitry? How did you even know where I was? Did Dmitry tell you?"

Just like my mum had earlier, he shushed me. "Slow down, and I'll tell you. I can't stay long. There's somewhere I need to be. Something I need to do." He laid a finger on my lips when he could see that I was about to break into another barrage of questions. When I conceded, his fingers trailed from my lips over my bruised cheekbone. For Valentin, it was surprisingly tender, especially coupled with the expression on his face. He looked vulnerable. He looked like he didn't know what to do or say. He looked like a man who was... "You love me?"

He chuckled quietly, his fingers continuing to trace over my skin, the touch so gentle I could barely feel it. "I thought you already knew that."

I turned my face into his hand. "I suspected. I didn't *know* because you never said. They're two very different things."

He leaned down, kissing my cheek, his lips lingering on the damaged skin. "Well, now you know."

"But you're still going to leave?" My words were imbued with the sadness I felt at having to say the words aloud. Was that what this was? A last goodbye before he flew back to Russia? But then why admit that he loved me?

He shook his head. "*Njet*. It has gone past that. If I leave, they will kill you." His lips twisted. "And as we have already established that I love you, then I cannot let that happen."

"You can't stop it."

He sat back, although he kept a tight hold of my hand. "I can. Hopefully." His brow furrowed. "I set something up a couple of years ago. Through a man I met at one of Dmitry's parties. He was a good man. He was only there because he was searching for a missing boy." Valentin's fingers tightened before relaxing again. "A boy who later turned up dead. Nothing to do with Dmitry. Dmitry wouldn't waste a perfectly good boy by killing him. Anyway, I have kept my eye out for useful information for years that I might be able to use to my advantage, and any I found I have been sending to him for safekeeping. It is time that Dmitry realizes that the majority of his secrets are not secrets at all, that he may have made a mistake in keeping me close all these years. I think that the information I have, in the right hands, could at the very least prove financially devastating to Dmitry and, at best, could ruin him completely. I believe he will want them to remain a secret."

"You're going to blackmail him?"

"Something like that." His gaze fastened on mine. "I am not a hundred percent sure that it will work, Max. It may be that I have nothing. If it doesn't work, then..."

He didn't need to say it. I already knew what the consequences would be. I tugged him closer. "Maybe you should just forget it. Leave. I want you safe."

His lips slowly curved into a smile. "I can't do that, because... it works both ways. The way you feel is the way I feel too. I want *you* safe."

For a moment, as we stared into each other's eyes, there was nothing in the world but the two of us, and I knew that there was no convincing him. He'd already made his mind up. "If it works?"

He bit his lip as if he was trying to temper its need to smile at the thought. "Then... if you want me, I'm all yours."

There was no hesitation on my part whatsoever. "I want you!"

"I figured you did."

I tried to laugh before realizing that the action would be way too painful. "Kiss me."

His head turned toward the door to the corridor. "Your mum is watching."

"I don't care." I didn't. The whole of the London Philharmonic Orchestra could have filed into the room, and I would have still demanded to feel his lips on mine. He was about to go and face the big bad wolf, so the least he could do was leave me with one last kiss. His lips slowly lowered to mine. As kisses go, it was fairly chaste, but even so, neither of us was in any rush to break it. We lingered, each of us content to simply breathe the other one in and maintain contact for as long as we possibly could.

Finally, he stepped back, letting go of my hand and putting some distance between himself and the bed before I could reach for him. "I hope to be back here later. If I'm not... well, then you'll know that I was unsuccessful."

I stared at him. "I'm scared for you. Is there someone you can trust? Someone you can take with you? That might be able to help?"

He shook his head. "*Njet*. There is only me. I wouldn't put anyone else in danger anyway."

The lump in my throat made it hard to form words, but I persevered. "I love you. Stay safe, Valentin."

His smile was blinding. "I love you too, Max."

And then he was gone.

Chapter Eighteen

Valentin

Max's mum was waiting outside the room, her eyes as round as saucers as she stared at me. I would have been able to tell they were related, even if I hadn't known, just from the similar bone structure and the color of their eyes. She finally seemed to give herself a mental shake. "Who are you?"

Given what I knew of her son's nonexistent dating status, I could well understand her shock at the touching scene she'd witnessed while peering through the glass partition in the door. I also knew that there was no way, given the nature and the time scale of our relationship, that Max would have told her anything about the two of us. I cast a surreptitious eye down the corridor, checking for anyone suspicious while I considered the best way to answer the question. She'd seen us holding hands. She'd watched me plant a kiss on her son's lips, so there was little point in claiming we were just friends. "I'm the man who's hoping to be able to call himself your son's boyfriend if the next few hours go well."

Her face lit up. "Really? Oh my God! You have no idea how long Max has been alone. It's been such a waste. I kept telling him to find someone nice, and he kept claiming that he was fine on his own. He was hurt a long time ago, you see, so..." She stopped midsentence. "You are nice?"

I grimaced. "I think the jury is still out on that one."

She was already shaking her head though. "No, you are. I can tell. And your accent is gorgeous. You're gorgeous." She seemed to be working herself up into a frenzy, and I could handle many things, but an overenthusiastic mother wasn't one of them. She advanced toward me, and I resisted the urge to take a step back. "Can I hug you?"

Before I could agree or disagree, she launched herself at me, and I found myself engulfed in motherly arms. She held on tight, and I was surprised to find that I liked it. It had been years since anyone had held me like this. Probably since my own mother had died. Max liked to hug too, but it wasn't quite like this. I disentangled myself reluctantly from her embrace. "I'm sorry. I have to go."

She beamed at me, seemingly completely undeterred that I was fobbing her off. "I'll see you later. I'm going to interrogate Max about you and probably have a go at him for keeping you a secret. Concussion or no concussion, there's no excuse for that."

I nodded. Poor Max. He wasn't going to know what hit him.

"Don't leave him alone, will you? Keep him safe for me."

She shook her head, confusion written all across her face, and I turned and limped my way back down the corridor before she could question my reasons for saying that.

* * * *

I kept getting halfway through inputting the number into my phone before panic would seize hold, and I'd have to stop and pace around on the lawn in front of the hospital some more, or at least as close as I could get to pacing in my current state. Putting it off wouldn't make it any easier. In fact, the longer I left it, the more chance I had of losing my advantage. I keyed in the rest of the number and pressed call before I could think better of it.

"Dmitry Gruzdev. Who is this?"

I forced my body to relax. It was imperative from this point on that I acted perfectly calm, supremely confident, and absolutely unflappable. If Dmitry suspected anything else, the battle was already lost before it had begun. "It's me."

"*You* are meant to be in Russia. How dare you disobey me? There will be consequences for your actions."

A car horn beeped. I headed in the opposite direction, needing quiet. "Like killing Max? Are those the sorts of consequences you mean? Oh wait, you already attempted that last night, didn't you?

You broke your agreement with me that he would be safe, Dmitry." I poured every inch of scorn I could into the way I said his name. "You are going to meet me today in *La Gelatiera*, and we are going to come to a new agreement."

His laugh was filled with disdain. "Who do you think you are, Valentin? Did you hit your head at the airport? Do you think that *you* now call the shots? Poor deluded boy. Have you forgotten who you are talking to? We will *not* meet there."

I kept my voice firm. "Yes, we will, Dmitry." I needed the meeting to be in a public place. Somewhere I was familiar with that only had one entrance and exit. I knew for a fact that he wouldn't come alone, so I needed to be in control of as much as I possibly could. "Five o'clock. I'll see you there. Goodbye." Then I hung up, the shaking of my hands belying the calm I'd managed to infuse into my voice. I was relying on his need to pull me back under his control to overrule his refusal to follow my demands.

* * * *

I was in place by four thirty, carefully positioned with my back planted against the wall so that I had a clear view of the entire café and any possible threats it might hold. Dmitry didn't do early; waiting was beneath him. I'd banked on that, naming an hour that would give me plenty of time to visit the print shop and get copies of everything I needed, and still be able to arrive early.

My hand reflexively reached out to touch the large brown envelope I'd placed on the table. It was tempting to check the contents again, but I'd already done it twice since my arrival at the café.

There was always the possibility that Dmitry wouldn't show after all. But if I knew him as well as I thought I did, then his curiosity would be piqued, and he would be chomping at the bit to put me back in my place. Not to mention reeling at my sheer audacity for daring to stand up to him. No. I couldn't envisage a scenario where he wouldn't come. I just needed to wait.

"More coffee?"

I shook my head at the pretty waitress hovering by the side of the table, my hand immediately moving to cover the top of the mug in case she got carried away. I didn't intend to drink the coffee I had, didn't really know why I'd ordered it. The last thing I needed was to make myself even more jittery than I already was. I should have asked for tea, but tea always reminded me of Max. My mind drifted back to the hospital. He'd been both the most dreadful sight I'd ever seen and the most beautiful. Dreadful because there'd been hardly any part of him on display that hadn't been covered in bruises, but beautiful because he'd been alive. That was the main thing, and it was my job to do everything in my power to make sure he stayed like that. I needed to make up for that moment where I'd invited him into my dressing room and set the ball rolling on the whole of this mess.

I smiled as I recalled admitting I loved him. Love had always been something that happened to other people. Sometimes I'd caught myself looking at couples holding hands—gay and straight—and I'd found myself wondering exactly what it was that had brought them together and then made it worthwhile to stay together. In some ways, I'd felt superior, imagining that their emotions made them weak.

Meeting Max had made me realize how far from the truth that was. Emotions didn't make you weak. They made you stronger. If it weren't for the way I felt about Max, I wouldn't be sitting here now. I wouldn't be preparing to take on a man who had a whole organization behind him, its tendrils sneaking into most countries in the world, its connections going back decades.

Two men entered. I tracked their movements out of the corner of my eye, watching as they took up seats close to the door. There was no doubt in my mind that they belonged to Dmitry. There was less than a minute before another two men passed my table, taking up a position on the far side of the room. It left me sandwiched between them. Neither pair had spared me so much as a glance. I tapped my fingers on the table. Now that the advance party was in place, it meant that Dmitry's arrival was imminent.

I didn't have to wait long, my eyes immediately drawn to him as he paused in the doorway. I kept my gaze fixed on him as he

266

made his way between the tables, the way a zebra might keep their eyes locked on an approaching lion. Only I didn't bolt. I stayed seated, and I kept my face expressionless, not even letting one iota of emotion escape.

He eyed the chair across from me with distaste before pulling it out and reluctantly seating himself in it, his blue eyes boring into me. Unlike Max's, which always radiated warmth, his were cold and calculating. I waited while he shifted his position and made himself comfortable, determined not to be the one to speak first. I wanted to show him that I wasn't going to be rushed. That this meeting was on my terms—not his. He steepled his fingers together. "I don't hear you apologizing, Valentin."

I lifted my chin. "For what?"

He snorted, his fingers automatically reaching into his jacket pocket to extract a cigar. Even when he couldn't smoke it, he liked to have one in his hand. It was an old habit of his. "For running off. For deliberately misleading Mikhail and Igor. For not being in Russia where you are supposed to be. For throwing around orders." He scanned the café, his lip curling with distaste. "For demanding we meet here rather than a place more suited to a man of my status."

I leaned forward, bracing my elbows on the table and studying him without so much as blinking. I caught a flicker of surprise before he masked it. "Maybe I'm waiting for *you* to apologize first."

He rolled the cigar between his thumb and forefinger, his face thoughtful. "All this rebellion for one man. I highly doubt he is worth it."

A muscle ticked in my cheek. "That's for me to decide. Not you."

He sighed wearily, as if I was a recalcitrant child whose attitude was becoming beyond tiresome. "You are not a teenager, Valentin. You need to stop acting like one."

My splutter of indignation was loud, even to my own ears. "A teenager! How dare you act like I'm not allowed to be upset!" I switched to Russian. "We had a deal that you would leave Max alone. Instead you gave orders for him to be killed. Why? What was the purpose behind that? He was no threat to you."

Dmitry shrugged. If it wasn't for the fury I could see lurking behind his eyes, he might have been able to carry off the bored act that he was trying to portray. He wasn't used to anyone talking to him the way I was. Especially not in public. He tapped the cigar against the side of the table. "Sometimes plans change." His head tilted to one side. "Did you enjoy your visit to the hospital today?" A smile tugged at the corner of his lips. "I hope you said your good-byes."

I curled my fingers around the edge of the table, using the pain of the wood digging into the palm of my hand to keep the rest of my body immobile, and I still didn't take my eyes off his face. His brow furrowed slightly, giving away the fact that he was less than pleased at my lack of reaction. I slid my free hand across the table, smoothing it over the envelope and reminding myself that I hadn't come without weapons. But how flimsy they were remained to be seen. "We're going to make a new deal."

A sneer appeared on his face. "I really think you're miscalculating your worth to me, Valentin. You have been nothing but trouble lately. You can't even dance. So I do not know what you think you have to bargain with." He leaned closer. "I will let you into a little secret. I am deciding whether I even let you walk out of here." He gave a pointed glance to where the four men were stationed as if I was stupid enough not to have realized they were there.

I ignored him. "How long have I spent with you, Dmitry? Ten years, right?" He didn't bother to acknowledge my question. I forged on regardless. "And you think I have spent that time doing what? Just dancing. You think I am oblivious to what you get up to most of the time? And it never occurred to you during all that time that I was alone in your house or waiting in the car while you had clandestine meetings. It never crossed your mind that I might have been tempted to collect information that would prove useful to me at a later date?"

I paused to see what effect my words were having—if any—on him. To an onlooker, he'd seem just as calm as he'd been from the moment he'd arrived. But I knew every mannerism, so I saw the tension that was apparent in his shoulders and the way his fingers tightened ever so slightly around the cigar.

He scrutinized me down his nose as if I was nothing more than an annoying bug that had landed on his windshield. Then he laughed slowly and deliberately. "You. Have. Nothing."

A buzz of adrenaline zipped through my body. "On the contrary..." I pulled the envelope toward me, pulling the flap open and extracting the first thing I'd had printed from the data Claude had returned to me that afternoon. I laid the photo flat on the table, turning it around so that it was the right way up for Dmitry to be able to get a good look at. "Do you remember this meeting you had last year? Do you recognize the man in the picture? I did. I was surprised when you met with him, considering that he works for a rival organization. Do your colleagues know that you regularly meet with him?" I pulled another piece of paper from the envelope, this one stamped with dates and times, laying it on top of the first. "I have more photos linked to some of the other meetings you had with the same man, but you know" — I gave a deliberate shrug — "printing costs." Dmitry still hadn't said anything. "Oh, and there's more. You really need to choose your passwords more carefully because" — I pulled out the third piece of paper — "you make it way too easy to get into your financial records. It's interesting how many payments you've received from this same man. Almost like he's been paying you for inside information or you've got some sort of deal going on the side with him."

"Is that it?" Dmitry's expression was so glacial that I was surprised that the remaining coffee in my cup hadn't developed an icy layer.

This was the moment of truth. Most of the evidence was circumstantial. If there was a valid explanation for the meetings and payments—something sanctioned by Bratva, then I had nothing. I was placing all my chips on the gamble that Dmitry's actions were for his own selfish reasons. If I was wrong, then I was dead, and so was Max. "That's it."

I watched him closely. He picked all three pieces of paper up again and examined them closely before lifting his head. My heart stopped at the smile on his face. "So, I take these. My men kill you, and then kill your boyfriend." He smirked. "I don't understand how you thought you could win here, Valentin?"

Sweat trickled down my back, but I remained outwardly calm and played my last card. "There is a man on standby who has several envelopes all containing copies of this same data. If I don't call him in"—I made a big show out of checking my watch—"an hour, he's under strict instructions to mail those envelopes."

"To where?"

"The press, the police, your colleagues in Bratva. And he's also under strict instructions to do the same if either Max or myself mysteriously disappear." I held my breath as Dmitry's head shifted to stare across the room as he considered the ultimatum I'd given to him. Then he did the worst possible thing he could have done, he laughed. My blood ran cold at the realization that I'd failed. His head swung back toward me, his eyes narrowing. "Oh, Valentin, I gave you everything you could possibly want, and you've thrown it all back in my face." He shook his head. "I treated you like a son."

I forced words out through lips that suddenly felt numb. "If you think that, then I'm incredibly relieved that you never had children. Yes, you gave me dance instructors, but that was for your own selfish purposes. A father doesn't take away his son's freedom. He doesn't hit him." I swallowed. "And he certainly doesn't pimp him out to the highest bidder." I had nothing to lose by not saying it now. I was dead anyway.

A flash of anger crossed his face and I realized that somewhere in that dark, twisted mind of his, he'd actually believed the things he said. The phone in my pocket vibrated and I pulled it out with trembling fingers, opening the message from an unknown number. I found myself looking at a short video, less than a minute long. I pressed play, the phone on silent, and then I started to laugh as I realized what it was. The video showed Dmitry fucking someone over a desk. The recipient was unmistakably male, a young blond whose face was twisted in what could have been agony or could have been ecstasy.

I even recognized him. He was a dancer from a previous show. I'd spent years trying to get hold of this sort of evidence to no avail, knowing that above all else, Dmitry wanted to keep his sexuality and preferences a secret. I wondered who Mikhail's mysterious friend was that he could succeed where I'd failed.

I quickly sent a copy to Claude, knowing that even without an explanation, he'd print off screen shots or copy the video to a USB and include it with the other evidence. I lifted my head to find Dmitry smirking across the table at me. I was about to wipe that damn smile off his face, and I'd enjoy doing it. Every damn second. "I have one more thing that I need to show you."

I didn't wait for his response, pushing the phone across the table as I pressed play again. His fist clenched, crushing the cigar within it, and his face rapidly lost its color. He stopped the video, staring at the frozen screen for the longest time, as if he couldn't comprehend what it was he was seeing. "Where did you get this?"

I shrugged. "It doesn't matter. If you're not bothered about the other information being sent to everyone, how about this? Are you ready for everyone to know about your predilection for young blonds? What would your colleagues in Bratva have to say about that?"

He finally raised his head, the hatred in his eyes taking me by surprise. "What do you want? You said you wanted a deal?"

Those words were my proof that I'd snatched victory from the jaws of defeat. I wanted to laugh. I wanted to cry. I didn't do either of those things. I continued to stare coolly at the man opposite, the man who had controlled every aspect of my life for the last ten years. "Not much. I get my freedom and the knowledge that you will never contact me again. You don't blacken my name in dancing circles. We both agree to say that we went our separate ways due to irreconcilable differences. And you leave Max alone as well. That's it. That's all I want."

He laughed, shoving the phone back across the table toward me.

"You threaten to ruin my life, and that is all you ask for? You disappoint me, Valentin. I thought I taught you better than that. Where is the demand for money? Where is the demand to know the names of the men who were hired to kill your beloved boyfriend? An eye for an eye. A tooth for a tooth."

I shook my head, exhaustion starting to creep in. "I'm not like you. I'm not a killer, and I don't want your money. I just want out."

He rubbed his chin. "It occurs to me that you could be bluffing. Who is this mysterious man who is supposedly ready to mail this evidence? You do not have friends. I've made sure of that. So, how am I supposed to believe this story of yours? Tell me this man's name."

I smiled at his last-gasp effort not to come out of this as the loser. "I'm not that stupid. And by all means, gamble if you want.

But" — I leaned forward for extra emphasis, putting every ounce of conviction into my voice that I could — "I'm not bluffing. He does exist." I gestured at the pieces of paper. "Where else did I get these from? Or do you think I've been carrying it around with me? You have my room searched regularly."

Dmitry's face had settled back into an unfathomable mask, but I'd had enough. "Do we have a deal or not?"

The seconds that ticked by while I waited for his response were the longest I'd ever experienced. Finally, he nodded. "We have a deal."

I stood immediately. "Then there is nothing left for us to say to each other." I pointed at the data and threw the envelope on top. "You can keep those... as a reminder." With one last glance, I limped away.

The two men closest to the door started to rise to their feet as if they were intending to block my path to the exit. They sank back into their seats at what I assumed had to be a signal from Dmitry. I didn't know for sure because I had no intention of looking back. I was free, and I had an awful lot of living to catch up on.

Chapter Nineteen

Max

Time had become my worst enemy. Each minute that ticked by was another minute of worry that Valentin's plan had failed. Even worse were all the minutes that added together and became hours. It had been five in total since Valentin had left the hospital, and I'd heard nothing. I'd only managed to convince my mum to go home and take a break about an hour ago. Her arguments about needing to stay had only been strengthened by Valentin's apparent request for her not to leave me alone. I'd known what his thinking had been. Of course I did. But if Dmitry was going to send someone to the hospital to finish the job, then the last thing I wanted was my mum getting caught in the crossfire.

Then there was the fact that, quite understandably, she wanted answers. Not just about last night's attack but also about the extensive bruising I'd already had prior to that. At the moment I couldn't give her any. My concussed brain still failed to come up with anything feasible that she'd believe. As if that weren't bad enough, she'd also been desperate to interrogate me with questions about Valentin. I'd had to feign sleep to get out of that one.

The door to my room opened, the burst of optimism that briefly flared into life quickly extinguished at the sight of the nurse's happy, smiling face. She picked up my chart and examined it, the doctor having paid a visit a little over an hour ago. "Do you need more pain relief?"

Truth be told, I did. But it made me drowsy, and I didn't want to risk the possibility of Valentin arriving, only to find me sleeping. "Not yet."

She frowned. "Are you sure? Your last dose should be wearing off by now. There's no point in suffering."

I glanced over her shoulder toward the door. "What time do visiting hours end?"

"In an hour."

"And no one's come to visit? You haven't turned anyone away?"

She shook her head. "Afraid not. I'm sure whoever it is you're waiting for will come tomorrow."

I knew the comment was meant to be reassuring, but it wasn't. If Valentin didn't come today, then chances were high that I'd never see him again. And who knew whether I'd even get to see tomorrow. Although it would be hard to pass off a murder in a hospital as anything but what it was. So I had an inkling that

277

they'd probably wait until I was discharged.

The nurse bustled around, checking my blood pressure and making a note on the chart while I did my best to pretend that each and every movement wasn't agony. Finally, she left with the instruction to press the button when I needed pain relief. And then I was back to solitude and watching the hand of the clock tick slowly around.

There were only thirty minutes left of visiting hours. It was time to face facts. Valentin wasn't coming. Tears pricked my eyes as I considered the fact that he could be dead. I remembered the way he looked when he danced, so vibrant and alive, like nothing could touch him. To think of that light being extinguished forever caused far more pain than the broken ribs and concussion ever could.

"You look sad, Max."

I looked up to find him standing by the edge of the bed. Various wild scenarios tumbled through my brain one after the other: he was a hallucination conjured up by the fact I'd been thinking about him; I'd fallen asleep and he was nothing but a dream; he was a ghost paying one last visit before he was claimed by the afterlife. Just like earlier, I reached out, only truly believing it was him when my fingers met solid flesh.

He pulled the chair closer to the bed and sat, his eyebrow lifting as I continued to drink my fill of him. He looked tired. No, scrap that. He looked exhausted. I made an effort to formulate words. "I thought you weren't coming."

He took hold of my hand without having to be asked, his thumb delicately tracing the lines on my palm. "Only reason I wouldn't have come was if I was dead." His face changed as he suddenly grasped my point. "Ah! I see. Sorry. Things took longer than I expected, and I spent all the money I had on printing. I didn't have enough for a cab to get back here." His lip curled. "I had to get the bus. It was not a pleasant experience."

Despite the fact I was having problems being able to tear my eyes away from his face, I couldn't help the smile that pulled painfully against my bruised flesh at the bus comment. It was so typically Valentin. The only thing missing was the cigarette in his hand. "Diva!"

He shrugged. "I guess I'm going to have to get used to managing without some of the finer things in life, you know, like five-star hotels, champagne, and being driven everywhere."

My heart started up a crazy rhythm in response to his words. The fact he was there should probably have been enough confirmation, but I needed more. I needed to hear the words. "It worked then?"

Valentin tilted his head to the side and looked reflective. "Eventually. Someone came through with something at the last minute." For the next few minutes, he filled me in on exactly what had happened in the meeting with Dmitry. I listened intently, not wanting to interrupt his flow by asking questions until he'd finished. I was left amazed, not only by the fact he'd been plotting for years but also that he'd been brave enough to go through with it, especially when I realized how close he'd come to failing.

I'd faced the real Dmitry during my first beating, had seen what a powerful and formidable opponent he was, yet Valentin had confronted him, armed with data that had turned out to be worth nothing more than the paper it was printed on. Whichever mysterious person had sent that video had my eternal gratitude. Valentin had said that he'd tried to call the number to thank them, but no one had answered. "Did you ask about your parents?" I regretted the words as soon as they were out of my mouth. "Sorry. You don't have to answer that."

Valentin's eyes closed. "I didn't ask, but" — when his lashes lifted, I was surprised to see his eyes shining with tears — "he didn't kill them. I don't know whether that makes it better or worse. Better, I guess."

I ignored the pain and managed to shift myself up onto the pillows into a more vertical position, gripping his hand tightly in case he had any stupid ideas about pulling away. "I don't understand. If you didn't ask, how can you know that?"

"Because" — wiped his free hand over his eyes, dashing the tears away before they could threaten to spill over — "he was furious that I'd won. If he'd had any ammunition to throw at me, any ammunition whatsoever, he would have used it. He would have looked me straight in the eye and told me that he did it. The fact he didn't has to mean it was nothing but an accident."

I wasn't entirely sure I followed his reasoning. It may not have been Dmitry personally, but that didn't discount Bratva from having been behind it in some way. As it was better for Valentin's mental health to believe it was an accident rather than cold-blooded murder, I said nothing. "So, you're free. What will you do?"

He exhaled. "I don't know. I have nothing. Even my suitcase was left at the airport. It's probably in Russia by now. All I have are the clothes I'm wearing, an empty wallet, and" — he pulled an old-fashioned phone out of his pocket — "this phone. Mikhail could have at least gotten hold of a decent one."

"Hey! Look at me." I waited until his head turned my way. "You have me. Tell me what you need."

I frowned at his subsequent look of amusement, unable to comprehend what he could possibly be finding so funny. "What do I need?" His smile grew even wider. "Same thing as I always need when my head is all over the place. A good fuck." His gaze traveled slowly over my prone and battered body hidden beneath the crisp, white hospital sheets. "Guess I'll have to wait a while for that one."

I dug my fingers into his hand. "Don't joke. Seriously."

He threw his head back and laughed. "Who's joking? I do need a good fuck. Sex is great therapy." He shook his head, his face switching to a more serious expression. "I guess... first and foremost, I need to find a place to stay." He toyed with the phone in his hand. "One of the dancers will probably let me stay on their sofa for a few nights. I don't think any of them have a spare room though, so I will have to—"

I cut him off. "You're still joking, right? What did you do with the real Valentin Bychkov? He would have swanned in here and, like the diva he is, told me that he would be taking over my house."

His eyebrow rose. "And would that have worked?"

It was amazing how I could feel the worst I'd ever felt but still want to tease when it came to him. "I don't know. Try it and see."

"Max?"

I smirked. "Yes."

He gave me his coldest and haughtiest look. I remembered it well from the first time we'd met and subsequent occasions after that. "I'm going to need to stay at your house."

The effect was somewhat ruined by the fact that we still held hands, but I played along. "Oh, are you?"

"Yes." There was a glimmer of uncertainty on his face, and I reminded myself that the majority of the hard shell he wore on the outside was nothing but a carefully cultivated act. And he'd also just experienced the day from hell. He was bound to be feeling fragile. I pointed over to the small cabinet where the nurse had told me she'd placed the few belongings that were salvageable from the attack. Most of my clothes had needed to be thrown away. "My keys are in there." I waited until he'd moved across and had them in his hand, hating how bereft I suddenly felt at the lack of contact between us. "I can't give you any money because they took my wallet to make it look like a mugging, so we're going to have to work out how we're going to get you from here to there."

He sat back down, staring at the keys cradled in his palm. "Are you sure about this?"

I closed his fingers around the keys. "Yes. I want you there."

He peered at me from beneath his lashes. "And your mum will be okay with that, will she?"

I laughed, grabbing my ribs as the pain tore through me, turning it into more of a strangled gasp. "Are you kidding? After you told her that you planned to be my boyfriend... all she's done is talk about you. That and ask loads of questions. Most of which I couldn't answer. She's going to be over the moon to discover that you're staying at my house."

The nurse poked her head around the door. "Just a heads-up that visiting hours are over in five minutes." She gestured toward Valentin. "I guess this is who you were waiting for." She took a few steps into the room, addressing her next comment to Valentin. "He was pining for you."

A smug expression appeared on his face. "I wasn't pining for you!" Neither of them looked convinced at my interjection. It was amazing how it had only taken one set of keys and a comment from a nurse to turn Valentin back into a self-assured asshole. I had half a mind to wrestle the keys back off him. There were only two problems with that idea: I was in no fit state to wrestle anyone, and there was nothing I wanted more in the world than to have Valentin waiting for me when I was discharged from the hospital. I didn't want him finding an alternative place to stay. I wanted him with me. That only left words with which to defend myself. "I wasn't. I was worried, as you very well know."

Valentin winked at the nurse. "It can be our secret. He can say worried, and we'll know the truth."

She smiled conspiratorially back at him, a faint blush on her cheeks, and I decided a change of subject was needed before she fell head over heels in love with the man I was already in love with. I was beginning to see a lot of benefits to the frosty facade that he normally showed to the world. "Nurse?"

Her head turned my way. "Is there any way we can organize a cab when neither of us has the money to pay for it? My wallet was stolen, and..." *He's spent years with a tyrant who wanted him to be completely beholden to him.* "Valentin doesn't have any either."

"Hmmm..." She looked thoughtful.

"I can pay you back when my mum comes in tomorrow." I gave her my most beseeching look for good measure.

Her face softened. "I guess for you two lovebirds I can sort something out." She inclined her head toward the clock. "Speaking of which, time's up. You better say your good-byes. I'll wait outside, and then we'll sort that cab out for you. And then" — her gaze lost the softness as she raised her finger in my direction — "I'm coming back to give you that overdue pain relief, whether you like it or not."

I nodded meekly, and she left the room, giving us a last few precious seconds of alone time. I was suddenly seized by panic at the thought of letting him out of my sight. "What if Dmitry hasn't really accepted it? What if he just pretended to and he's biding his time and — "

"Max." He laid his hand against my cheek. "It's going to be okay. I can feel it."

"Are you sure?" My gaze searched his face, looking for any signs that he might be hiding something. But there was nothing. I relaxed slightly, noting that the time on the clock showed that it had already passed the hour. Given the nurse's generosity with offering to help with the cab fare, I didn't want to risk upsetting her. "You better go."

Valentin leaned over, planting a lingering kiss on my lips similar to the one from earlier, except that where the other had been filled with longing, this one held more of an air of optimism. He drew back, and I stared into his hazel eyes. He really was beautiful. "Are you going to be okay?"

He nodded. "You?"

"Yes." There was one more thing I needed to clarify if I was going to get any sleep that night. "When you said you needed a fuck..." I hesitated not sure how to phrase it.

"Are you asking if I'm going to pick someone else up?"

"I mean... if you were, I guess..." I wanted to say it would be okay, even though it wouldn't be. The mere thought of him with someone else made me feel sick. But we hadn't hashed out any relationship details, given that having one had only been a possibility for a little over ten minutes. The nurse knocked on the door, giving the universal sign for winding something up through the glass. "...if you did, then..."

Valentin continued to stare.

I sighed. "Fuck it! Don't. Please."

He tilted his head to one side. "I had no intention of doing so. I'll wait for you." He smirked. "But watching you work yourself up to saying what you really feel is so entertaining." He dropped another kiss on my lips and then stood up. "I'll see you later, *lyubov moya*."

I frowned. "What does that mean?"

But he'd already gone.

Chapter Twenty

Two months later

Valentin

I leaned back against the wall, taking a long drag of the cigarette in my hand and enjoying the familiar feeling as the nicotine began to work its way through my body. I hadn't had a cigarette for two weeks, something to do with a certain someone finally getting around to offering me something far more interesting. My cock stirred at the memory of how much fun that night had been. So the cigarette in my hand was most definitely overdue and tasted all the better for it.

Being on my own gave a rare opportunity for reflection. There had been zero contact from Dmitry, which meant his desire to keep his tastes secret was as important as I'd always suspected. I sometimes found myself wondering exactly what the relationship had been between him and the dancer. It would have been easy to dig a bit deeper, to locate him and ask, but the burning temptation was squashed by the sensible part of my brain reminding me that

I'd gotten Dmitry out of my life. There was absolutely no sense in poking the sleeping lion. Some things just weren't worth it.

I even thought about Mikhail and Igor on occasion. Were they still working for Dmitry in another capacity? Or had my absence effectively terminated their employment contracts? It was strange to think that the perpetual shadows had been the key to my salvation in the end. Well, more Mikhail than Igor, but the latter had gone along with it, so I was grateful to him too. Unanswered questions plagued me as well. Who had Mikhail's mysterious friend been? How had they gotten hold of that evidence, and why? And what was Mikhail's connection to it? Was he more than he'd seemed to be? I guessed I'd never know.

I stared at my foot, still getting used to the sight of it without the protective boot. After six weeks, the doctor had pronounced me ready to walk without it, and I'd started physical therapy. It was still a long road back to being able to dance again, but I was beginning to feel that I'd get there eventually.

"Valentin?"

I smirked at the sound of my name being called, particularly given the note of complete and utter confusion in it. What did he think I was doing—playing hide and seek? I stayed silent and took another long drag of the cigarette, watching the tendrils of smoke travel into the air and disperse, and thinking that I really should learn to blow smoke rings. Max would find me eventually, especially when I'd left the back door open as a huge clue.

"Where are you?"

I waited, Max finally rounding the corner and appearing next to me, his eyes narrowing as he took in the scene. "I mean... I guess I should have known that you'd be outside"—his eyes drifted down my body, taking in the fact that all I wore was a pair of jeans—"half-naked, trying to catch your death, and smoking. I thought you'd given it up?"

"Being half-naked or smoking?"

He pulled his "you're an annoying little shit" face. "Smoking."

"I did, and then I started again. And as for the half-naked bit, I am used to the climate in Russia. It is warm here."

He moved to stand in front of me, concern written all over his face. "Why are you smoking? What's wrong? What are you stressing about?"

I smiled, reaching out and linking my arms around his waist to pull him toward me. Despite the clear look of disgust pointedly aimed in the direction of the cigarette, he didn't protest, moving closer until we were pressed chest to chest, his shirt rasping against my bare skin. "I am not stressing, *lyubov moya*. Simply taking some time to reflect." He smiled at the Russian endearment, the way I'd known he would. He knew what they all meant now: *lyubov moya*—my love; *malysh*—baby; *dorogoi*—darling. He even, on occasion, said them back, although his Russian accent was still terrible, so I usually pretended to have no idea what he'd said.

The last couple of months had been quite the learning curve. Neither of us was used to being part of a pair or having to take someone else's feelings into consideration before we did or said something. That fact alone had led to many rocky arguments, particularly in the first few weeks of Max getting out of the hospital. He'd not only been struggling to heal physically, but he'd thought he could hide his fear of leaving the house.

But at the heart of it, there'd been genuine love on both sides that had only grown week by week, so we'd overcome everything. Together. And we'd found a way to navigate around those difficult parts of our relationship and make the weaknesses into strengths.

He linked his arms around my neck, his lips hovering by my ear. "Did you do your exercises?"

I stubbed the remainder of the cigarette out on the wall, letting it drop to the ground. It would give Max something to moan about later when he discovered the butt on his beloved lawn. "Yes, nurse Max, I did my exercises." He was referring to the home support program that the physical therapist had set up to rehabilitate my ankle. Nobody wanted my ankle to heal quicker than I did, especially when there was still a question mark hanging over whether I'd ever dance again. Or even if I did, whether it could ever be to a standard anywhere near where it had been before the injury. Max was the only person who knew how scared I was that that could be a possibility. I hadn't needed to tell him; he'd just known.

Hands came up to cup my face, and I leaned into them as soft lips brushed against my own. Max pulled back enough that he could look into my face. "It's a shame you're not stressed, really. Because we both know what the best cure for that is."

I slid my hands down to grasp his ass, pulling his lower body flush to mine and already feeling the stirring of a hard cock against my thigh. "Are you offering to fuck me, Max? That's very sweet and self-sacrificing of you. Tell me what you had in mind?"

A glint appeared in his eye. "Well, I'd say we could go back to bed, but you'll accuse me of being dreadfully vanilla and unimaginative. Maybe one of us could hang from the light fitting in the living room, and the other one could..."

His brow furrowed as he left himself with nowhere to go with that scenario. I burst out laughing and reached into his pocket to see if he had his wallet with him. He did. His eyebrow arched as I pulled it out and extracted a sachet of lube. We'd dispensed with condoms a few weeks back after getting tested. I gave him a look of challenge. "How about here?"

"Here?" His voice came out incredibly high-pitched, and he looked as if he was about to choke.

I almost took pity on him. Except that we were tucked far enough back that nobody could see unless one of the next-door neighbors was determined enough to open their window and hang out of it precariously. And if that were the case, well, I'd be more than happy for them to enjoy the show for their efforts. Max was so much fun to push out of his comfort zone. The longer we spent together, the fewer ways that was possible. So discovering he wasn't quite on board with the idea of outdoor sex was ramping up my arousal to such a degree that there was suddenly nothing I wanted more. I regarded him silently while I made up my mind. It was the flush on his cheeks and the fact his pupils were dilated that made the decision easy. His mind might be balking, but his body was already one hundred percent sold on the idea.

I lowered my voice, channeling the old Valentin, the one who had to grab sexual opportunities of his choosing whenever and wherever he could—including dragging poor befuddled sound engineers into his dressing room to have his wicked way with them—and knew exactly how to get it. "You mean, you don't want to fuck me hard against this wall, Max? Like you did in the dressing room when we first met?"

His cheeks flamed even more, his dick so hard against my thigh it might as well have been a rod of steel. Max's gaze darted to the windows of the neighboring houses. "I do, but—"

I wriggled out of his grasp, one hand fumbling at the fastening of my jeans as I turned my back to him. There was something to be said for ballet tights in comparison to jeans. I finally got them undone and dragged them down, along with my underwear. I pressed my chest against the cold brick of the wall, enjoying the interesting sensation of the rough brick against my nipples as I wrapped one hand around the solid length of my cock.

I tipped my bare ass up in clear invitation, waiting for the feel of his hands on my skin. When it didn't materialize, I glanced back over my shoulder to find him staring hungrily at my ass as if he'd never seen it before. "I'm getting cold here, *malysh.* How about a bit of attention?"

The struggle between lust and common sense was written all over his face. Finally, he shook his head, one hand going to the fastening on his trousers. "I wish I had more self-control when it comes to you. Reckon I ever will?"

I smirked. "Hopefully not. I like things just the way they are." I turned back to face the wall, listening to the telltale sounds of lube being applied. I spread my legs a little and braced myself.

Warm lips descended on my neck at the same time as hands grasped my hips, pulling me back against a very hard cock. "One day, you're probably going to get me arrested."

There was probably some truth in that statement. "But that day is going to be one hell of a day! And I'll be right there with you."

He laughed against my neck. "Tell me if this hurts your ankle at any point."

Max was so sweet. Even horny and with a hard cock sliding between my ass cheeks, he was still first and foremost concerned about my ankle. "I will. Don't worry."

Then my ankle was the last thing on my mind as Max shifted position and pushed his cock inside me, his sigh of satisfaction mixing with the strains of my panted exhalation. He knew I didn't like slow. I liked to feel the burn. I liked to reach that point where I was almost at the brink of begging him to take it out before pain finally gave way to pleasure. So he kept pushing as I bit into the back of my hand, leaving teeth marks on my skin.

Then he was fully seated inside me, his fingers digging into the tops of my thighs as he plastered our bodies together. I turned my head to the side, seeking his lips, our mouths joining together in a passionate kiss.

Max's lips trailed down over my neck, his hands caressing every inch of skin he could reach. "I love you, Valentin."

I never got tired of hearing those words. Nobody since my parents had ever said the words and meant them. "Even though I talk you into doing stuff like this?"

His breath was hot on my neck, his teeth tracing a mark he'd left there the previous night. "Especially because you talk me into doing stuff like this."

I smiled, a feeling of warmth seeping through my body which had absolutely nothing to do with the cock up my ass. "*Ya tebya lyublyu.* I love you too, Max. Now for God's sake, fuck me. You are *so* slow."

I got exactly what I'd asked for as he took hold of my hips and withdrew, only to slam back into me. My toes curled as he nailed my prostate, and I gasped. No one had ever told me that a great cock felt a million times better when it was attached to someone I loved, someone who loved me equally in return. Although I probably would have mocked anyone who'd dared to tell me such a thing, claiming that all I needed was the hard cock part. But I could see now that I'd always needed more. I just hadn't known it until I'd met a man capable of letting his own barriers down and breaking through mine at the same time. He'd offered me something that no one else had: a future, with him at its center.

I arched back against Max, taking everything he had to give, our bodies finding a rhythm that we'd fine-tuned over the last few weeks while we'd learned as much as we could about each other. I knew that he loved it when I was loud; something about being able to force emotion out of me. He knew that I liked it rough, that fingermark bruises and hickeys were marks I wore with pride.

I gave him what he wanted, groaning loudly and repeating his name over and over as his cock pegged my prostate mercilessly. He pushed me harder against the wall as he pounded into me, wrenching my head to the side, a possessive tongue tangling with my own. When I would have moved away, desperate for oxygen, he held it there that little bit longer, demanding that little bit more. And I loved it.

I hadn't touched my cock, and already there was a tightness in my balls, warning that my orgasm wasn't far away. I tuned myself into Max, listening for the telltale hitch in his breathing, the slight jerkiness of his hips that would precede him being moments away from reaching his climax. I didn't have to wait long. His teeth fastened on my neck, his hips thrusting faster and his cock pushing deeper as he came close. I reached down, fisting my cock and unleashing my orgasm at the same time as he cried out, pulling me back against him, his twitching cock embedded to the hilt as he shuddered against me.

"Fuck! So good." His muttered exhalation in my ear made me smile. He withdrew from my body and turned me around to face him, his eyes perusing my cum-splattered abdomen with a look of smug self-satisfaction. Then he wrapped his arms around me and leaned us both back against the wall, my face tucked into his neck. I licked at a bead of salty sweat, the resultant quiver of his skin making me want to lick him all over. Although that might not be an option when he heard what I was about to say. I picked my moment carefully, bracing myself for the predictable reaction. "*Spaseebo*. Thank you. I've never had sex outside before."

Max reared back, open-mouthed. "What? But... you made me think... you... I don't... I can't... Jesus!"

I laughed, my hand stroking his chest through the shirt he still wore. "I thought you might want to share a new experience with me."

He laughed, his hands struggling to pull my jeans up, having apparently decided that my bare ass had been on display for long enough. "You're nothing but trouble. I should have known that from the first moment I saw you."

I winked. "You did." I slid my hand between our bodies, finding a cock that was still half-hard, even though he'd only just come. He bit his lip as I stroked the sensitive head. "You just kept thinking with this, so you didn't care." I wrapped my fist around it and stroked harder, watching the initial discomfort slowly give way to renewed arousal. Max had amazing stamina when it came to being ready to go again in no time at all. A fact I never ceased to take full advantage of. I inclined my head toward the door. "I'm not done with you yet. Bed or light fitting? Your choice."

Epilogue

Six months later

Max

I sat there stunned as the curtain went down after the final encore, able to breathe for the first time in what felt like hours and barely aware of my mum chattering away next to me. "Oh my God! He was amazing. I know you told me he was good, but I didn't realize he was *that* good. I could hardly take my eyes off him. He was stunning. He was..."

My head turned toward her as she finally ran out of superlatives. "He is amazing." And I wasn't just talking about the dancing. But on that stage, he'd been something else. He'd been truly alive for the first time in months, every perfectly poised leap filled me with a strange mixture of elation and fear. It had been a long road to get to this point. Even when Valentin had been given the go-ahead to start dancing again—his ankle sufficiently rehabilitated—he'd found it difficult.

Valentin being Valentin, had struggled with the realization that, of course, he was going to be rusty, that it was going to take time for him to reach the dizzy heights that he'd been operating at before. Given our close proximity, it hadn't come as too much of a surprise that Valentin had taken it out on me. I knew it hadn't been personal. Dancing was Valentin's whole world. He'd made sacrifices in order to be able to carry on doing it that other people wouldn't even consider, like spending ten years under Dmitry's control. And then, of course, there was the fact that I had to expect things like that when your boyfriend was a highly strung diva.

I'd simply gritted my teeth, bitten my tongue, and concentrated on being a supportive boyfriend. Work had proved my salvation, Valentin always seeming to gain a little more perspective when we were separated for a few hours.

Next had come the struggle for Valentin to find a show willing to give him a chance. Dmitry might not have blacklisted him, but their names were very much still entwined. It didn't matter how many times Valentin assured them that he no longer held any association with the man, still he was met with the same wall of reticence. It seemed that if Dmitry wasn't bankrolling the show, then the threat of the man's reputation was enough to put anyone off.

Then this show had come along, and for whatever reason — possibly naivety on the part of the theater manager — Valentin had been given an audition. As soon as they'd seen him dance, there was no question of them not hiring him. They'd all but begged him to star in it, Valentin joking that if he wasn't so desperate to get his foot in the door, he could have held out for more money.

Tonight's show had been the opening night. Valentin had received a standing ovation, and I couldn't have been any prouder.

My mum squeezed my arm. "Awww... you're emotional. You two are so sweet together. You should go and see him in his dressing room."

I took a deep breath, trying to shake off the feeling that it could all be a dream. "I'm not going to leave you on your own."

She tutted. "I'll be fine. I'll have a drink at the bar, and then you can come and collect me from there before we go to the party. Go and see your lovely boyfriend and tell him how wonderful he was."

I stood up. "I suspect he already knows that. In fact, it'll probably be him telling me rather than the other way around."

I'd visited Valentin a couple of times during rehearsals, so I knew where his dressing room was. I wasn't sure whether I'd find him alone or surrounded by throngs of people. If it was the latter, well, I'd congratulate him and then back off and let him have his well-deserved moment of glory. The door was closed, so I knocked, thinking back fondly to another time when I'd waited for the enigma that was Valentin Bychkov to open the door. On that occasion, he'd been all clipped words, insults, and naked skin that I hadn't been able to resist.

It was a very different man who opened the door this time, his face breaking into a huge smile as soon as he saw it was me. He grabbed my arm and hustled me inside, his arms wrapping around me as soon as the door had closed. I squeezed him tight, breathing him in, his body almost vibrating in my arms with excitement. He pushed me away, too excited to stand still for longer than two minutes. "Max, did you see? They loved me. I'd forgotten what it was like to dance in front of an audience, to look out and see hundreds of faces all watching me. And I got a standing ovation. Did you see that? Even though I didn't reach perfection. Which gives me something to work on. I don't think that anyone noticed." He grabbed a bottle of champagne from an ice bucket, pouring a glass and handing it to me. "Aren't you meant to be congratulating me?"

I stared at him, loving how happy and carefree he was with the adrenaline of performing still coursing through his veins. "I would if I could get a word in edgeways."

His brow furrowed. "But you liked it?"

"Of course I liked it. You were fantastic. But then I already knew that. I think I fell in love with you the first moment I watched you dance."

He smiled. "That explains why you couldn't even manage to press a button at the right time." His face suddenly shadowed. "I have news."

I didn't like the expression on his face or the fact that he'd gone from ecstatically happy to worried, all in the space of a matter of seconds. "Bad news?"

He crossed his arms over his chest, half of the glitter that had been on it, now smeared all over the front of my shirt. Not that I cared. "I guess that depends on your viewpoint."

My mind started to race. *Had he heard from Dmitry? Was it something about his ankle?* "Tell me."

He leaned back against the wall, still wearing a somber expression that did nothing to ease my panic. "I knew before the show, but I wanted to wait until after." He grimaced. "I don't know why, really... it just seemed better."

I wasn't used to my boyfriend fumbling for words. He was usually the epitome of calm and collected. "Valentin, whatever it is, just tell me."

"They signed a contract to take the show to New York for six weeks, with a good chance of a possible extension, and they want to keep me in the lead role."

I stared at him, shaking my head slightly when that was all he had to say, a smile breaking out on my face. "That's fantastic news! Congratulations."

His face didn't change. "Is it? I mean, I know it is, but we are going to be apart for six weeks." He looked even sadder. "I know we talked about the fact that this might happen, but I'm going to miss you, Max, so damn much. I'm not used to feeling like this.

Aren't you going to miss me?"

I grabbed his hand, pulling him back into my arms so we swayed together, my heart bursting with love. "Like you wouldn't believe. But we're going to talk on the phone every night and think of the reunion we'll have when you get back."

Valentin smiled, but he didn't look any happier. "We wouldn't get out of bed for at least a week after."

"Bed!" I did my best Valentin impression in an effort to cheer him up. "You're so vanilla." For once, it didn't work. "Hey! Don't be sad. This is your big night. You should be enjoying it. This is not for a few weeks anyway. Don't start missing me while we're still together."

He nodded. "I know." He paused. "Unless..."

"Unless what?"

"Unless you come with me?"

"To New York?"

"*Da*. For the whole six weeks. Longer, if it is extended. When I am not dancing, we could go sightseeing, and you could come to rehearsals. They're paying me good money, and the hotel is already paid for, so you will not need to worry about the fact that you will not be working. Your work is flexible so you can take the time. Right? What do you say?"

It was on the tip of my tongue to say no, to say that I couldn't live on his money, but if he'd done the same while his ankle was healing, we'd never have gotten anywhere as a couple. He hadn't liked depending on me, but he'd done it. So really, it would only be returning the favor. I imagined six weeks without being able to see him or touch him, wondering constantly what he was doing and who he was with. Not that I didn't trust him, I did. Neither of us was interested in anyone else. We'd found the person we wanted to spend the rest of our lives with and that was it for us.

Thinking of it that way, recognizing that our lives were inexorably entwined and that what was mine was his and vice versa, left only one possible answer. "Yes. Yes, I'll come to New York. For however long you want me—"

I didn't get a chance to finish my sentence due to the eager pair of lips pressing against mine and the enthusiastic tongue looking to get better acquainted. We kissed until we were both dizzy, our cocks straining together. I forced myself to stop. "You've got a party to get to so that everyone can tell you how fabulous you are and fawn over you all night."

He backed off a few steps, a mischievous look on his face, his arousal clearly evident in the ballet tights, which made me want to get down on my knees and worship something very different from his dancing talent. "That does sound fantastic, but I think there's enough time for you to fawn all over me first." I didn't need asking twice. I dropped to my knees, peeling the ballet tights down over the muscular thighs and preparing to demonstrate just how much I loved Valentin Bychkov.

He might be an insufferably arrogant diva at times.

But he was *my* diva.

<u>Afterword</u>

For those of you that are annoyed that Dmitry didn't get his comeuppance, all I can say is that I wasn't too happy myself, but it just didn't fit with this book. Maybe he'll pop up again though in another book, and hopefully then he might get what's coming to him.

Watch this space.

Thanks, from H.L Day

Thank you so much for choosing to read this book. You've made me really happy. How could you make me even happier? Well, you could leave a review. Then, I'd be ecstatic. :)

About H.L Day

H.L Day grew up in the North of England. As a child she was an avid reader, spending lots of time at the local library or escaping into the imaginary worlds created by the books she read. Her grandmother first introduced her to the genre of romance novels, as a teenager, and all the steamy sex they entailed. Naughty Grandma!

One day, H.L Day stumbled upon the world of m/m romance. She remained content to read other people's books for a while, before deciding to give it a go herself.

Now, she's a teacher by day and a writer by night. Actually, that's not quite true—she's a teacher by day, procrastinates about writing at night, and writes in the school holidays, when she's not continuing to procrastinate. After all, there's books to read, places to go, people to see, exercise at the gym to do, films to watch. So many things to do—so few hours to do it in. Every now and again, she musters enough self-discipline to actually get some words onto paper—sometimes they even make sense and are in the right order.

Finding H.L Day

Where am I? I often ask myself the same question.

You can find me on Twitter as hlday100

You can find me on Instagram as hlday101

You can find me on Facebook. Send me a friend request or come and join my group Day's Den for the most up-to-date information and for the chance at receiving ARCs

You can find me on my website: www.hlday.author.co.uk

Or you can sign up to my newsletter, through my website for new release updates.

More books from H.L Day

A Temporary Situation (Temporary series; Tristan and Dom #1)

Personal assistant Dominic is a consummate professional. Funny then, that he harbors such unprofessional feelings toward Tristan Maxwell, the CEO of the company. No, not in that way. The man may be the walking epitome of gorgeousness dressed up in a designer suit. But, Dominic's immune. Unlike most of the workforce, he can see through the pretty facade to the arrogant, self-entitled asshole below. It's lucky then, that the man's easy enough to avoid.

Disaster strikes when Dominic finds himself having to work in close proximity as Tristan's P.A. The man is infuriatingly unflappable, infuriatingly good-humored, and infuriatingly unorthodox. In short, just infuriating. A late-night rescue leading to a drunken pass only complicates matters further, especially with the discovery that Tristan is both straight and engaged.

Hatred turns to tolerance, tolerance to friendship, and friendship to mutual passion. One thing's for sure, if Tristan sets his sights on Dominic, there's no way Dominic has the necessary armor or willpower to keep a force of nature like Tristan at bay for long, no matter how unprofessional a relationship with the boss might be. He may just have to revise everything he previously thought and believed in for a chance at love.

A Christmas Situation (Temporary Series; Tristan and Dom #2)

Love conquers all. But can it survive Christmas?

Dominic and Tristan have been together for almost a year. So everything's got to be plain sailing, right? Not quite. Not if you ask Dominic. Tristan's a bundle of energy and crazy ideas at the best of times. Add in Christmas, and it's a recipe for disaster.

That's not the only issue. There's also Tristan's mysterious absences and secret phone calls to contend with. Dominic might be insecure, but he's not crazy. His boyfriend is definitely up to something, and neither family nor friends seem interested in listening to his concerns. He won't jump to conclusions this time though. He'll talk to Tristan. Only what do you do when you can't get a straight answer out of the man you love?

When Tristan's secrets are revealed, will their first Christmas together also be their last? Or is Dominic about to discover that all his worries have been for nothing?

Only time will tell.

A story containing Christmas snark; a drunk Tristan; snow; and absolutely no mention of spiders — well alright, maybe a few mentions.

Time for a Change

What if the last thing you want, might be the very thing you need?

Stuffy and uptight accountant Michael's life is exactly the way he likes it: ordered, routine and risk-free. He doesn't need chaos and he doesn't need anything shaking it up and causing him anxiety. The only blot on the horizon is the small matter of getting his ex-boyfriend Christian back. That's exactly the type of man Michael goes for: cultured, suave and sophisticated.

Coffee shop employee Sam, is none of those things. He's a ball of energy and happiness who thinks nothing of flaunting his half-naked muscular body and devastating smile in front of Michael when he's trying to work. He knows what he wants — and that's Michael. And no matter how much Michael tries to resist him, he's not going to take no for an answer.

Sam eventually chips through Michael's barriers and straight into his bed. But Michael's already made some questionable decisions that might just come back to haunt him. He's got some difficult choices to make if he's ever going to find love. And he might just find that he's too set in his ways to make the right ones quickly enough. If Michael's not careful, the best thing that's ever happened to him might just slip right through his fingers. Because even a patient man like Sam has his limits.

Kept in the Dark

Struggling actor Dean, only escorts occasionally to pay the bills. So, his first instinct on being offered a job with a strange set of conditions is to turn it down. No date. Don't switch the lights on. Don't touch him. I mean, what's that all about? What's the man trying to hide? Dean certainly doesn't expect sex with a faceless stranger to spark so much passion inside him. It's just business though, right? He can put a stop to it whenever he wants.

When Dean meets Justin — a scarred, ex-army soldier unlucky in love. Dean's given a chance at a proper relationship. He can see past the scars to the man underneath. He's everything Dean could possibly wish for in a boyfriend: kind, caring and sweet. All Dean needs to do is be honest. Easy, right? But, Justin's holding back and Dean can't work out why. But whatever it is, it's enough to give him second thoughts.

They both have secrets which could shatter their fledgling relationship. After all, secrets have a nasty habit of coming out eventually. The question is when they do, will they be able to piece their relationship back together? Or will they be left with nothing but memories of bad decisions and the promise of the love they could have had, if only they'd both been honest and fought harder.

Refuge (Fight for Survival #1)

If you no longer recognise someone, how can you possibly be expected to trust them with your life?

Some might describe Blake Brannigan's life in the small Yorkshire village of Thwaite as bordering on mundane. His job in a café doesn't exactly set the world alight. But, he's got his own house, a boyfriend, and a close-knit group of good friends. For him, that's more than enough to lead a contented life.

Then in one fell swoop, everything's ripped away when he's forced to flee the village with only his boyfriend for company. He doesn't know why they're leaving. He hasn't got the faintest clue what's going on, and he's struggling to understand the actions and behaviour of a man he thought he knew. A man that it soon becomes clear knows far more about what's happening than he's letting on. A man hiding a multitude of secrets.

When the true extent of what's happening comes to light, Blake is rocked to the core. Peril lurks around every corner. The smallest decision suddenly spells the difference between life and death. If Blake's to have any chance of survival in this new and frightening world, he's going to have to unearth buried secrets, figure out whether love really can conquer all, and face emotional, physical, and mental challenges the likes of which he could never have imagined.

One thing's for sure, when life suddenly boils down to nothing more than the desperate need to find refuge, priorities change. Blake's certainly have.

Taking Love's Lead

Zachary Cole's new personal shopper is stunning in more ways than one. Gone is the staid, professional Jonathan. In his place is sexy, whirlwind Edgar, whose methods and lifestyle are less than orthodox. Still reeling from the experience, Zack can't get him out of his head. He needs to see him again. Even if it does involve dragging his heavily pregnant sister and her dalmatian into his cunning plan.

Sick of being dumped yet again, dog walker Edgar's pledged to stay single and put energy into finding a career more suited to an adult instead. Zack might be extremely tempting...and just happen to pop up wherever he goes, but that doesn't mean he's going to change his mind. He's got bigger priorities in life than a website designer who's after a brief walk on the wild side. Edgar's heart has taken enough of a bruising. He's not prepared to get dumped again.

Zack wants love. Edgar only wants friendship. Can the two men find common ground amid the chaos of Edgar's life? Or is Zack going to find that no matter what he does, there's no happy ending and he'll have to walk away?

Warning: This story contains dogs. Lots of dogs. Big ones. Small ones. Naughty ones. Ones that like ducks, squirrels, and lakes and ones that like to be carried. No dogs were harmed in the writing of this book.

Edge of Living

Sometimes, death can feel like the only escape.

It's been a year since Alex stopped living. He exists. He breathes. He pretends to be like everyone else. But, he doesn't live. Burdened by memories, he dreams of the day when he can finally be free. Until that time comes, he keeps everybody at bay. It's been easy so far. But he never factored in, meeting a man like Austin.

Hard-working mechanic Austin has always gone for men as muscular as himself. So, it's a mystery why he's so bewitched by the slim, quiet man with the soulful brown eyes who works in the library. The magnetic attraction is one thing, but the protective instincts are harder to fathom. Austin's sure though, that if he can only earn Alex's trust then the two of them could be perfect together.

A tentative relationship begins. But Alex's secrets run deep. Far deeper than Austin could ever envisage. Time is ticking. Events are coming to a head, and love is never a magic cure. Oblivious to the extent of Alex's pain, can Austin discover the truth? Or is he destined to be left alone, only able to piece together the fragments of his boyfriend's history, once its already too late?

Trigger warning: Please be aware that this story deals with suicidal ideation and other dark themes. If this is a subject you find uncomfortable, then this book is not recommended.
Despite this, there is a guaranteed HEA.

Made in the USA
Las Vegas, NV
27 February 2021